I0823979

A Guide To FALLING Off The Map

A Guide To FALLING Off The Map

ZANNI L. ARNOT

SCHOLASTIC PRESS / NEW YORK

Library of Congress Cataloging-in-Publication Data available

ISBN 978-1-5461-3844-0

10 9 8 7 6 5 4 3 2 1 25 26 27 28 29

Printed in Italy 208

First edition, September 2025

Book design by Maithili Joshi

To Kiah

Part One

A Map of Our Universe

CHAPTER 1

VINNIE: *The Wizard of Oz*

The crowd surges.

"Stand, Vinnie. We're standing!"

"What? Oh."

Lilah helps me up by the elbow. I clap along with the rest of the audience. At first, I'm a puppet. But soon, my head gets its act together and I'm in the room.

"That was Molly's best performance yet," I shout-whisper into Lilah's ear.

"Agreed!"

My fingers make pistols in my mouth and my whistle pierces the applause. Lilah covers her ears, laughing, embarrassed.

"That's so *loud*, Vinnie! Sheesh."

"You know you love it." Mum was a whistler too. But since missing her is a punch in the throat, I snap the memory closed.

The director, our drama teacher Ms. Montague, strides onstage in denim overalls and bright white sneakers to raise Molly's hand. She grabs the Tin Man's too because my ex-boyfriend, Jez, also kicked some serious *Wizard of Oz* butt.

Molly catches my eye and waves. I wave back in a cheesy fangirl way, because she's the best actor and singer in our school. Also, this year's Drama Captain, aka my Queen. I can't believe this is her last performance at Murwillumbah High.

Lilah and I ride the audience wave toward the lobby.

"Let's wait by the dressing room," I say, yanking her through the throng. She thinks this is me being excited, which

I totally am, but right now, I need her to keep me upright.

I've been wobbly ever since I woke up this morning. Tired too. Unreasonably so. Then the double vision kicked in at lunch time. It's not my period, nor a cold, as much as I wish it were.

"But they'll think we want to crash their cast party," says Lilah, trying to hold me back.

"So? Don't you want to crash their cast party? I want to crash their cast party." Then I have an excellent thought. "I bet Freddie will be there! He's never missed a party." I kiss the back of my hand as if I am Lilah and my hand is Freddie.

"Oh, stop!" she says, but she's laughing. She's been in love with Freddie Sinclair since we started at Murwillumbah High. Not a bad choice, either. Freddie has Thor's proportions. Also, he appreciates the dramatic arts. You can't say that for every player in the Rugby Firsts.

Now that I've offered up Freddie, Lilah lets me drag her toward the dressing room door. When Jez opens it, I wrestle him in a bear hug.

"You were so great, Jezzie!"

"Thanks, Vinnie." His grin reveals the big gap between his two front teeth. He pushes back his blond hair, streaked silver from colored hair spray.

"Are you guys coming to Lu's?" he asks.

"Lilah?" I make prayer hands under my chin.

She rolls her eyes, but I can tell she's pleased. I would have been happy to gate-crash, but she's the kind of person who likes things in writing. Gold embossed, preferably.

"I thought you'd never ask." I hand him my phone. "Type the address in Google Maps for me? Thanks!"

I text my other best friend, Roo, on our way to Lu's via Lilah's place. I know what he'll say, but I'm going to try anyway.

Party at Lu's. Promise me you'll be there and I'll buy you waffles tomorrow morning. Plus whipped cream. Plus iced coffee! 26 Ostrich Avenue. Mwah.

His reply pings immediately.

No.

I reply,

Waffles? ☺

Then . . .

Your commitment to parties is pathological, Vinnie Smith. Besides, I have this interesting thing happening right now called W-O-R-K.

I grin, imagining Roo in Brad Whitelaw's photo lab, placing undeveloped negatives in a solution bath. His lopsided smile as images emerge. I'm glad he's found his calling because school wasn't his bag.

I send him a kissy face, which I know will make him want to throw his phone out the window.

He also hates parties. He thinks they're second only to torture. I tell him he's being offensive to torture victims and that he's probably just an introvert, stop being so dramatic.

He says, Who's being dramatic, exactly?

And I punch him in the arm. Kindly. A gentle, friendly punch. Because that's how we roll, Roo and I.

CHAPTER 2

ROO: Upholding the Pavlović Brand

Daniel Pavlović isn't being nice. But because he's my boss, I have to be polite.

"Scrub harder, Roo Bean," he says, in his thick accent. He lights a cigarette and leans against the garage door.

I hate how he calls me that: *Roo Bean*. It's Rueben. Or Roo will do. I really don't care. Just don't call me Roo *Bean*.

I dip the window squeegee in the dirty water, let it drip, then smack it on the windshield of Pavlović's Prius.

"Careful!" he says. "You know how much this car costs, huh? You want me to dock the scratches you make from your pay?"

Yeah, funny, Pavlović. Of course I don't want that. You know that. I know that.

I tenderly caress Pavlović's precious Prius windshield with the squeegee, then wipe the excess liquid from the rubber with my sleeve.

Pavlović groans and presses his ciggy butt into the ground with his boot.

"Now your sleeve is wet. What are my customers going to think about being driven around by a kid in a wet shirt, huh?"

"Customers?" I say.

"Yeah, dumbo, customers. You know, the ones who pay to sit in the back of a taxi and be driven around Murwillumbah? Those ones."

I'm quiet. Chew my cud.

"I can't," I say eventually.

"What do you mean, *can't*?"

"I can't drive."

"I've seen you drive. You drive fine."

"I mean, I *can't*. As in, I can't be seen driving your car."

Now he's quiet. He frowns, his graying brow so low his eyes are buried.

"You kidding me right now? Are you actually kidding me?" He's a small guy, but his anger makes him bigger.

"Not really." I almost call him sir, but that is one step too far. Even for me.

"So what? You embarrassed or something? Embarrassed to drive a Prius? You want something a little more fancy, huh? A Lamborghini?"

I shake my head.

"So, not embarrassed? Then good. Tonight, you're my new driver. Mullins is chucking a sickie."

Pavlović doesn't get that I can't drive his car because someone will see me. And someone will tell Mum, for sure. This town isn't that big.

But he has me by the short and curlies—all ten thousand of them. Not that I've ever counted.

I put away the bucket and squeegee. When I return, Pavlović is waiting in the passenger seat.

"Oh. You want me to drive now?" I say.

"Sure. We do a block. I want to see your ability. Your cheery nature. Make sure you uphold the Pavlović brand. Roll up your sleeve."

"Huh?"

"Roll it up. Your sleeve. So the customers don't see the wet patch."

I hold my sigh and do as he says. Short and curlies and all that. My wrist is skinny like a kid's.

"Okay, okay. Now, give me a smile."

Inside my head, my eyes are rolling. On the outside, they're demonstrating a cheery attitude.

"Teeth," he says. "Show your teeth. Be genuine. Yeah, that's better."

Oh, man.

I put the stick into reverse and check my mirrors. I drive Pavlović down Pavlova Hill. It isn't really called that. But his house is all creamy and frouffy. A couple of years ago, he was a cleaner at our school. Now look at him. A house made of meringue and a fleet of cars. Nothing suspicious about it.

At the end of the drive, I go to do a U-turn, but he shakes his head at me.

"That was not a proper test drive. We go farther."

I turn into Urliup Road and head into the countryside.

"Okay. You drive fine. Smile more, though. Ask about my night."

"How's your night?" I say, my tone flat.

He grins. Slaps the dash. "My night is good! And yours?"

I return the cheesy grin. "Really great! Thanks!"

I hope he doesn't hear my sarcasm.

As much as I don't want to drive Pavlović's customers tonight, I don't really have a choice. Because at the end of the shift, he'll pay me a wad of cash, which I'll give to Mum. Her shoulders will relax and she'll feel less like covering that shift for Vicky or Rah or whoever. Instead, she might actually put her feet up and give her effed-up back a rest.

If I don't play the Pavlović game, Mum will go back to

feeling the bite, the one that makes you take every bit of work you can because you don't want them to chuck you and your kid out of the only apartment in town you can still afford.

CHAPTER 3

VINNIE: Guard Dogs in Marble

Lilah and I are going to Lu's party *Reputation*-meets-*Lover* style. I'm dressed in a plaid crop top with hot pants and Dad's work boots. Lilah wears a cute baby-pink sports coat with metallic shorts and heels she ordered online from ASOS. I give her hair a fluff, then bunch it on top of her head in a high pony. When we examine ourselves in her mum's full-length mirror, I think we look pretty darn smoking.

"You sure you're okay, Vin?" Lilah asks my reflection. "You look kind of tired."

"Gee, thanks!" I stretch the skin under my eyes. Pat my cheeks.

"Oh, I didn't mean it badly. I'm just worried."

"I'm seriously fine. Couldn't be finer." I widen my eyes and shoot her some classic Vinnie sparkle.

But she's right. I do look exhausted. She can't see inside my head, thankfully, so can't tell that the floor's swirling and the mirror swims.

"What do you reckon Freddie will be wearing?" I ask, applying yet another layer of lip gloss. "My bets are on his usual: sleeveless tee. You have arms like that, you show them off."

Her cheeks flare at the mention of Freddie's arms.

"Come on, girls! I want to get back for the end of the game. The Wallabies are finally up on the scoreboard," one of Lilah's mums, Kathomi, yells from the front door.

When we arrive at Lu's place, Lilah and I saunter arm-in-arm down the long driveway, which is lined with weeping birch. Lu's place looks like it should be hosting a *Gatsby* event, not a *Wizard* event.

"I had no idea Lu's family is loaded," says Lilah. "Lu's so understated."

"Humble," I agree. "And in love with Kmart sweatpants. They could wear pure designer if they wanted. Life's unfair."

"Should we steal a statue on our way out? For your dad's garden?"

"Good plan." I smile at her under the porch light. "Let's take the Great Dane. I reckon Dad would appreciate it."

I pretend to lift the stone Great Dane that guards the front steps. Fat lot of good is a guard dog made of marble. Still, it gives off the overall whiff of money and power, which is the point.

"Vinnie! Lilah! You came!" Molly is first to greet us and embraces us simultaneously. She smells of musk stick, which adds to my overall love for her.

"You were amazing, Molly!" I say.

"Aw, shucks. Coming from you, that means the world. Hey, guess what? You guys are doing *Grease* next year! I'm so jealous. Ms. Montague told me tonight. Are you going to try out for Sandy?" She looks at me but must feel bad so includes Lilah in the question.

"Vinnie was born to be Sandy." Lilah hooks her arm through mine. "Look at you, Vin! All Olivia Newton-John in her prime."

Technically, Lilah has a better voice than me. She started lessons when she was four. Plus, she's got more natural talent and a wider range. But she prefers supporting roles because she needs to leave plenty of room for her psychology brain—the one she's fine-tuning to help teenagers manifest their futures.

"I'll try out, for sure," I say.

"And Drama Captain, huh?" Molly looks first at me, then Lilah, knowingly.

I laugh. "Not yet! Announcements aren't until Tuesday."

"Totally. But Drama Captain!" She squeals and claps her hands. "I have had literally the best year. Like, what can I say? You're going to love it!"

I glance at Lilah, who squeezes my arm. I try swallowing my excitement. I have been fantasizing about being Drama Captain ever since I played Matilda in Year Seven. I redirect my enthusiasm toward Molly, as this is her night, not mine. Also, I don't want to put the cart before the horse, as Dad likes to say when he's feeling old-fashioned.

"Oh, Mol, I don't want you to leave!" I say. "I am going to miss you soooo much next year. When is your drama school audition anyway? What monologue are you doing?"

The twinkle in Molly's eye fades.

"Ah, I've applied for Melbourne University," she says.

"They do drama there? Or are you going to the Conservatorium?" The Melbourne Conservatorium of Music has a good reputation. Molly could totally focus on voice instead of drama. I'd respect that.

"Neither."

Dua Lipa music pumps so hard that I barely hear Molly. It's making me disoriented. If I am not mistaken, the floor is in the process of rising up to punch me in the nose.

"What?" I lean closer, gripping Lilah's arm tighter.

"I'm applying for medicine," Molly yells through cupped hands.

Lilah, too, looks shocked.

Medicine? But Molly's amazing. At acting. At singing. Neither of those things are required to study medicine.

Molly shrugs. "I always wanted to be a pediatrician. Pretty sure I'm going to get the grades I need to get into Melbourne."

I fix my disappointed face. "That's great, Molly." I hug her to show I believe my words. "You'll make a great pediatrician."

Molly's ripped away by her girlfriend, Jayde, while a conga line weaves between Lilah and me.

I'd like to say I'm enjoying the festivities, but my vision is in the process of splitting in two. There are two Mollys. Two Jaydes. Way too many of everyone else. I squeeze my eyes, urging my head to get its freaky self together. This is neither the time nor the place.

It takes me a moment to register that Freddie Sinclair is asking me something.

"Sorry?" I murmur. "You're looking for Lilah?"

Where is she? I need to find her too.

"You okay, Vinnie? You're looking out of it."

I squeeze past his giant shoulders and make my way through the throng. *Not out of it. Fully with it. Need air.*

I spot Lilah talking to Tiger Someone from Year Ten.

"There you are!" I clutch her arm and drag her away from the Dua Lipa fest, into the fresh night.

CHAPTER 4

ROO: Lorraine and the Wrecking Ball

I get a pang of satisfaction at the lack of power Pavlović's Prius has getting up his steep driveway. He's so proud of this car. He keeps opening up the screen on the dashboard, which shows how much battery is being used and how much money he's saving on gas. Fact is, his Prius is a wuss. Judging from his scrunched-up face, Pavlović is lamenting.

"Remember," he says, getting out of the car, "take all the calls. Be polite. Chatty. More chatty than you were just now. Ask about weekend plans. That kind of thing. Don't do that weird frown face you have going on. Give my customers a bit of cheer. And take off that damn cap." He rips it off my head and flings it on the passenger seat. My glasses dislodge in the process. He slaps the roof, and I give him the cheesiest grin I can muster.

"That's it, Roo Bean. Better."

As he swaggers up the steps, the automatic lighting pings on and, for a moment, I marvel at his strange beauty, perfectly framed by a black background. His jeans slung around his hips. His gray hair patchy and thin. Could be a Gregory Crewdson photo.

Framed like this, he's so small. Vulnerable. A kind guy, even. A character you feel sorry for and want good things to happen to.

His front door slams and I get my first ping of the night. Let's hope they have no idea who I am.

Lorraine. I don't know a Lorraine. That's promising. Even so, I put my cap back on and pull it low before pulling up in front of Myrtle's Laundry. Pavlović won't like this look—doesn't fit his *brand*. But hey, what Pavlović doesn't know won't kill him.

Mum, on the other hand, might kill me if she sees me driving this car. As far as she's concerned, I'm busy studying Photography at vocational college. The only reason I was allowed to drop out of school was because she believed I had a chance to be some kind of hotshot photographer or something.

Myrtle's isn't a laundry, but probably was at some point. Now, it's an award-winning restaurant. Murwillumbah doesn't have a ton of fancy restaurants. There's this and there's a fancy-schmancy rustic thing set up in someone's shed just out of town. Claremont, I think it's called.

You'd barely know Myrtle's was a restaurant. It looks like a shop with a few tables inside. Everything's white, steel, and glass—more like a clinic where they cut up dead people.

I peer through the passenger window, looking for so-called "Lorraine."

Oh crap. Lorraine is Ms. Parker, my ex-principal. I should pull away. But pulling away is losing my job.

Instead, I yank my cap lower as she opens the back door of the Prius.

She's tall, for a lady. Nearly as tall as me. At school, she wears linen suits and a dozen rings on each finger. Here, out in front of Myrtle's, she's in a frilly dress. Looks like an oversized cup-cake. Teeters on skinny heels, which make her tower over the guy she's with.

"Good, you're here." She slides in, not noticing it's me. Laughs her head off as she gets caught on the seat belt buckle on her way past.

"Shove over, Lorraine." Her date is jovial. He could be a foot-baller or a wrecking ball. Broad-shouldered. Thick-necked.

You don't often think about your teachers' private lives, let alone your principal's. Watching these two in my rearview mirror, I understand why.

"Old Ferry Road?" I make my voice deep.

They ignore me and continue laughing and chatting about the night.

"Miriam's absurd, right?" says Lorraine. "Did you hear she's planning to flip her house? Is she actually serious? *Miriam?*"

They cackle. Poor Miriam. If only she knew.

It occurs to me that Miriam might be Ms. Barkley from the art department. Miriam Barkley. I feel even more sorry for her now that I can give the butt of their joke a full name.

Lorraine makes herself cough with too many guffaws and takes a swig from a water bottle. I let my guard down and make the mistake of watching her in the rearview mirror. She catches my eye. Grabs the back of my collar.

"*Reuben?* Is that you—Reuben *Carpenter*?"

Damn it.

"Hi, Ms. Parker."

"Dave, Reuben is that kid I told you about the other night!" Oh, man. "What are you doing now, Reuben? You're a taxi driver?"

What's the worst that can happen? She bumps into Mum at the shop. Tells her how proud she is of me, that despite my shockingly bad grades at school, I ended up driving an eco-friendly car, and Mum walks off confused and disoriented. Confronts me. I lie. Tell her I haven't seen Ms. Parker since I dropped out of Murwillumbah High at the end of last year.

"Good on you, Roo. Like I always say, the final school certificate isn't everything."

I squint, watching her in the mirror. Well, she certainly didn't say *that* when I bid my farewell at the end of Year Ten. Instead, she let out a long, exhausted sigh. I still hear it. It was the same sigh I'd been hearing the whole way through school. It sounded something like: "Roo, you screwup. You no-hoper."

I pull up in front of a 1930s weatherboard house tucked behind a row of skinny pines.

"Okay, here we are! Have a great night!" I say cheerily.

She grins in the mirror and climbs out. She makes me jump when she leans through the driver's window.

"Sooo nice bumping into you, Reuben. Stay out of trouble, won't you!"

She and the wrecking ball trip up the stairs to do god knows what principals and demolition balls do in their private lives.

I exhale and consider uninstalling the booking app from my phone, which would mean I won't get any more call-outs.

Pavlović's face pops up on my screen, as if reading my thoughts.

Cheery! Big smiles! Remember!

CHAPTER 5

VINNIE: Three Marty Oxenburgs and a Shit Ton of Flamingos

I let the clean night air wash over me. Squeeze my eyes tight. I'm getting dizzier as the night progresses, which isn't good.

"Vinnie, are you okay? Do you want to go home?"

It takes me a tediously long moment to open my eyes and reassure Lilah that I'm fine. That I'm not seeing double. That I'm not freaking out about what all this means. Especially since this is not the first flare this week.

"I'm fine, okay?" I snap. She looks hurt. I cover my tracks with the biggest smile I can summon and clutch her hand lovingly. "Sorry. It's just all this . . . noise. Hey, I saw Freddie." I coo his name.

"What? Inside?" The distraction works. My health is forgotten as she flutters her eyelashes against her finger as if to catch excess mascara. "Do I look okay?"

"You're a smoke show," I say. "Hey, isn't it tragic Molly's not auditioning for NIDA? I'm gutted. She's so talented."

A splash makes us look across Lu's emerald lake, also known as *the swimming pool*. Marty Oxenburg from Year Ten, who played the delightful munchkin Boq, is lying fully dressed on a flamingo floatie, a cocktail balanced on his stomach. His patent-leather shoes trail the water's surface. Traces of munchkin makeup make his complexion milky.

"Not everything revolves around the performing arts," says

Lilah. "If Molly wants to be a doctor, we should support her. I bet her parents are pleased."

"What if it's her parents who are making her be a doctor?" I'm suddenly worried.

Lilah shrugs. "Who knows? Maybe Molly's been manifesting doctor stuff her whole life. She seemed pretty happy about the idea of studying medicine. Aggie was a doctor and she wasn't so bad." She pauses and bites her bottom lip. "Uh, sorry, Vin." She watches me, waiting for my reaction.

I want to be able to talk casually about my mum, Aggie. I really do. But it literally hurts bringing her into the conversation.

"Aggie was first and foremost a creative person." I keep my voice as relaxed as possible. "Being a doctor was her side gig."

Lilah laughs louder than warranted. I wonder if she's relieved that the Aggie gates are open, even if it's just a smidge.

Thinking about Mum makes the dizziness worse. I blink hurriedly, which does nothing except make it seem like there are now three Marty Oxenburgs, instead of two, plus a shit ton of flamingos floating in the pool.

I pull Lilah down with me so we can sit on the edge before I topple in. I unlace my boots, chuck them behind us, and drop my feet into the water. The cold shocks my giddiness to a standstill. For the first time all evening, I feel almost human.

I lean against Lilah's shoulder. "Okay, I hear you. I support Molly one-hundred-percent. Now, tell me about our apartment in New York."

CHAPTER 6

VINNIE: Two Saint Bernards Called Lemon and Lollipop

Lilah eyes me suspiciously as if assessing my physical state. Thankfully, though, manifestation is too tempting. If she could pick one thing to do for the rest of her life, it would be to stand in front of our vision board and manifest us in a two-bedroom apartment in New York with our two Saint Bernards, Lollipop and Lemon.

"So, our place is four stories," she says. "But we are on the third floor. Close enough to the street that we can watch the comings and goings. But we still can see glimpses of the park from our bedroom windows."

Lilah and I have visualized our New York apartment a thousand times. We have very specific requirements, like needing retro appliances and thrift store–only furniture. But of course the apartment is just one part of the vision. Another is me acing my Juilliard audition and Lilah receiving her letter of acceptance from NYU so she can do a bachelor's in Psychology. Without these two events, an apartment in New York is redundant.

Occasionally, I privately manifest Roo getting on a plane and visiting us. In my vision, he sleeps on a mattress in our living room and walks our Saint Bernards while we're at college. It's hard to imagine a future without Roo living in the same zip code. We've been each other's person since we could garble baby gibberish at each other. We shared a camping mattress when we were little kids. Slept top-to-toe when the adults drank too much and couldn't drive home. He was there the night Mum died and the only one who ever understood what that did to me.

Meanwhile, Real Life Roo refuses to visit us in New York. Says he can't justify that amount of carbon emitted into the atmosphere by his plane trip just so he can look at a city he can already see in movies. I tell him he can plant trees to offset the carbon if he's so worried.

The truth is that Roo won't ever leave this town because he hates leaving his mum. Also, he's scared to step outside his comfort zone.

"We'll go thrifting on Saturdays to look for cool old-lady paraphernalia like biscuit tins and crystal vases," continues Lilah. "We'll collect signed Broadway posters and have a room dedicated to theater. We'll invite friends over for long brunches on Sundays. And share a bed Sunday nights because we fall asleep watching *Little Women*."

Lu calls to us from the doorway. "Vinnie! Lilah! Come partay!" Their voice is singsong. "We're doing a dance off!"

I grin, happily noting that the dizziness has subsided as I rise. My vision is pretty normal too.

"Let's see if we can find Freddie," I say. "You and he can *dance off*." I may as well have said, "*have sex*."

Lilah slaps my arm but says, "Well, it would make this the best night of my life."

CHAPTER 7

ROO: Toasted Cheese Sandwich

I haven't had a call-out for the last fifteen minutes. Nor have I had a message from the (not so) big boss. I checked to see if Mum's at work so I am safe to pop home to get something to eat.

My key gets stuck again in our lock. I should get it fixed. I've got a grand total of $157 in my bank account plus this week's pay. I still need to pay the electricity bill, which is due next week. I hope I have enough to cover a locksmith.

Using serious muscle, I manage to unlock the door and push it open with my shoulder.

We live above a liquor store, which is mostly not an issue, until a drunk dude yells obscenities at the cashier for refusing to sell him booze. It's the smallest apartment in Murwillumbah and possibly not even legal. But it's all we've ever been able to afford on Mum's single-parent salary.

Our apartment is furnished with stuff from the thrift shop and things Mum inherited from her nan when she died. Wall space is crowded with paintings Mum did before she had me. They're still lifes—but not your usual bunch of flowers and fish on a silver platter. These are quirky arrangements. The lighting and style is traditional enough. Flowers, yes. But also a chewed-up cork she found on the beach, a snapped cucumber, a little porcelain dog wearing sunglasses.

She's also framed a couple of my photos. The one of Vinnie facing the waterfall, where she's just a silhouette—a ghost of the valley. The one of Aggie's turquoise Kombi Volkswagen bus disappearing over the horizon. I recommended Mum shouldn't waste hard-earned money on frames or the cost of printing. But she insisted.

I don't mind the photo over the couch. It's a water dragon's shadow, weirdly exact and recognizable, even though the lizard itself is invisible.

I make a cheese sandwich and lay it in the sandwich press. I have a special interest in collective nouns, so I look up if there happens to be a collective noun for sandwiches. There isn't. The best I can find is a collective noun for toasters, which are neither sandwiches nor sandwich presses but are called "burnouts." I can't imagine it's used very often, though. How many times do a group of toasters get together? I think about this and very little else as I scroll Instagram, waiting for the cheese to sizzle.

Surprise, surprise, Vinnie is out at that party, posting pictures of her and Lilah by a freakishly blue pool. She's pouting into the air like a goldfish.

Cast parties rooool! 🔥 reads the caption. I sigh, scroll another minute, then jam my phone into my pocket. I hate Instagram and social media. If it weren't for Vinnie updates, I'd probably ditch it altogether.

I never post stuff myself. But I have the idea now to post a photo of me and the sandwich press.

Toasted sandwiches rooool! 🔥

Or maybe

Doing burnouts! 🔥

Everyone will think I'm being an awkward loser, as usual.

As if I care. I don't post anything. Mainly, I can't be bothered.

My phone buzzes.

Feed yourself. I'm home late. Love you. Hope studying is going okay!

Mum.

Have a good night. Hope shift is going all right. X

I'm not lying directly. Just not telling the bare and honest facts: Not studying, Mum. Making a toastie while I wait for a call-out. Yep, that's right. I'm driving for that guy, Pavlović. You know, the one who used to clean toilets but now does some dodgy stuff? Yeah, that one. So not studying. The college doesn't even offer that course anymore. Arts budget cuts, you know. And remember that studio gig? Well. It fell through, didn't it? Can't believe I thought someone would pay me money for my talent. How did that dumb idea get in my brain?

But I'll never tell her that. Can't bear the look of disappointment. The same one she would have had opening my kindergarten report card. One minute full of hope and expectation. The next? Fizzle. I'm not exactly the sperm donor kid she'd ordered.

Mum's an optimist, so she tries to see the best in me despite the obvious indicators. Yet I keep letting her down, time and time again. A series of screwups and bad report cards, no matter how much hope she pours into me. No matter how many hours tutoring and late nights spent sitting with me, helping me do homework.

Me leaving at the end of Year Ten was not her choice, obviously. But the photography diploma at TAFE was the draw card.

"I can see you doing that!" she'd said. "You take beautiful shots."

Also, you can't mess up a photography diploma. All you have to do is hold a camera and press a button. Not much to it, right?

Melted cheese crackles. I burn my tongue when I take a bite, wince, and fling the toastie onto a plate.

I use my phone to take a photo just in case Mum wonders what I have been working on tonight.

I call this one: *Still Life in Dairy.*

CHAPTER 8

VINNIE: An Homage to "Stayin' Alive"

"I think I might go soon," says Lilah when Lu and Henry Jorgensen finish their homage to John Travolta's "Stayin' Alive" dance.

"What about Freddie?" I wiggle my eyebrows in Freddie's direction.

She lifts a half-hearted shoulder. We glance over. Freddie's dancing with Jayde, Molly, and Tara. It feels like he's danced with everyone except Lilah.

"I want to finish my Astronomy essay before Mr. York's class on Monday. Are you coming?"

"Noooo! We can't go. Didn't you love how Lu managed to do the Swayze lift? Like, what the hell? Where did they get those muscles from in the last twenty-four hours? Anyway, we've still got to see Molly's group do the dance they've been practicing."

"You can stay. No one's making you leave." She texts her mum.

"You can't go! I'm lift dependent!" Now that my body is finally behaving itself, I figure I should make the best out of the situation. Also, Vinnie Smith *does not* leave a party before midnight.

"Call Roo," she says. "Then you can stay as long as you want."

"True." I know Roo won't like me using him for lifts. But hey, what's a girl to do when her bestie has use of his mum's

Corolla and her other bestie is about to ditch her for an Astronomy assignment?

Can you pick me up from Lu's about midnight? Lilah's abandoning me. Worst friend ever. JK.

I can practically hear Roo's groan as three dots appear.

Fine. Be out the front at midnight. I won't wait for you.

Thanks, baby cake. 😘

Nothing. Then a head explosion emoji comes through. I laugh and show Lilah our exchange.

"I swear you provoke him," she says, shaking her head.

"It's our thing. Him grumpy. Me happy."

"It just seems like our whole life makes him crazy," says Lilah. "Like he can't think of anything worse than two drama dorks."

"We make him crazy. But that's okay. Crazy is a break from the malaise of the rest of his life, which is probably good for him."

Kathomi is waiting for Lilah in the driveway. Lilah hugs me, then holds me at arm's length.

"Whatever you do, have fun," she says, all mum-like. "But don't get drunk. There are lots of boozy people in there."

I laugh her off. "As if! You know I can't drink for shizz."

"Exactly," she says.

"Are you sure you aren't coming with us, Vin?" Kathomi leans across the gearshift. "I don't like the idea of you staying out alone."

"I'm not alone." I wave toward the party. "There are a thousand people in there. But thanks for being worried about me."

"Have you told your dad where you are?" she asks.

"Yep—I texted him. Thanks, Kathomi!"

"Be safe!" she calls from the driver's window at the same time Lilah yells, "Don't have too much fun without me!"

"Enjoy Astronomy!" I yell after them.

CHAPTER 9

ROO: Noodle

I kill time until the next call-out by flicking through old photos on my phone. There are a bunch of arty shots: Shadows on pavements. Grates. Drains.

There aren't many photos of people. Unless you count the folder delivered by the Apple gods called "Vinnie." Most of the photos are pretty old. Trips Vin and I used to take with our families when things were *normal*.

I land on a cluster of photos taken at Crystal Shower Falls near Dorrigo. Most of them are of Vin trying to get the perfect headshot. But there's one of her looking upward that she didn't know I'd taken. Vapor gathers on her freckled nose. Her eyes are closed. Her smile goes on for days.

Just after that sequence, I land on a pretty good photo (composition-wise) of Vinnie's mum standing on the rocks at Iron Peg, years ago. You're not meant to go out that far. But Aggie was always doing stuff like that. Crawling to the last rock on the outcrop. Not just crawling. In this photo, standing, like freaking Jesus Christ, her arms outstretched, the ocean at her mercy.

The real-life moment made my stomach plummet. The photo has roughly the same effect.

I swipe on but stop again on a rare photo of the five of us sitting on a rock, Minyon Falls raging behind us. Look at us here—college besties Aggie and Carla (aka Mum). Aggie's husband, Mike. Their daughter, Vinnie. And me.

We'd been campaholics for years by the time this photo was taken. Every weekend, just about, we'd head off in Vinnie's mum's Kombi, the holiday breeze in our hair.

Vin and I are scraggly preteens in this photo. I was way more scraggly than her back then. Aggie was still muscly and lean. She had MS flares, but most of the time, no one would ever have known.

A memory kicks in, then. I think it was the same trip that we camped at Rummery Park. Vin and I were carving sticks by the van when we overheard Aggie talking about her depression. I don't think she realized we were in earshot because she was telling Mum and Mike she'd been having some really bad thoughts. Suicidal, even. I remember being shocked. This was *Aggie*. Aggie didn't struggle. She charged at life, full speed. Vin held her carved stick in one hand. Her other clutched my arm so tightly, her nails broke my skin. Who could blame her?

Mum told Aggie depression was a very expected symptom. She gave Aggie her counselor's name. Mike wrapped Aggie in a tight hug and told her that the lot of us would get her through anything, whatever it took. And I told Vin that she had nothing to worry about. That Aggie would be fine.

Little did I know.

I shove my phone away, furious at its power. But it immediately pings with another call-out.

I make my way toward the Great Northern on Wollumbin Street. Neither Wandalicious nor her partner are even vaguely familiar, so I let them climb aboard.

"How's your night?" I ask, friendly as cream cheese on crackers.

"Great, thanks!" I decide this is Wandalicious. She looks old enough to be my gran. Wears a sports jacket and jeans. Suede loafers. Her partner (let's call her Liz) also looks too glam for the Great Northern in a long velvet dress, her gray hair bunched on her head like a bao bun.

The women sit in the back seat, their shoulders together. I can't see via the mirror, but I guess their hands are clasped.

"Did you feed Noodle?" asks Wandalicious.

"Yep," says Liz.

That's it. Simple. Where do you find this easy kind of love? IKEA?

Liz and Wandalicious are lucky. I don't reckon I'll ever have someone like they have each other. I'm a faulty sperm donor kid, after all.

Vin's face lingers in the crevices of my brain for a moment before I remember to push her away. There's no way in a billion years that Amazing Vinnie Smith will ever be my girlfriend. We are eons apart—she's Venus and I'm the little planet that got booted out of the solar system because it couldn't even do Planet right.

Noodle comes out to greet Wandalicious and Liz as I roll into their driveway. I feel an irrational sense of emptiness seeing this dog wag his tail and jump all over his owners as they amble through the front garden.

I sigh.

On North Arm Road, my fingers fizz against the steering wheel. Next stop, Vinnie Smith's location: Ostrich Street. I know they shouldn't do that.

But you can't always prevent a tingle.

CHAPTER 10

VINNIE: Greek for "Dance Like No One's Watching"

I melt back into the party, relieved to feel mostly human. Jez and I dance for a bit, then his girlfriend, Perry, and her friend with a diamanté nose stud and cool rainforest Docs join in. Molly sashays over at some point and finally, thank the lord, she, Tara, and a bunch of other Year Twelves do the dance from the Barbie movie, which is literally the best moment of my life.

"I can't believe it's all over!" says Molly, handing me a paper cup. "Drink up!"

I probably (definitely) shouldn't drink whatever this is because me and alcohol aren't exactly friendly at the best of times. I've never tried drinking while being symptomatic, but instinct tells me it won't be the best concoction.

But this is Molly asking, and it's her night, not mine. I take a tiny sip. Just one. Then one more.

"Vin, join in!" says Tara as "Macarena" blares. "Molly, hold Vinnie's drink."

"You are kidding me. This is so nineties right now," I say.

"Of course! You got it, bae." She knocks my hip with hers on the "Aiii!" and we both turn, beautifully in sync as if we have been dancing the Macarena our entire lives.

"There you are." Freddie Sinclair sidles up to me as the song ends. He brushes back his dark, sweaty hair. "I've been looking for you."

"You have?" I take a sip. Crap. Probably shouldn't have done that. The alcohol burns my throat. "Did you like the musical?"

He leans in to hear me better. So close, I smell his alcohol-meets-coconut breath. I should draw back.

"Yeah. It was great. Why weren't you Dorothy, though? I would have thought you would be the obvious choice."

Is Freddie Sinclair complimenting me?

"No way, man." I bat his shoulder. "Molly was born to be Dorothy. Anyway, I have another play on. *The Great Gatsby*."

"I bet you're Daisy," he says.

I am.

"That's pretty good you remembered her name," I say.

"Why wouldn't I? I read the book a bunch of times, even before we did it in English. So, is that a yes for Daisy?"

I shouldn't be surprised. Freddie is a smart guy as well as everything else. He generally tops most classes. He could probably write *Gatsby*, given half a chance.

I nod, basking in his attention. A thread of guilt weaves through me. But Lilah's not here. I can bask for a tiny minute. No one will ever know, except Freddie and me.

He reaches one sculpted arm over his head and scratches his back. My eyes linger on the dark patch of hair in his pit for a moment too long. I breathe in.

"Is that a tattoo?" I force my gaze to the markings on his upper bicep. "What's it mean?"

"Greek for 'dance like no one's watching.'"

I try not to smile. *Dance like no one's watching?* The saying seems too corny for Freddie Sinclair.

"Why Greek?" I ask. "I thought you were Samoan."

"My grandma's Greek. Anyway, it looks way better than English."

"It does. I didn't know you were part Greek."

"There's a lot you don't know about me, Vinnie Smith." His teeth glow white against his dark skin.

Oh man.

He produces a flask from what could be his underwear and sloshes something golden into my cup.

"No, thanks!" I cover the opening. "I don't drink. Take it away from me."

"What do you mean, you don't drink? Everyone drinks. It's mandatory." He demonstrates "everyone" by emptying his cup into his mouth and refilling it. "Cheers, big ears." He taps my cup with his.

I sniff. The liquid is sweet. I dip the tip of my tongue and it's weirdly delicious. Maybe this kind of alcohol will be okay. Maybe I can make an exception for Freddie. Those biceps. That tattoo.

I sip. Then slug. He tops me up. "That's it, Vinnie. Now you're a real party person."

"I was always a real party person. I'm ninety-eight-percent party, baby. It's officially confirmed in my DNA test."

He laughs. I laugh, shaking away thoughts of Lilah, best friend Lilah, and ignore the grogginess cloaking me and weighing me down.

When I realize Freddie and I have drifted away from everyone else, I drag him over to the dance floor because I don't want people gossiping in the corridor on Monday.

"It's your turn to dance like no one's watching, Freddie," I say.

"On my own? No way. You and I are dancing together."

Before I can resist, he pulls me into a Fred Astaire–Ginger Rogers twirl and of course he can dance. Like he can do everything else. We're hip to hip, heat rising between us. I shouldn't be as invested in this dance as I am. Lilah would hate me if she could see us now.

"Go, Fred!" someone yells.

My phone vibrates against my butt. I swing away from Freddie to check.

Ten minutes. Remember, this taxi waits for no one.

Except me.

Especially not you.

I give Roo a virtual thumbs-up before Freddie hauls me onto the dance floor and whips me around like clothes drying on a windy day, which is exactly what you want when you're staving off a dizzy spell.

"Come upstairs," he mumbles into my hair.

I pretend I can't hear him and tug away.

"Upstairs. With me." He drags me across the dance floor toward Lu's staircase.

My heart races.

CHAPTER 11

ROO: A Freaking David Attenborough

Look at them. People hanging off one another. Sprawled in the grass. Sitting on one another's laps nursing booze, their hair as messy as their heads. I'm freaking David Attenborough studying the life of teens. Normal teens who still go to school and have loads of friends and don't muck up their lives.

Do I miss all this?

Who am I kidding? I never had this. None of it. I was the kid who had to sit close to the teacher so they could make sure I was paying attention. I was the kid who walked home alone from school. Who spent weekends taking photos of drainpipes instead of playing ball or hanging at a friend's house. There's no way I'd be invited to a party at one of the cool kids' houses.

Now that I'm a school dropout, the chances of blending into this chaos are even slighter. Mum warned me; she said, "Roo, leaving school's not all it's cracked up to be. Do you know how hard it is to make friends in the real world?"

Little did she know, I didn't really have friends at school. I don't count Vinnie because she was too busy hanging out with more interesting people. She always made an effort to talk to me and tried to include me, but her friends thought I was weird and awkward. Fair enough.

One of the Normal Teens comes toward me—a guy in a jock jacket, with a confident strut. He taps my window. I sink into my seat but turn on the engine so I can wind down the glass.

"You waiting for someone, mate? Or just lurking?"

It's Christoff, who finished school last year. He clearly doesn't recognize me.

"Waiting for Vinnie Smith?" I say, my voice coursing upward. *Honestly, Roo. Stand your ground, man.*

His expression softens. "Vinnie—the hot one? Cool. You guys dating, are you?"

I shake my head, mortally offended on Vin's behalf. She could date anyone she wanted.

Christoff's bored now that he's realized I'm not a kidnapper nor dating a hot girl, and wanders back to the mansion.

I let my chair go back, tip my hat, and sink into an alternate reality where I can concentrate in class and understand class texts; write faster and neater so teachers don't think I'm lazy and stupid; where I don't drop out of school, because I blend in with the Normal Teens. In this world, Christoff slaps me on the back and invites me to kick a ball with him after school.

CHAPTER 12

VINNIE: Ebby Staircase

I draw back. Freddie and I part sweaty hands.

"My friend's here to pick me up. Great dancing, though! You should do it more often!"

He looks disappointed. But I can't go upstairs with Freddie. I could never, ever do that to Lilah. It would be the end of my life as I know it.

No Juilliard. No NYU.

No apartment by Central Park.

No Saint Bernards called Lollipop and Lemon.

My cheeks burn. Dancing has made the alcohol race through my system so of course the dizziness is back. Tenfold. I desperately want to lie on cold ground and curl into a tight ball.

"Don't go, Vin!" Tara grabs my arm to pull me back.

"Got to!" I yank away, jogging through the party before anyone else can stop me. By some miracle, I don't fall over. Bursting through the front doors, I seize the sides of my head, demanding it to get a grip.

The stairs ebb under me. I steady myself with a Great Dane. When that doesn't help, I sink to the porch steps and hang my head on my knees, wishing my Milky Way brain would still.

Flashing headlights make me jerk up. It's not Roo's Corolla, though. It's a Prius.

I let my head plunk back onto my knees.

"Vinnie?"

All of me exhales, seeing Roo's face at the car window.

"I was about to drive off," he says.

"Nunchucks, you only just got here." I slowly make my way to the car, my legs struggling to cooperate, and somehow maneuver myself into the passenger seat.

"Whose car is this?"

"My boss's."

"Nice."

"You're drunk?"

"Nope. Not drunk."

The Milky Way froths. Bass thuds in my ears.

Why did I drink, exactly? Why didn't I go home with Lilah? I don't understand myself sometimes.

Roo says, "I'm taking you straight home."

"Not home," I plead. Dad can't see me like this. He'll panic and send me off to Brisbane Neurology Specialist Unit in a package marked *EXPRESS! FRAGILE!*

"Your place," I murmur, letting my head sink against the window.

CHAPTER 13

ROO: Festoon Lighting

I see you back here at 12:30. Do not be late. I have early start. I want to see car locked away before I go to bed.

I check the time on the dashboard clock, swipe Pavlović's message away, then start the car.

"How was the party?" I ask Vinnie.

She mumbles incomprehensively. Her head rests against the window, eyes closed. I glance at her. She's all sweaty. I press the back of my hand against her forehead but she shoos me away, eyes squeezed shut. I want to be angry at her for drinking so much. But it's impossible to be mad at Vinnie Smith.

Forget Pavlović and his darn early start. I only have one job now. Even though she doesn't want me to take her home, I have to.

I drive grandma speed through Murwillumbah until we reach Vin's end of town. The streets are as empty as always. I spot a couple of kids spray-painting under the bridge by the river. Idiots. They wear hoodies, but I can tell from their posture that it's Adam Roland and Zinc Patterson—the other school dropouts, who make me look presidential.

As we turn onto Vinnie's street, my autonomic nervous system clicks over. My heart speeds up, triggered by the poincianas. The speed bump. The fire hydrant. My palms sweat.

Her house used to be my happy place. I'd glow warm as

soon as I saw the festoon lighting strung across the veggie patch. These days, though, Vinnie's house conjures up the night Mum and I watched the ambulance lights paint the night blue and red as two big men walked the stretcher to the van, a sheet covering Aggie's face. I can remember the exact pitch of Mum's wail. I'd never heard it before and hope I'll never hear it again.

I glance at Vin, who's still out of it. What's it like for her? How do you drive up to your house over and over and not get your guts kicked in as you realize your mum's never going to open the front door for you again?

She might be my best friend, but I have no idea what she thinks about any of the Aggie stuff because she refuses to talk about it. She's too set on being Happy Vin. Bright Bubbly Drama Princess. Life's Amazing Vin. She refuses to drop the act for even a second.

I take a breath in. Breathe out. Slow my heart rate so I can focus on the job at hand.

Getting Vinnie out of the Prius is a delicate art. Opening the door, I use my body to catch hers, then bend at the knees to unbelt her and lift her to standing.

"We're home. Lean against me. That's it." I sling one of her arms across my shoulder.

"Gah," she mumbles.

"Vin, can you walk a bit? I've got you. But you've gotta do the walking."

"Argh." Her voice is slurred. I really wish she hadn't drunk. She knows how bad alcohol is for her. Like when she drank a single bottle of Mountain Goat and spent the night vomiting in my bathtub . . . What was she thinking?

Her eyes spring open. "I can't go inside," she slurs.

She tries sidestepping me and grabs the car door handle. Shakes it with surprising and vicious energy, before sinking to the ground.

"Calm down, Vin. This isn't helping." I crouch next to her. "You're really drunk, aren't you?"

"I'm not. I swear."

Vinnie's usually fireworks. She can do air somersaults on the trampoline. This isn't her.

"Let's go inside. I'll get Mike."

"No!" she calls after me. By now, I'm in parental mode. Vin is not making healthy life decisions.

"Roo?" Vinnie's dad, Mike, is reading *Scientific American*, his horn rims perched on his broad nose. His crossed ankles rest on the coffee table. "What are you up to, mate?"

"It's Vinnie. She's had too much to drink."

He flings the magazine and hurries outside to help. He's ruffled, his eyes wide under his bushy eyebrows. "Vin—talk to me. What's going on?"

"It's nothing, Dad. I'm fine. Just . . . drunk."

Now she admits it.

We prop her between us, which isn't easy because she's trying to make a getaway.

Somehow, we octopus it upstairs and Vinnie slumps on her bed.

"I swear, I'm fine. Leave me alone." She turns away from us and curls into a ball.

Mike and I watch over her until I realize we're being creepy and I head downstairs. Mike follows.

"Thanks, Roo, for looking out for Vinnie. You know I always appreciate it." I take his meaty hand and shake it. He salutes me as I get back in the car. Check my phone. Pavlović.

5 min late. Not happy.

Jesus. I still have to get across town. I text Vinnie before driving toward Pavlova Hill.

Text me when you're up. I need to know you're okay.

CHAPTER 14

VINNIE: Closing Walls

"Here, drink this." Dad looms over me with a glass of water. "It'll make you feel better."

I manage a thanks and a sip, then pull my blanket over me to black it all out.

"It's not like you to get this drunk," I hear him say somewhere in the distance. I'm not sure when he leaves, but at some point I know I'm alone.

I'm glad Dad thinks this is just alcohol. Because if he connects the dots like I have done—double vision leads to dizziness, leads to Dad shipping me off to Brisbane Neurology Specialist Unit for MRIs, reflex tests, and vision tests—next thing you know, I'll have an MS diagnosis hanging around the neck of my beautiful future.

I can't put Dad through that again. Not so soon. It's been fewer than five years since Mum's diagnosis.

Two, since she took too many sleeping pills.

I need water. I need to throw up. I try to steer myself to sitting, but I'm the *Titanic* and this ship's sinking fast. I cannot. Lift.

Cannot.

"Dad," I hear myself rasp. "Dad?"

But my voice is as useless as the rest of me.

Finally, I haul myself to sitting, then standing. Blackness hems me in like closing walls. I'm tiny, distraught, and on the floor.

Just me in a private hell.

CHAPTER 15

ROO: Omission Is Not a Lie

Pavlović is like one of those cartoons with steam piping out of his ears.

"I put my trust in you, Roo Bean! You let me down, boy. You think my trust is easily gained? Well, you got things to learn."

I hand him the keys, my head low.

"My friend had a medical emergency—"

He cuts me off. "Pah! Stop. I don't want to hear this bollocks. You let me down. Don't come in tomorrow." He walks away.

"Pavlović! Please. Wait!" I jog after him. "I need this job. I'm sorry. Really. My friend . . ."

"Lies." He spits on the concrete next to him.

"Your customers were happy." I try another angle. "They thought I was friendly. I really made their night great."

He stops and eyes me slowly. "Happy, huh?"

"Yeah, real happy. Wandalicious gave me a ten-dollar tip." I pass him the bill from my pocket.

He fingers it slowly, stretching it, refolding it, and pocketing it.

"Six a.m. tomorrow," he says gruffly. "I need the Land Cruiser cleaned for a job. Mullins will be here by eleven to take it out, and it's not been cleaned properly for a week. Needs the works. Tires. Hubcaps. Full detailing."

"Six a.m.?" I check.

"Six a.m." He strides up the path toward the house.

I can't believe my future is in his tiny hands.

*

I check my phone a billion times that night, at five thirty the next morning, and every five minutes after that. Vinnie still hasn't replied, which is unlike her. She's the type of person born with a phone attached to her finger pads.

At work this morning, Pavlović's still cross at me. Tells me to stop getting distracted and get his bloody Cruiser polished before pickup. By eleven, he finally lets me off shift so I can sleep.

I'm climbing into bed when—"Roo! Get your gear on! We're going for a run!"

I groan. Mum's at my bedroom door looking excited about life.

"No, we're not." I turn over in my bed. "I had an intense night of . . . studying. Need sleep."

I feel her hyperactive energy change the cellular construction of my bedroom. She plunks onto my mattress, making me bounce.

"Exercise boosts endorphins," she says, as if tempting a child with a head-sized lollipop.

"I know," I mumble.

"So?" She slaps my hip. "You can get a happy high just by running around the park."

"That's a negative," I say. "I worked until one or something then got up early to take more photos and stuff."

"I love that you are giving this course and job your everything. Didn't I tell you? You just had to find something you're passionate about. Look at you now. Sucking the marrow out of life."

"Ew, Mum."

She laughs. "You realize it's nearly midday, right? If you sleep now, your circadian rhythm will be messed up. How about I set you up a workout on YouTube? You like YouTube."

Mum is so *trying* sometimes. Like, literally trying to make me be a different person.

"Fine," I say. "But no YouTube workouts. I'll run with you."

"You will?" She beams, then starts chucking gym clothes at my bed.

We're halfway out the door when she says, "Don't bring your phone. I want to spend time with you, not your phone."

"I need it. I'm waiting for Vin to get back to me."

"Important, huh?" She cocks an overly curious eyebrow.

I roll my eyes. "It's not like that. I dropped her home after her party and she was pretty wasted. I'm waiting for her to tell me she didn't end up in the hospital."

"Oh my gosh! Is she okay?"

"Yeah, she drank a bit too much, is all."

"Okay, okay. Just a big night. Promise me you'll never consider nursing. You'll frighten the patients to an early grave with your worst-case scenario outlook."

We jog up Tombonda Road and around the cemetery. I'm way too overdressed in sweatpants and a cotton sweater. My glasses keep fogging up. Sweat dribbles down every side of me. It's hot. But it could also be the ridiculous lack of fitness. And exhaustion.

Mum keeps pulling ahead. Since her back got better and she started Pilates, she's been jogging a few times a week. Even though there are nearly thirty years between us and Mum could barely walk six months ago, she's currently making me look like I've escaped from the palliative care unit. She slows to let me catch up. Very kind.

"Nice to hear you and Vin are hanging out," she says, casual as can be.

"Yeah," I manage between pants.

"You always had such a lovely friendship. Now, you're taxiing her home from parties. So grown-up."

I frown through the sweat. "Mum."

"What? Just saying. I think it's lovely."

I stop. Wipe my glasses. Bend at the hips to let my godforsaken burnt-up brain hang between my wobbly legs.

"You okay? I'm going too fast." Mum jogs on the spot next to me.

"What's the big assignment you're working on?" she asks as we set off again. "Is it due soon?"

"Ah, yep." No details. Omission is not a lie. If I stay vague enough, I can give Mum the general impression I spent a whole day and night editing photos on my phone.

"I'd love to see some of your work sometime."

"Yeah." I squat next to a patch of clover. "You. Keep. Going." I pant. "I'm holding you back."

"See you back home!" She sprints off, a flash of neon orange in New Balance sneakers. I, meanwhile, jog home to text Vin.

Please call. WTF? Are you okay? What's going on??

I will the reply dots to appear. They don't.

I should go to her place right away. Find out what's going on. If only Mum hadn't tried to murder me with fitness.

Still in my sweaty clothes, I rifle around Mum's handbag for her keys and head out to the Corolla.

CHAPTER 16

ROO: Heaving with Waffles and Whipped Cream

I hammer the door. Once. Twice. Flat palm on paneled wood.

"Vinnie? Mike?" I call. Nothing.

It's after lunch. Maybe they're out. Grocery shopping? A bush hike? A father-daughter lunch at the Bowlo?

My thoughts quickly escalate. Vinnie hooked up to a drip. Mike hunched by her side. The monitor beeping ominously.

It takes me five minutes to drive across town to the Murwillumbah hospital. The building is old, but I love the hill it's on. Vin and I often come up here and look over the town. She tells me it's our special place. It's just a bench with a view . . . a few rosebushes dotted around. But if Vin calls it special, it's special.

I take the stairs two at a time. A smoking woman hooked to an oxygen canister growls at me as I pass. Like I'm the worst thing she's got going on right now.

"Vinnie Smith," I say at reception.

"Room?" asks the receptionist. She's about sixteen and should be playing volleyball on Saturday, not working at a hospital.

"No idea," I say.

I take in the surroundings. Artificial flowers on the bench. Oversized clock ticking morbidly over the receptionist's head. A row of plastic chairs intended to torture those waiting while they linger to see if their loved one lives or dies.

"My mum works here. Nurse Carpenter. Carla Carpenter? She's asked me to check on Vinnie."

The girl studies me suspiciously. She must decide I'm telling the truth because she consults her computer.

"No patient with that name."

She's blunt, I'll give her that.

The best news is, there's no person of that name and, as usual, I've had a freak-out with no cause. I bet Vinnie's just in bed, sleeping with her pillow over her head to drown out her hangover.

It's nearly two p.m. and I haven't eaten, made clear by the announcement echoing from my stomach.

I park right out front of Jo's Waffles, which isn't far from the hospital, and stop dead at the window.

So, maybe I can be mad at Vinnie Smith after all.

"What the actual . . . ?" I loom over Vinnie and Lilah's table, which heaves with waffles and whipped cream.

"Roo! I am soooo sorry. I totally promised you waffles and iced coffee. On the other hand, you didn't come to the party. So not my bad, dude."

"No, I mean—*this*." I show her my phone screen and my unanswered messages.

She fumbles for her phone. "Sorry, okay! I had it switched off." She looks like she's about to say something else but changes her mind. "Oops?" She shrugs, palms up, and grins at Lilah as if this is hilarious. It's not.

"You realize I've just come from the hospital, don't you?"

"What? Are you okay?" Vinnie grabs my hand, her eyes full of concern. I rip it away.

"Am I okay? No. I'm not okay. I left you semiconscious last night, and I've been checking my phone ever since. I was this close—*this close*”—I demonstrate with a small gap between my thumb and forefinger—“to calling the morgue.”

“You were semiconscious?” gasps Lilah.

Vinnie pats her hand reassuringly and says, “Roo’s being dramatic. I’m totally fine. I literally had three sips of alcohol. No biggie.” She wrestles a forkful of waffle from her plate and shovels it into her mouth. “What do you want, Roo? I’ll order for you.” She waves her phone over the QR code fastened to the table.

“I’m not hungry,” I lie and sink next to Lilah, opposite Vinnie. I stare at her through narrowed eyes, willing myself to hate her. But the more I look at her, the less I hate her, which is the usual way this goes. Even though she and Lilah banter about the boring cast party last night, I grip every word like it’s a handhold on a terrifying cliff face.

The waffle special Vinnie must have ordered lands in front of me with a hearty bang. I flinch.

At the same time, someone slaps the window next to our booth. Damn it. It’s Freddie from school. I roll my eyes and turn my back to him. Freddie’s one of those football blockheads who swaggers around being beautiful and beloved. Easy for some.

“Freddie!” Lilah calls through the glass. Vinnie’s looking uncharacteristically uncomfortable. Does she also hate Freddie?

“Hey, kids!” He eases his huge self into the booth, and slings a giant arm over Vin’s shoulder. My protective instincts prick up. I want to rescue her, but she won’t like me being her knight in shining armor.

“Hey, Freddie!” Lilah perches her chin in her hand. “How fun was last night?”

He grins at Vinnie rather than Lilah. Vinnie stares intensely at her phone. I’ve known her since she wore diapers and can see that either she's got the hangover of all mofos or she really wants this Freddie guy blasted to Mars.

"You should have seen Vin dance. Amazing!" Freddie runs a palm down Vin's bare arm. I hate how he calls her "Vin." How he touches her like he owns her. Vinnie's tensing, I can tell. I feel Lilah also turn to stone beside me as she watches the spectacle. Um, what's going on?

"Did something happen after I left?" Lilah asks Vinnie.

"Everyone danced. You know! Lots and lots of dancing, hey, Freddie?" Vin waves her hand.

He raises an eyebrow, a smile playing on his lips. "Yeah, lots and lots of dancing. Really nice dancing," he says.

"So, assembly on Tuesday, hey?" Lilah cautiously addresses the table as she changes the subject. "You realize you're the top pick for Sports Captain, Freddie?"

"Yeah, totally." He laughs easily. "You voted for me, I hope?" He does that Boris Johnson smile that makes me want to puke. Lilah is all for it, her doubt swept aside.

"Course! Who else would I vote for? Importantly, did you vote Vinnie for Drama Captain? We all think she's going to get it. Right, Vin?"

"Ha, yep. Maybe!" Vinnie grins.

I think I'm done. With waffles. With high school peacocking and captain this and that. If I wanted all this, I would have stayed in high school.

"Roo, where are you going?" asks Vinnie. "Don't go! You haven't eaten."

"Later, gaters," I say. I need a shower. I need to get out of these skanky gym clothes. I need to not be at Jo's watching Vinnie sink under Freddie's bicep.

CHAPTER 17

VINNIE: Our Map of the Universe

Freddie finally leaves and I can breathe.

My body still aches after yesterday's symptoms. Crushed by steamroller might come close to describing it. But I am used to scraping myself up from the floor and resuming life as usual. To the naked eye, I am a fully functioning teen out to a late lunch at Jo's.

"He's so hot I could die," murmurs Lilah as we watch Freddie cross the road and climb into his truck.

"Please don't die," I say. "I'd miss you too much. Here's a better idea: Do you want to come to mine and hang out for a bit? I need your help running lines for *Gatsby*."

"Sure!"

After we go through the script twice, we lie on my bed and gaze up at our vision board. Our map of the universe. It's a forty-by-forty-inch Officeworks corkboard covered in pictures of New York apartments we've cut out from real estate magazines. A postcard of the Statue of Liberty. The Juilliard logo. The NYU logo. Lilah's top five psychology goals:

1. Set up her own practice
2. Write for Mind Magazine
3. Do a PhD in manifestation
4. Meet Joe Vitale
5. Meet Deepak Chopra

My top five actors to meet in person:

1. Zendaya
2. Saoirse Ronan
3. Timothée Chalamet
4. Emma Watson
5. Scarlett Johansson

We've added flourishes cut out from crafty mags, the Saint Bernards Carla drew for us, and fake flowers I bought from Silly Solly's.

"Manifestation time?" I say to Lilah, playing the game of "Future" for the millionth time this year. After a day like yesterday, I need this more than ever. To make our future real.

"Hells yes." What else is she going to say? She lives for her next manifestation ritual.

I set the timer on my phone to one minute. We kneel on my bed and stare at our board. Part One of the ritual.

Today, it's the brownstone in the bottom corner that's drawing my focus. It's the apartment block with a geranium in a pot on the landing and a lady walking past, smoking a cigarette. I let the image plant into my brain. Feel it sink right in and form significant ditches in my neural pathways. *Dear Universe*, I plead, *let this be our home*.

The timer beeps. I reset for another two minutes. Part Two of the exercise: Imagine yourself existing in this moment. Like, really existing. The more you inhabit this moment in your imagination, the stronger the neural pathways leading to this eventual reality will become.

We sit cross-legged on my bed, facing each other, eyes closed. I rest my fingers on my knees and manifest the crap out of our lives together. The two of us making percolator coffee, leaning against a rugged breakfast bench that's etched with decades of markings by students like us, who moved to New York to Live (capital *L*). I bring to life the secondhand blender on the bench. The framed drawing of roses on the wall. The retro wallpaper. Specificity is the key to successful manifestation.

Here with Lilah, legs crossed on the bed, I deeply believe that all this will happen. That I don't have MS. That I will get into Juilliard. That I will have a Saint Bernard called Lollipop.

This is the life I choose.

No surprise, Roo's a big Law of Attraction skeptic. He says it's nonsense. Lilah meanwhile swears the science behind it is real. She's spent a lot of hours visualizing her future as a big-shot manifestation expert. Doing a TED Talk. A podcast!

The timer jolts me back to my room and my eyelids flutter open.

"Do you reckon you can manifest your mums into letting you fly to New York without them?" I ask.

Lilah plasters on a smile. "Trust the process, Vinnie!" I can tell, though, she's trying to convince herself.

And this is where I remember how lucky I am. Even though Mum died, even though my body betrays me, my dad is super cool and supportive and is all for Lilah and me flying to New York in January for the audition. Even better, he's giving me early access to the money Mum left in her will, which easily covers the fare. He's constantly printing off stuff like subway maps and Tripadvisor restaurant recommendations. I figure I'll be letting him down if I don't go.

It's not just that Dad wants me to live my best life. He doesn't say it, but he knows as well as I do that New York was pretty special to Mum as it's where she caught the acting bug. She lived there with her best friend, Ruby, the year they finished university. They'd sneak into Broadway shows they couldn't afford to see. Ruby encouraged Mum to sign up for an acting class, which led to her first role. She didn't muck around either. She went straight to the top as Christine from *Phantom of the Opera*.

When I was little, Mum would tell me New York stories while she bathed me or braided my hair. The same stories over and over, never boring because I could see and smell and hear the city through her words.

It's another reason why I need this manifestation to work. Walking Mum's path is a way to breathe her in and keep her close.

CHAPTER 18

ROO: Some Turd-like Behavior

"What do you call this, huh?" Pavlović is hassling me again, this time pushing my head inside his Prius. I should sue the guy for physical abuse. Report him to the authorities at the very least.

"What am I looking at?"

"This!" He points to what looks like a line of mustard as thin as a fingernail. "Someone ate in my car."

"Well, it wasn't me."

"You let customers eat in my car."

"I didn't." I had three customers the other night, and other than Vinnie passing out, my customers were very well behaved. No eating. No puking, even though it was a Friday night.

"You have no respect for other people's property. I should fire you."

All I can picture is me vacuuming the Land Cruiser at six the other morning with Pavlović's half-assed vacuum. Or me driving slowly up his crummy driveway so as not to get dust on the hub-caps. Or me wiping spider crap off the left-side mirror of the RAV4 using a cotton ball that barely covered my finger.

No respect at all.

"Please don't fire me," I say. "I need the money."

A smile twinges the corner of his mouth. I really am stupid. I have given him power, again. The last thing he needs. Now he knows I am putty. He knows he can treat me like spider crap on a side mirror and I won't do anything because I need him more than he needs me.

I may as well shove my own head into his stupid Prius and give the mustard a lick.

Times like this, I wish Brad Whitelaw had done me a solid and said, "Yes, please, Roo. Be my sidekick. Follow me to weddings and promo shoots in fancy hotels," rather than what he actually did, which was humiliate me and tell me there was never a job in the first place. That I'd misunderstood the arrangement.

I envision myself, shoulders back, standing up for myself for once. Telling Pavlović where to shove it. Maybe I could shove *his* head into the Prius. Get *him* to lick off the mustard. Instead, I pick up my bucket, careful not to let the water slosh.

"Do you want me to do the hubs on the RAV?" I ask, weak as milky tea.

*

Mum's off work when I get home. She's painting her toenails, her feet against the coffee table with scrunched-up bits of toilet paper between her toes.

"Hi, sweetie. You been at Brad's?"

"Yep." No details. No specifics. "Two-minute noodles?" I fill the kettle.

"I've already eaten. Thanks, though."

"How was work?" I ask.

"Fine. Linda was a turd. But what's new?"

Linda is Mum's Pavlović. One of her supervisors. She has an IQ of about two and is very insecure about it. She takes all her insecurities out on Mum, who she probably suspects is a better nurse than her and all the patients like her a lot better. Wouldn't be hard.

"Anything specific?" I ask.

"Well, she filled out one of the patient's bedside forms

incorrectly. Had the wrong medication, can you believe it? I was tempted not to say anything. Just quietly fix the form myself so the patient isn't murdered by Linda's stupidity. But no. I did the right thing, went to Linda, who basically felt humiliated, and spent the rest of my shift undermining me, pointing out everything I was doing wrong. Like, who cares if I don't roll up the bandages in a perfect scroll? No one does."

"Very turd-like behavior," I say.

"So, what are you doing at Brad's right now? Anything cool?" She lowers her feet from the coffee table and wiggles her turquoise toes. "I've started following him on Instagram to see the kind of shoots you might be working on. Did you go to that wedding at Claremont on Saturday? It looked beautiful."

Yikes. This lie is going to get a whole lot harder to maintain if Mum is tracking my whereabouts via Whitelaw's Instagram.

"Nope," I say. Simple as anything. Keep it cool. "Just backroom stuff. I mainly work on edits."

"Can I see some of the photos?"

"Nah, not really. Brad's really cagey, you know. Client confidentiality."

"Totally!" She walks across the carpet, her toes turned upward. "It's good to be cagey if your clients are paying you top dollar for a few photos. Hey, I'm just going to lie down for a bit. My back is being a jackass. I start again at six p.m."

"I thought you had tonight off," I say. "We were going to go to Jo's, remember? Then we were going to watch *Shawshank Redemption* again." Our joint favorite movie is on SBS at the moment.

"Sorry, baby boy. It's Sandra's birthday, so I said I would cover for her." She yawns and waddles, toes up, to the bedroom.

She says it's for Sandra. But I know Mum will take any shift on offer. Being a single mum, it's habit.

I open the drawer and pull out the Extra envelope. It literally has *Extra* written in permanent marker, which is why I call it that. It's our savings. Mum says it's for a rainy day, but I'm kind of hoping she'll use it on herself. One of those art courses she likes circling in the community college brochure, maybe.

I tuck fifty dollars inside from my pay. Then another. The envelope is fattening like a pig at Christmas. Makes a happy thump against the table when I slap it. I'll put the rest of my pay into our joint bank account in the morning.

Pavlović is a jerk, but it's nice to be able to help Mum with the bills and everything. She's been doing this by herself for so long. Twelve-hour shifts, six, sometimes seven, days a week.

There was no Extra envelope when her back went last year. Six whole weeks without Mum being able to work. Rupert, the landlord, thumping on our door on the first Wednesday of the month, shoving red-striped letters through the slot.

Even with our fat pig envelope, I understand why Mum feels the need to take every shift.

CHAPTER 19

VINNIE: I'll Cling to You Like a Connector Pen

"Good luck with announcements today, Vinnie!" calls Tara on our way to assembly. She blows me a kiss. I catch it, squish it against my heart, then push it in my pocket. My future in New York might be a tenuous dream. But if Molly's right about what Ms. Montague says and my gut instinct is anything to go by, then Drama Captain is in the bag.

It's been nearly three days since the party, and so far, no one's told Lilah they saw Freddie and me dancing together. It might be optimistic, but I'm hopeful I'm in the clear. When I see him lingering at the lockers with Blake Pike and Billie Jones, though, I worry my luck's run dry. He's smiling a bit too hard. I can tell it's for me, but Lilah thinks it's for her.

"Aren't you guys going to assembly?" she asks them, hip tipping in Freddie's direction. "The parents are already here."

Freddie chortles. "Course! Some of us have been waiting for this assembly for months. Haven't we, Vin?"

"Come on, Lilah! We need good seats!" I drag her away.

The whole school and most of the Year Eleven parents are gathered in the gym. Dad couldn't come because he has to teach at St. Martha's. Both of Lilah's mums made it. They wave as we pass and join the rest of our grade in the front three rows.

When everyone's finally settled, our principal, Ms. Parker, strides onstage, wearing a rust-colored suit and strappy sandals. She lifts the mic from its cradle—a slow, tedious event that makes me want to get up there and do it for her. Her sloth-like slowness gives me that feeling you get when you're stuck in a bad dream and your limbs are chalky.

"With our Year Twelves graduating next week, we embark on a new chapter. The people we are about to bring onstage will be your leaders next year. A good leader is not a boss. Nor the most popular student. A good leader is someone who listens. Who cares. Who pays attention." I squeeze Lilah's arm, wishing hard that Ms. Parker could talk a bit faster.

"The vote was democratic," she goes on, "but teachers leaned in with their advice and input, as they always do. We will be collaborating with your leaders, so it's important we get along. Now, without further ado . . ." She clears her throat. Lilah and I tip forward, clutching each other like connector pens. "Melaleuca House Girl Captain: Sherry Rogers."

We clap. Someone whoops. Sherry trots onstage. She's full of bubbles, which I completely understand.

"Melaleuca Boy Captain: Nadeem Ali."

She rattles off names and the honorary person comes onstage and lines up next to Sherry. Being the Arts, we're way down the list. After Sports, obviously. Probably after Music. Just before the School Captain announcement, most likely.

Ms. Montague sits onstage on a yellow plastic chair with the other subject heads. I try to catch her eye, but she's focused on the procession of captains, clapping ceremoniously for each.

"Sports Boy Captain—" Lilah and I both mouth Freddie's name. But Ms. Parker says, "Jake Windemere."

"Huh?" I say just as Lilah says, "What?"

Someone shushes us. *What?* We are genuinely shocked. Freddie's clearly Sports Captain. There must be an error. He's captain of the Rugby Firsts. Captain of the cricket team. State champion swimmer *and* state champion javelin thrower. All-around nice person too.

I spin in my chair to catch his expression through the heads behind us. He lowers his eyes. His shoulders are noticeably hunched.

"Poor Freddie!" I write on Lilah's arm with my nail.

She draws a sad face on mine. You don't expect this kind of stuff to happen to Freddie Sinclair.

Jake jogs onstage and pumps Ms. Parker's hand. He beams out at us, clearly stoked. Seeing him there, eyes twinkling with sporty energy, I realize that of course he's an obvious choice for Sports Captain. The system never lies. Jake will be fine. Freddie will be fine.

The knot of nerves tumbles in my belly—if Freddie didn't get Sports, is there a chance I'll be overlooked for Drama? *No, Vinnie, you're being stupid.* Ms. Montague told Molly I was Captain. I've had my sights set firmly on the position since playing Matilda in Year Seven.

Sports, Debating, Music, finally . . . Drama. Lilah squeezes my hand so hard it hurts. I press both our hands to my knee to stop it from jiggling.

"Next year's Drama Captain is . . ." I nearly bite off the tip of my tongue. "Lilah Gatwiri."

My best friend's name drifts. She lets go of my hand, squeals, and rushes onstage. Only halfway up does she think to look back at me, a *sorry* carved into her expression.

I smile for her. Because that's what best friends do. We shine for each other. This is a huge moment for Lilah. She's never the lead. Always the B+. It's Vinnie, then Lilah, when choosing sporting teams, improv teams, and Biology groups.

Tears sting the corners of my eyes, while Lilah shakes Ms.

Parker's hand. She looks out at us and smiles her beautiful heart out. She seems taller onstage. I'm not used to seeing her up there. We're either onstage together or in the audience together. Always.

But there she is—next year's Drama Captain.

I am happy for her. I really am, I tell myself urgently.

The rest of the announcements are muted. I am sure names are called and people certainly come onstage. None of them are me.

What just happened? Did the manifestation break?

Then a thought occurs—*Could I be School Captain?*

Vice, possibly? I'm giddy, just imagining it. Okay, okay. Vice or School Captain would be a fair compensation for Drama Captain. I slide crossed fingers under my thighs.

Tilda Rohanson is Vice Girl Captain. Okay, that makes sense.

Shan Lee is Vice Boy Captain.

"Boy Captain is Freddie Sinclair!" says Ms. Parker. She claps like he won an Oscar. Everyone roars like crazy. They stomp their feet. Wolf whistle. Freddie high-fives a few people on the way up. He's confident and smug, as if he knew this was the universe's plan all along. He winks and waves at me. I squirm but lift a hand to show I am happy for him.

Lilah's all eyes on Freddie. The two of them are school royalty up there, waving and smiling at each other. I try to visualize myself and Freddie as co-captains. Will that be weird for Lilah, if, by some crazy chance, I am elected School Captain?

There's only one role left to announce.

"Finally, our Girl Captain for next year is . . . Verity Barrigos. Come to the stage, Verity!"

The auditorium is a vacuum. I slide back in my seat, numb.

CHAPTER 20

ROO: Sinewy Legs and Untied Laces

"You're covering a driving job for Mullins while he's at a doctor appointment." Pavlović throws me the Prius keys.

In broad daylight? With Mum not yet at work?

"No." I push my shoulders back. Assertive, you might say.

"What you say, huh?"

"I'm not employed to drive for you. I'm your cleaner."

I know I am pushing it. He's a head and shoulders shorter than me but he gets right up close. His pointed nose is angled up at me. I can see the gray hairs growing inside. A booger clings to one, desperately.

"You drive for me when I ask you to," he says quietly. "No discussion." His breath is tinned fish.

I could work at Macca's. Tell Mum it's a side gig. Tell her I'm making extra money for a new camera. That Brad doesn't pay me enough. I could pick up a cheap secondhand camera on eBay. Tell her it cost an arm and a leg. Meanwhile, I'd siphon money into the bills before they turn red.

Instead, I take Pavlović's keys because I am a rotten coward and he's in charge.

Fifty-six Green Street is a ramshackle unit in blond brick. A wonky cactus fights for its life out front. A blue bucket is upturned on the overgrown lawn.

All the things you notice.

I don't recognize Smarty76 at first. He's hunched over, wearing an oversized flannel. Orange hair puffed out to one side.

As he gets closer, I see Timberland boots with untied laces and know then who Smarty76 is. My stomach twists.

He gets in the car without paying attention to me. He's tapping stuff on his phone the whole time. I feel his knees press into my back through the car seat. He's a giant of a man—too large for the Prius. I subtly pull my seat forward, hoping not to attract attention.

I could go an entire car ride without Brad Whitelaw realizing it's me driving him across town, and I won't have to live through the humiliation of our last conversation again.

Brad's my first silent passenger. Doesn't say hello or how are you. It begs the question of why he ended up as a school counselor. But maybe his silence was construed as listening. Students thought they were being heard, meanwhile Whitelaw was checking Facebook under the desk.

I wasn't mentally unwell or anything. But all my teachers from Mr. Ambrose to Ms. Lee thought I should see Whitelaw. Maybe they thought he'd run some tests, check to see which parts were screwed loose. Uncover the great mystery of Useless Roo.

He didn't do tests or check for loose parts. Instead, we did a lot of sitting around in silence, just as we're doing now. One day, for whatever reason, I commented on the photo of the lighthouse hanging behind his head. Said I loved how somber it was and how it made me feel that the world was infinite and empty. At first, he looked at me long and hard. Then he said, "Good. You see it too. You clearly have an eye, Roo."

I wondered what sort of an eye he thought I had. A somber eye? A lighthouse eye? The eye of empty infinities?

Turned out, he meant I had an eye for photography. We spent the next few sessions talking about lighting effects, white balance, and saturation. He showed me his latest work on his phone and even brought in a few printouts. He gave me a small lithograph he'd made that morning from soil rustled up from his dad's grave. Morbid.

I started looking forward to chats with the guidance counselor, despite telling Mum I'd see a counselor over her dead body. Didn't tell her that Whitelaw and I never talked about me, or about my head and all its faults. We never mentioned what happened to Aggie. All we ever talked about were photos.

I watch him now in the rearview mirror, his head bent, frowning at his phone like the world is scheduled to end this Thursday.

It's my fault. I let him draw me in. I let myself fall down a rabbit hole of apertures and shutter speeds.

It was my fault for getting excited when he told me to visit his development lab on a Saturday. For riding there on my bike, a dumb grin on my face.

It was my fault for not understanding that the phrase "photography apprenticeship" meant doing crap for Whitelaw unpaid. And here was me being a dumb-ass, thinking it might be a good moneymaking option while I completed my diploma at TAFE. Here was me thinking Whitelaw's so-called apprenticeship was a viable reason for leaving school in Year Ten.

I pull up now in front of Freckles, a café opposite the supermarket.

Out he climbs—long, sinewy legs in cargo pants, laces untied. He lopes toward the café without once lifting his head.

Sometimes it pays to be invisible, I think as I exhale and drive back up to Pavlović's to finish vacuuming the RAV.

CHAPTER 21

VINNIE: Once a School Counselor

I've never ditched school before. Not even for a minute. In fact, my school attendance record is so spotless, you can see through it. But here I am, fast-walking during school hours toward Roo's apartment because he's the only person I want to see right now.

I bang on his door, hoping he's not at work.

"Roo?" I call. No answer.

He must be at the photography studio in town. I guess he could be at TAFE. But the studio is closer, so I head there.

My phone pings on the walk.

Where are you? Are you okay? Xx

Lilah. I can't. I turn on airplane mode.

The center of town's stone quiet with everyone doing their thing. The faster I walk, the less I can cry. And that knot in my chest? That's something I can use for a future part, for sure.

I trawl through what I did wrong. Not trying out for *The Wizard of Oz* surely didn't help. What was I thinking? At the time, Ms. Montague swore community theater was necessary for my Juilliard application and if I had to choose, choose *Gatsby*. But the other students wouldn't know or care about that.

Could I have been nicer? Verity Barrigos is nice to everyone. Too nice, maybe. I once saw her hugging a kindergarten kid the whole lunch break. Like, is that even appropriate? She's also ridiculously nice to teachers, helping them carry stuff and always staying back to pack up the classroom long after everyone else leaves.

I should have done that.

Did I do something to annoy Ms. Montague? Try too hard? Talk too much?

I don't understand. I've been manifesting *Drama Captain* my whole life.

I think back to what Molly said at the cast party, when she got my hopes up that the decision was already made. Was she talking about Lilah, not me? Maybe she meant we should be excited about *Lilah*.

A brand-new sob wells inside me, making me feel like the world's worst friend.

I'm pretty sure I know where the photography studio is. I go down the wrong alley at first, then find the right one.

Our old school counselor, Brad Whitelaw, has his name in white cursive on the shop window. It's the smallest pane of glass you've ever seen. But *studio* implies small.

I never saw Mr. Whitelaw for counseling. He seemed like a bit of a loser to me. I couldn't understand why Roo spent so much time in his office. Like, how's this dude helping exactly? When Mum died, I told Dad I'd see him. I didn't, knowing Whitelaw couldn't bring her back. Nor could he cure heartbreak. If his hallway demeanor was anything to go by, he would have only made the mess in my head worse.

The bell tinkles as I push open the studio door. The person at the desk looks up from his phone.

"Hi, Mr. Whitelaw," I say.

"Hello?" He looks confused, then his eyes settle as if adjusting to the dark. "Vicenza Smith?"

"Yes, Vinnie. Um, I'm looking for Roo?"

Half his mouth lifts, which could be happy. Something tells me it's not.

"Roo? He hasn't dropped by in months."

"He hasn't?" I'm confused. "Isn't he doing his apprenticeship here?"

Mr. Whitelaw laughs. "God, no."

I bristle, mama hedgehog style, hating his tone.

"He's great at photography. You don't need to scorn him," I say.

"Not scorn, just . . ." He sighs. "Anyway. He's not here."

Mr. Whitelaw goes back to his phone. Great guidance counselor. How he got let into a school to support students, I'll never understand.

Outside in the alley, I switch off airplane mode, slide away a million messages from Lilah, and call Roo.

"Vinnie?"

"Where are you, Roo?"

"Work."

I'm quiet. Should I tell him?

"What's up?" he says. "I thought you weren't meant to have phones at school anymore."

"I'm not at school." My voice catches. I know Roo hears it. He hears everything.

"Wait, are you okay? Where are you?"

I could tell him I'm out front of the Brad Whitelaw Photography Studio.

"Walking to your place. When are you home?"

"Give me thirty minutes."

"'Kay." I hang up.

Holding my phone, I stare at his name and the picture of us

as kids. Seeing us together—Roo and Vinnie—I know why it's him, of all people, I want to talk to right now. Not Dad. Not Lilah.

Roo.

I pick up the pace so I can be there when he arrives.

CHAPTER 22

ROO: Marching to a Pathetic Tune

"I need to leave early," I tell Pavlović. He ignores me and carries on eating his fishy lunch at the coffee table. The smell of smoked mackerel clogs my nasal passages. Bread crumbs and strands of sauerkraut cling to his stubbled chin. Oil leaves a trail down his white T-shirt. He washes down each bite with a slug of lager. There are already four empty bottles lining the table.

Four empty bottles hanging on the wall, I sing in my head. I also happen to remember the collective noun for mackerel, which makes me laugh silently. A mess of mackerel.

"Pass me the mayonnaise," he says, remembering I'm in the room. He gestures toward the kitchen bench behind him. I pass the jar. He slathers mayonnaise in slabs across what's left of his bread and shoves it in his small mouth. A chunk of mackerel slides toward the carpet.

"Well?" I say, hoping this eating spectacle hasn't put me off food for life.

"Well, what?"

"I'm done with those three cars. I need to head off."

He laughs. Takes another bite and wipes his sleeve across his mouth.

"You done, huh? Clean out my fridge. It hasn't been dealt with in years."

"Daniel, I need to head off. Sorry." There we go again, slumping shoulders. Diminishing.

He slams his glass on the table and leans his elbows on his knees.

"You kidding me, huh?"

"What? No. I have a . . . family emergency."

He checks his watch. "Where I'm from, you work ten hours, not three. You think you fancy? A rich kid, right? Don't like a bit of elbow grease? If I had knocked off after three pathetic hours, you wanna know what my boss would have done?"

No. No, I do not. I shake my head a fraction.

"Cut off my hand!" He waves his un-cut-off hand at me, waggling his small, hairy fingers.

"Really?" I say.

He laughs, mean and thin. "Oh yeah, really. Anyway. No."

"No?"

"No, you can't quit early. Clean my fridge. And after? Sort out the tools in the shed. It's a mess. You knock off when you're meant to knock off. Hear me?"

I never had a dad. If I had, this isn't the kind I'd want. The kind that bosses you around. Has you marching, dancing, even, to their pathetic tune.

I don't say anything as I slide silently toward his fridge. Vinnie is sitting by my door, waiting for me. I need to get to her.

But Pavlović hasn't cleaned out his fridge in years.

I lay mustard, soy sauce, and fish sauce on the bench. Milk, with chunks floating at the surface like icebergs. I open the lid, sniff, and nearly throw up. There's a banana on the back shelf that's so small and black it could be a leech.

Meanwhile, Pavlović finishes his lunch and watches daytime telly, a talk show about sex with monkeys or something. I pitch leech-like bananas and other out-of-date goods from his fridge into the full bin by his sink. Other than the bin and his fridge, his house is a vacuous mausoleum.

If I am quick, I won't be much longer than thirty minutes. Pavlović will no doubt conk out on his couch from all the fish and lager. I'll head out to his toolshed, but really, I'll head home to meet Vinnie.

I pull a wet sponge across the shelves, dry them with a tea towel, and place only five items back, including the mustard, because the rest is long past its use-by date.

As predicted, Pavlović is soon snoring, his head lolling backward. I let myself out.

CHAPTER 23

VINNIE: Maple Syrup

"Where have you been?" I say as Roo approaches. His dark curls are more tousled and messier than usual. I instinctively want to brush them off his face.

"Work. I told you. You okay? You look like yesterday's tacos."

"Thanks, baby cake." I lurch at him. *Squeeze* him. He smells like Windex and familiarity. I let his lie go. Roo will have his reasons.

"Well, what's happening?" He lets us in, reaching behind me to unlock the door. He jiggles it hard then pushes it open. "Is it . . . ?"

He doesn't finish his sentence. I wonder if he wants to ask about Mum. But Roo knows me better than anyone.

Emotion surges. I grab him again.

"Drama Captain," I say into his chest. He's trembling. Wait—is he laughing? I step back.

"No, you don't."

"What?" he says, pushing aside a grin. "It's just—really? This is about being Drama Captain? You ditch school. Drag me out of work for . . ." He chortles now. Hysterical.

"Not Drama Captain!" I slap his chest to stop him from laughing. "I'm *not* Drama Captain! Lilah is! That's what I am trying to say!"

I collapse on my knees, to bury the sobs.

"Oh geez, sorry, Vin." He kneels next to me.

We sit, hunched like this, for ages. He strokes my back as I cry.

"Damn. That's not in the plan, is it?"

"No," I manage. "I mean, am I happy for Lilah? Of course I am. She's amazing. She'll be an amazing captain. But I just thought . . . I thought . . ." The blubs recommence.

This isn't the first time I've cried with Roo. I'm pretty sure I bawled my eyes out that time he hit me on the head with a wooden train when we were tiny. And I definitely cried with him the night Mum died, plus once more at her funeral. He was the only one who didn't feel the need to say anything. He knew that just being with me was enough.

"You know there's no such thing as a predictable life, don't you?" he says after a bit. "And if there was, you wouldn't want it. You'd be bored."

"Not predictable. Just . . . meaningful. A life that makes sense. Like, I'm not Drama Captain. Okay. What else is there, though? Sandy in *Grease*? A place in Juilliard? What if I muck up my audition? What if they hate Australian accents?"

"You don't need any of that to have meaning. You know that, Vin."

I look at him, shocked. "Are you crazy? I *need* all that stuff. It's all there is! Who else am I?"

"So much more."

The terrible truth dawns on me. If I managed to screw up the Drama Captain manifestation, maybe I'll do the same to my New York manifestation. Maybe there will be no place in Juilliard or an apartment with Lilah. Maybe there'll be no dog walks through Central Park. What if I can't manifest my way out of an MS diagnosis? What if this is actually real and the future in my head is the mirage? I'm locked in a dangerous spiral.

Roo patiently strokes my back.

"Pancakes?" he says after a while. I nod and even manage a furtive smile as if pancakes are the actual answer.

*

We sit on his bed, his laptop between us, scraped plates discarded on the floor.

I'm indulging in my maple-syrup-and-too-much-butter-on-my-pancake haze. We debate the collective noun for pancakes for a while. "A pile of pancakes" sounds too boring, in Roo's opinion. Especially as a group of fruitcakes gets to be "an indestructibility of fruitcakes" and donuts are called "a holiness of donuts," which is pretty fabulous.

Meanwhile, Jo March from *Little Women* is telling Teddy she can't marry him because she can't love him the way he needs. I've fast-forwarded through the movie so I can capitalize on this scene.

"Oh no," says Roo, watching me. "You're going to cry again."

"I'm not!" I say. But he's right. The tears beat me to it. I can tell he doesn't really mind. Me, Saoirse Ronan, and Timothée Chalamet—we've done this a bunch of times before.

"How about something cheerful?" suggests Roo, as Saoirse sinks into the grass. "I dunno. *Paddington 2*?"

I light up, thinking of my favorite bear. Then get a better idea.

I type *Rewrite the Stars* into YouTube. It takes Roo a moment to catch on. He groans.

"No. That is not cheerful."

"Shhh," I command, as Zendaya lurches skyward, leaving poor Zac Efron gazing up at her.

"Seriously?" Roo wipes fresh tears from my cheek with his thumb. I smile without taking my eyes off the screen.

"What? It's so *tragic*. But she's so bloody awesome, you know what I mean? Look at her."

He's not looking at her. He's looking at me. I can tell he thinks I am a total blubber fish, which I'm not. I'm just deeply connected with my emotions, and Zendaya is the combination code that works every time.

Roo takes over the keyboard and types *Paddington marmalade scene* into YouTube.

As I watch him chuckling to himself, I wonder why he didn't tell me about Brad Whitelaw. Was he embarrassed?

I can't help myself. "Why didn't you tell me about Brad?" I say when Paddington is done plating up.

Roo's quiet, his eyes glued to YouTube, even though the clip is over.

"Mr. Whitelaw's a slob," I say. "You could have told me it didn't work out with him."

"It didn't work out with him," he says. "There. I've told you now." He still won't look at me.

"We used to tell each other everything." I try not to sound too whiny.

"Ah-huh."

I sense Roo retreating into a shell.

"You didn't like working for him?" I start gently. "I totally get it. Like, how does he even think he's going to make a living with that bad attitude? Who wants to hire a guy like that to drip on their wedding day?"

"It's not that. It was . . . a misunderstanding."

"Okay."

We sit quietly for a while until I decide to leave it. I take the plates to the kitchen to rinse them in the sink.

CHAPTER 24

ROO: Sipping Coffee from Metal Cups

"Here, I'll do that," I say.

"It's fine!" Vinnie looks and sounds a lot chirpier than when she first arrived. I'm gutted that she didn't get Drama Captain. Not that I personally care about that stuff. But I know Vinnie does.

"So, next year . . . is there a Plan B or something?" I ask.

That makes her really smile, just as I knew the word *plan* would. She and Lilah love a good scheme. I'm more "How about we wait and see?" Look how far that got me . . . all the way into the arms of a freaking sadist. Makes you wonder if I should start a vision board or some other form of manifestation rubbish.

"Well"—she puts her hand on her hip and holds a fork in the air—"my new and brilliant plan is to support Lilah one hundred percent. I'll be her supporting role, for once. I can do it. I just need to get into the right headspace."

"There's the Vinnie I've always loved." The word slips out before I can retrieve it. She doesn't seem to notice. It's as if I have just told her she's my favorite T-shirt.

"Yeah, I guess I'll also focus on the role of Daisy and give it my everything. I have to learn resilience and bounce-back if I'm going to make it in the industry anyway." I smile at her rising optimism. Her expression suddenly changes. "You booked your tickets, didn't you?"

I'm blank.

"To *Gatsby*?" she gasps, all panicky. "Tell me you booked! You know their shows always sell out."

"Um . . ." I fumble for my phone, press a few buttons, and show her the "allocation exhausted" message. She groans.

"Leave it with me. There will be a cancellation and I'll get you a ticket. Or the promo seats! They usually come available a couple of nights before the show. It'll be fine. You can't miss it, Roo. I'm Daisy!"

"Of course I won't miss it," I say, kicking myself for not signing up for the community theater's newsletter or whatever I needed to do.

"Can I see that?" She reaches for my phone. "That photo on your home screen. It's one from Crystal Shower Falls, right?"

"Yeah." I open the Vinnie folder for her and locate the original. The one of her with vapor gathering on her nose, face up toward the cliff face, a secret smile on her lips. Pretty much my favorite photo ever.

"Wow, I look pretty hot here." She grins.

I laugh. "Down, boy. Yep. You look hot." I press a palm to my cheek, hoping it's not flaming. The last thing I need is Vinnie working out that I have an insane crush on her.

She swipes through, biting her lower lip, her eyes bright. I can tell how happy this makes her, seeing pictures of beautiful her, in beautiful parts of the world. I wonder if she thinks it's weird there's so many of her on my phone. That I've kept them all. If she does, she doesn't say anything.

"I haven't thought about all this in forever," she says.

"I know, right?"

She's still looking at my phone as she moves toward my room and drops onto my mattress. I sink next to her and look over her shoulder. I should go back to Pavlović before he wakes from his stupor. But leaving Vin feels impossible.

"This one—" She holds up the phone so I can see. "How fun was that day?"

"At the weird amusement park?" I say. "Yep. It was fun."

Green Valley Farm is an outback amusement park where you can risk your life on homemade rides, including a roller coaster. Riding it was possibly the most dangerous fifteen seconds of my life. They have a museum where you can see animals with too many heads and too many legs. It's an unusual place. But Vinnie's right. We had fun.

We always had fun.

"How about this?" I move closer. "Girraween?"

"Place of flowers," she says. "I love how you captured the light here. You're really good at this, aren't you?"

"What, snapping photos on my phone?"

"Nah, dude. Capturing more than photos. Capturing . . . I don't know . . . It's hard to describe. But that's the whole point. You don't need to because you have these." She stabs the screen.

"What are you doing?" I ask.

"AirDropping these to myself. Is that okay?"

"Yeah, it's okay. Sure."

There's no method to her selection process. Some feature her. Some don't. All harness that feeling we used to have, though. That feeling me, Mum, Aggie, Mike, and Vin used to get when we camped together. Waking up in foggy fields. Adults sipping coffee from metal cups. Mike and Aggie singing around the fire. Mum trying to harmonize. Me and Vinnie belly flopping into muddy water. Plucking leeches from each other's backs as we lay on towels in dappled sunlight.

It's so painful whenever Aggie dips even a toe into my memory. I guess it's not that surprising, since she was Mum's oldest friend, Vinnie's mum, and basically my second mum. Now I let that old camp feeling gush through me so hard, it could be Ebor Falls after the rain; so hard, I'm not even thinking about Pavlović or my lack of worth as a human, or any of it.

I'm just here, with Vinnie, and a folder made by gods.

CHAPTER 25

VINNIE: The Curve of Her Calf

I haven't looked at pictures of Mum in forever. I close my eyes to her wherever she is. But here I am, on Roo's bed, looking at pictures of her. Because in these photos, it's not really Mum. Here, she's a tiny, smiling shape of a person somewhere in Phone Land.

Then I stop flicking because in this photo, I see her properly, and my chest constricts.

She stands on Bald Rock, in Girraween National Park, mostly shadow and hiking boots. The curve of her calf grows out of the stone like a tree. It's a strong calf, like ironbark. Here, she's resistant to everything.

I remember this day clearly. Mum was in one of her manic "Let's walk faster!" moods. She had us charging up Bald Rock, sweating like crazy. The whole time, she sang Andrew Lloyd Webber's songs. If we were close enough to join in, we would.

All of a sudden, the photo makes me angry. Why'd she have to die? She was strong. She should have held on. She would have aced MS. Learned to live with the pain. Gotten whatever support was out there. She was A+ at everything, so why not try to ace this?

Even though the photo twists my guts, I select it and AirDrop it to my phone.

Roo's close, his breath warming me. "What are you thinking?" he asks softly.

My vision blurs. Not this again. It's only been a few days

since the last bout of symptoms. But with the intensity of this afternoon . . . I breathe in hard, hoping to relax my nervous system and outwit it before it outwits me.

“I should go,” I say.

“Oh.” He sounds disappointed. “You want a lift?”

“I’ll be okay. Fresh air will do me good.”

I walk until I can’t walk anymore because my legs are jelly. I sink onto the bench on Hospital Hill and close my eyes. I recite my lines for the play over and over, the evening air cooling my skin and making me new again.

CHAPTER 26

ROO: Dog Toy Lost Its Juice

After Vin leaves, I drive up Pavlova Hill and sneak around the house toward the toolshed. I refrain from peering through Pavlović's living room window. I've been hoping and praying to someone that he's still in a drunken mackerel coma.

I'm kneeling on the dusty concrete, putting mismatching drill bits in a pile, when cigarette smoke announces his presence from the doorway.

"Where were you, huh?" he says. I swallow without looking up.

"When?"

"Earlier. You weren't here. You weren't inside. Look at me when I'm talking to you."

"Bathroom, maybe?" I push myself onto my haunches to face him. He comes closer and kicks the small pile of drill bits. They scatter with a tinny clink. I flinch despite myself when he taps ash into my hair.

"You know what I don't like, Roo Bean?"

"No, what's that?"

"A liar." He's a confusing guy. He's smiling, but I know he's not happy.

"Nor do I." I stand and dust my knees. Shake out my hair.

"Then why lie, Roo Bean, huh?"

I shrug. "I told you—"

He cuts me off and grabs my shirt collar. I don't have room to breathe.

"It's a girl, isn't it?" Still smiling.

"What?" I wheeze.

"I tell you I cut off your hand. You leave anyway. My guess is it's a girl. No other reason than a girl. She good-looking or something?"

I try to shake my head, but the whole guy's-got-me-by-the-collar thing isn't making it easy. I try to pull away, but he grips harder.

I could kick him—right there where it'll definitely hurt. Sink a knee into his balls. It would be easy. Then I'd walk out of here with some dignity.

Instead, I let him hold me. All I do is wheeze like a pathetic dog toy that's lost its juice.

At last, he releases. I stumble backward and try to recover my breath.

"Show me your phone," he demands.

My brain's too deprived of oxygen to think clearly. I hand it to him. He holds it up to my face for facial recognition and smiles smugly as he scrolls through my private life.

"Vinnie, hey. Strange name for a girl. You gay, are you?"

I hate him.

"She's a girl," I say. "My best friend."

His smug smile deepens as he keeps scrolling. I wish I could see what he is looking at. I want to grab my phone back but instead I'm motionless, watching.

"This her?" He turns the screen to me. Vin smiles back, her cheeks pink with life. She's waist-deep in the water hole near Girraween, wearing a cute floral bikini. I feel sick. "Well?" he says.

I nod, not knowing what else to say or do. Somehow, I know I'm letting her down. Letting myself down.

He whistles through his yellow teeth. Vin mightn't be able

to hear him, but I can. I see his look too—his leery, greasy gaze traveling over her body.

My fist disconnects from my thoughts and surges at his eye socket. He stumbles back, shocked.

"What the hell?" he murmurs, casing his eye in his palm. "You *hit* me?"

Yeah, I did, I guess. I've never hit anyone or anything in my life, except my pillow. Rage, though, flickers through me, making me think I could do it again.

"Don't you ever look at Vin like that again," I say, before I return to previous pathetic shades of Roo. I snatch my phone and stride away, wondering if someone can please tell me where they put Roo Carpenter.

CHAPTER 27

VINNIE: Shine for Her

Later, when the symptoms subside and the light fades, I find Dad at home, at the kitchen bench, marking papers for St. Martha's Secondary, where he teaches English.

"Hey, Dad." I prop myself against him.

"Vin!" He checks his watch. "You're home early. I thought you said you'd be at Lilah's this afternoon."

I shrug. Ah yes. Lilah.

"She had something on. What's for dinner?" I survey the assortment of ingredients strewn across the bench. Dad's an Uber Eats guy at heart. A HelloFresh guy at best. It's rare to see a Coles bag in our kitchen.

He beams at me. "Fried rice."

Fried rice was Mum's thing. Dad's favorite dish, sure. But Mum was the chef. She studied YouTube channels to learn how to crisp tofu to perfection and sourced what she called "real" ingredients from an Asian grocer on the Tweed.

An hour later, the ingredients remain on the bench because Dad's still marking. *The 7:30 Report* drones in the background.

"Shall I get dinner started, Dad?" I reach for a knife.

"Oh, darn. Sorry, Vin. Got waylaid. Let's do it together."

Shoulder to shoulder, we slice onion, crush garlic, grate ginger. The ingredients make a Venn diagram on the board.

The day's events press against my chest. I want to tell him everything. About how disappointed I am. How mad I feel. How worried I am that I will resent Lilah. That she and I will drift apart. But also, that I missed the signpost saying, "Drama Captain this way!" and now I don't know where I am.

It's only when the dishes are done that I at last have the guts to say, "Dad?"

"Yeah?"

"I'm not Drama Captain."

"Oh, Vin."

He hugs me because he gets it. The tears brim. But it's okay. I've wanted this so bad. *Of course* I am disappointed. I'm allowed to cry.

"You know, I was never Drama Captain either, and I turned out okay."

I wipe my cheek with my sleeve. "You hate acting. Why would you— Oh, it's a joke."

"I was never an anything captain. Never got decent grades. Rarely picked for the team. But I kept doing what I love, reading what I love, listening to what I love, and look at me now! Married my dream girl, had a beautiful, talented daughter, and just the other day, completed a cryptic crossword in under an hour."

I laugh. Neither of us say that the dream girl died, and isn't an hour kind of long to spend on a crossword? Because Dad has a knack for making me feel less dramatic, and that's exactly what I need right now.

It's on the tip of my tongue to ask, *What would Mum have done in this situation?* But I let it slide. Dad's as bad as I am at Mum conversations. We leave them on the floor like dirty laundry, stepping over little piles to get to where we're going.

In my room, I finally let Lilah's messages flood in.

You hate me.

I'm so so sorry.

Vinnie?????

Please reply!!!!!

I'm the worst friend eva.

I love you.

I am so so sorry!!!

Are you okay?

Where are you?

Please reply! I've tried to call you a billion times.

I hate myself.

Going to Ms. Parker right now to resign.

She sent that last message more than an hour ago. I call her immediately.

"Please tell me you didn't."

"Didn't what? Where are you, Vin? What happened to you? I've been trying to reach you all afternoon! Are you okay?"

"Please tell me you didn't find Ms. Parker."

"She had a medical appointment. Ms. Montague made me feel heaps better, though, telling me that you'll be okay, because you have so much else great going on. But don't worry. I'll go see Ms. Parker before class tomorrow. Everything will be fine!"

"Take a breath, Li," I say. "It's already fine. In fact, it's more than fine. I am so stoked for you. You're Drama Captain! And I get to be your second in command."

"Really?" she says softly.

"Really."

As I say it, I feel a burn in my chest for Lilah. I can shine for her. It's completely plausible. This is what being an actor is all about, right?

CHAPTER 28

ROO: Feeling Good about Ramen

I drive away in a delirious stupor. Baker Boy's "In Control" is at full volume. I thump the beat on my steering wheel.

By the time the song's finished, I've landed, metaphorically speaking, in reality with a bang. I pull over and slump against the wheel, half laughing, half crying, wondering what the hell just happened.

A cow in the paddock beside me looks through my window then takes a dump.

"Yeah, that's it, Cow. Tell it how it is," I say aloud. She walks off as if I've offended her.

So, this is me—one part knight in shining armor, one part unemployed. I could be cocky about this whole event if Mum and I didn't have an electricity bill clipped to the fridge.

Mum will pay it. She always does. But that's not the point.

I'm going to have to work at McDonald's. KFC. The gas station. At this point, I'm about ready to slink over to Mum and tell her what's what: I didn't get the studio gig. I've been doing crap work, but because I am forever screwing things up, I can't even do that. So now I am going to go look for more crap work.

She'll look at me with those big round eyes of hers, half hidden under her home-cut bangs. Then she'll say something along the lines of: "Roo, you aren't a failure. But you need to finish school."

Which isn't exactly an option, is it? Because who then is

going to make enough money for us? What if Mum's back goes again? What if we lose the apartment?

The only option is to pull up my big boy pants and get a job. Ideally, not working for a creep.

It would be nice to tell Mum. But it isn't possible.

I could tell Vinnie. She already knows Whitelaw's gig didn't work out. My fingers punch out a draft message: Funny story. Punched my boss to protect your honor. Now, no longer have a job.

But I delete it. She already knows I'm a loser for blowing the Whitelaw apprenticeship. I may as well let her go on thinking I'm putting my energy into the photography course. At least that way I'll still have fully-fledged human *potential*.

So I text:

Fun hanging out with you today. Sorry you missed out on the captain thing. You're better than that anyway. Oh, and sorry I didn't book in time. My bad.

She's replying. I wait. Then,

Yeah, you should be sorry. JK. I'm sorry you didn't book in time too. But I'm more sorry the promo seats I tried to score fell through. You could sneak in the back door once the show starts?

The Citadel

7 p.m. Thursday

I could sneak in. It'd be fun to see Vinnie do her thing. It always is. Once, she was Rafiki from *The Lion King*. She was amazing. So funny.

I envy her, that she knows who she is and what she wants. I make fun of her and Lilah's manifest crap, but in truth, I'm jealous. They have a map and they know where they are going.

I decide to head home and make dinner for Mum. It's nice to have some kind of a plan.

*

"You been out taking photos?" Mum eyes the SLR camera on my shoulder. No. This is just part of my elaborate ruse. "I'd love to see what you've been doing."

"You know how I feel about sharing personal stuff," I say. "How do *you* feel about ramen, on the other hand?"

"I feel excellent about ramen, thank you very much." She pops the lid off a Corona and sinks into our mustard velvet couch. She tucks her feet under her butt.

"I have some news," she says.

"Oh yeah?" So do I. But I'm sure as hell not sharing.

"You know that course at the Murwillumbah Community College? Guess what?" She waves her phone at me. I abandon the onion I'm slicing, wiping my eyes with my sleeve as I approach. "I actually enrolled."

"The Art of Still Life," I read from her phone. "Good on you, Mum. I've been telling you for ages to do something like that."

"Yep. You inspired me with your photography course and everything. I figured with that savings in the drawer, why not? The teacher sounds amazing. You know he studied at the Royal College of the Arts in London? He's represented by Schneider Galleries."

I gulp when I hear the word *savings*, especially when I see the cost of the course: $1,650. That's more than 130 hours working for Pavlović. *If* I was working for Pavlović. Which I'm not. Because I punched him in the eye.

Just when Mum finally wants to do something for herself. Something she should be doing. Something that isn't working her back into literal submission, doing twelve-hour shifts to keep us afloat.

With me no longer cleaning cars, it won't take long for the buffer to thin and for us both to feel poor and useless again. Certainly no still-life courses with the Royal College of the Arts guy.

I could plead for my job back, I suppose. Tell Pavlović I'll do anything. Clean out his fridge for the rest of his life. Open his beers. Drive whatever car he wants wherever he wants. Smile at his customers and keep up the Pavlović brand. Never abandon a shift no matter how much Vinnie needs me.

I feel ill just thinking about it.

So I focus on ramen, and intermittently scroll through Jobseeker on my phone. I'll take anything I can before Mum notices the envelope is getting thin and she decides not to do her course.

CHAPTER 29

VINNIE: Mannequin, Poised and Waiting

I have the day off from school because it's the final dress rehearsal before *Gatsby* opens tonight.

"Everybody thinks so—the most advanced people." I do Daisy's monologue into the dressing room mirror. "And I know. I've been everywhere and seen everything and done everything. Sophisticated—God, I'm sophisticated!"

I hold her gaze for a moment, then smile.

No matter how many times I do this part—any part—it feels like everything else melts away and all that's left is the naked mannequin ready for anything. The original form, standing strong and silent in the shop window. No adornments. No accoutrements.

An MS-free, dead-mum-free body, poised and waiting for her next outfit.

"Feeling ready for tonight?" Lilah missed Physics to help me with my costume. She grins at my reflection. It's been two days since the Captain announcement, and I have done nothing but be a supportive and awesome friend. I've shone for her like a freaking star.

"Ready!" I let her fix my headpiece onto my curled wig. She fastens it with bobby pins.

"You look amazing. How great is this dress? So perfect."

I'm wearing Daisy's crystal ball gown. It could have been handpicked by Catherine Martin herself. But, in fact, Lilah and I found it on the Lifeline thrift shop costume rack.

I twirl and heel-kick my silver shoes, which are also perfect.

"You shouldn't watch," I say. "Save yourself for tonight. I don't want you getting bored."

"I'll never be bored!" She slaps my wrist. "Oh, I have a surprise for you for tonight."

I clap my hands. "You do? You have to tell me! You know I hate surprises."

"If I told you, it wouldn't be a surprise. Anyway, it's more about me than you, this particular surprise."

"Now you have to, *have to*, tell me!" I grab her shoulders and get her to face me. She's shorter than me by nearly a head. She rolls her eyes, smiles, and tries to pull away. "Pleeeeease! I can't perform if I know you're holding something back from me. I need Pure Concentration, and this is going to mess with my neural pathways. You can't do this to me!"

"Can you guys be quiet?" Samantha, the stage director, appears at the dressing room door looking more severe than usual. "We're trying to do a scene, and all we can hear is squealing from the dressing room."

"Sorry, Samantha!" I say.

"Sorry," whispers Lilah.

She frowns at us and marches back to the stage.

"Anyway," I whisper, "you were about to tell me the big surprise?"

I can tell by the brightness of her eyes that she's as desperate to tell me as I am desperate to know.

"Okay." She steps closer so there's barely any air between us. "I'll tell you. But you have to promise not to make too big a deal of this."

"I promise." I grab her finger in a pinkie promise.

"Freddie's coming to the play."

"Oh?" I'm confused. Why is this exciting? Does she want him to see me perform? Is she trying to matchmake or something? What happened to her enormous crush?

"Why aren't you more excited?" She looks hurt.

"I'm sorry. Yeah. That's great! Freddie Sinclair!"

"Do you realize how much courage it took for me to ask him to come?"

At last I get it. She's asked Freddie on a date. To see *The Great Gatsby*. Okaaaay. I guess this is good?

"Wow!" I feign the excitement I know I should be feeling. *Supporting role, Vinnie*. "That's amazing! You go, girl."

"I saw him in Biology, and knew I had to ask but felt sick. Like I was going to properly throw up. But I made myself do it. Ask him. By note." She face-palms herself.

"A note? Really, Lilah?" I grin.

"I know. Lame. But, hey! I did it!"

"I'm proud of you," I say.

Samantha reappears. "Daisy, cue."

"Break a leg!" stage-whispers Lilah.

CHAPTER 30

ROO: Wilted Chrysanthemums

There's not a lot going on Jobseeker. Nothing in this town. Not even Macca's has an opening. There is a job as a boner and slicer at the slaughterhouse in the next town, but I can't stomach all that death, not as a vegetarian. Also, transportation would be an issue, as Mum and I only have one car. I have to think creatively if I'm going to make enough of a buffer to keep us afloat.

I remember then that Terri, who used to go to our school, manages Steiner Brothers supermarket. I never spoke to her at school because she was a few grades above me. But desperate times call for desperate measures.

It's still an hour until Vinnie's performance so I have time to drop in.

At the supermarket, I ask for Terri and am sent out the back. She's in an office on the phone when I come through the store. She signals for me to wait, and when she's off, stands and shakes my hand. She's only twenty or something but looks way older. Like me, she left school at the end of Year Ten. Unlike me, she's a successful person.

"Hey, Roo. How's things?"

"Good. I'm just swinging by to see if there's any work going. Happy to do whatever. Cleaning. Stacking. You name it. Out the back is best if you've got it." I don't want to run into Mum in the aisles. That would be awkward.

"Sorry, buddy!" She perches on the corner of her Real

Grown-up Desk like a Real Professional. "You're out of luck. I did need someone to help me with stacking, but filled the role last week. You should have come to me sooner!"

"Yeah." Sooner. How much nicer it would have been working for Terri than Pavlović.

"So is this an after-school thing? Need a bit of pocket money?"

"Ah, I don't go to school anymore. Want to focus on other things." If anyone gets it, it's Terri. Sure enough, she grins.

"That's cool. There's plenty out there beyond school. Look at me!" She sweeps her arm through her office. It is pretty impressive. Terri's running a supermarket.

"Well, if you hear of anything . . ." I say.

"Here, write your number on this. I'll give you a call if anything comes up."

On the way out, I double back past the flowers. I look for the cheapest ones I can find. A slightly wilted bunch of orange chrysanthemums will have to do. Hopefully, Vinnie will be too giddy from her theater high to notice the details. She'll just notice that I thought to bring her something.

"Hey, loser!" It's Zinc Patterson. He's sitting on a skateboard, on the edge of the bowl, defying the laws of gravity. His sidekick, Adam Roland, tic tacs on the path.

"Hey, Zinc." I wave.

"You wanna skate?" he calls.

"Nah." I keep walking toward the theater.

"Hey, Roo! Are you deaf or something? I'm talking to you."

I feel his heat from here. I stop. Turn around. He and Adam approach. Their boards hang from their fingertips. Their walk is slow and deliberate. I note Zinc's new frizzy mullet that he wears with undue pride.

“What? You too good for us?”

“No. I just have somewhere to be. Have a great night.”

He grabs Vinnie’s flowers, sniffs them, and laughs. “Bootiful. Who’s the lucky lady?”

“Just a friend.”

“A friend? Sounds pretty special.”

“She’s fine.” *She’s special.*

“Hey, ask him, Zinc.” Adam elbows Zinc in the ribs.

“Huh? Oh yeah. Adam wants to know—”

“Zinc wants to know—” They’re like Beavis and Butt-Head, these two. A real duo.

“You want in?” Zinc pulls out a little Ziploc bag of pills from his pocket. “We heard you were between things.”

“I’m good,” I say.

“Nah, mate, you don’t understand,” continues Zinc. “We’re making good dough. Just hear me out, brother.”

“I said, I’m good.” Zinc once beat me up at school. It was after a rugby game, and he and his friends were drinking under the grandstand. They thought I was going to rat them out. I wasn’t. Still, he kneed me in the nuts and busted my eye. Now, I instinctively take a step back.

“You still with Pavlović?” asks Adam.

“Not really. Can I have my flowers back?”

Zinc considers them, then pelts them over my head. They land in a sorry mess on the pavement. I sigh, pick them up, and try to straighten them out, but several of the stems are broken or bent.

“I really have to keep going,” I say. “But thanks.”

Zinc’s right. I’m a loser, thanking those bastards.

CHAPTER 31

VINNIE: She's Every Emotion under the Sun

"Here, Vin." Dad looks nervous as he hands me a parcel wrapped in brown paper. We're having a pre-show meal at Yuli's, the dumpling place up the road from the Citadel.

"What is it?"

"Open it."

The paper makes a satisfying crunkle. I fold it carefully so we can reuse it for something else.

There's a photo of young Mum on the cover of a clothbound book. My arteries ice over, protecting themselves. I'm grateful I primed myself by looking at Roo's photos from our trips the other day, otherwise I'd be a sobbing mess.

As I flick through the album, I realize this experience is very different from going through photos I already know. These are pictures of Mum before she had me, being her best self and doing the thing she loved most.

My eyes pool. Dad puts both hands over one of mine. He doesn't say anything for a bit. Then, "I made the album for her when we first got together. I found lots of old photos from her acting days on a hard drive and put them into a book for her. You probably haven't seen most of these."

I don't want to, but I peel open each page, absorbing Mum as Eva Perón from *Evita*, Christine Daaé from *Phantom of the Opera*, and Maria Rainer from *The Sound of Music*. She's every emotion under the sun.

Immediately, I'm swept back to that moment when I was about six or seven, sitting on the bathroom bench studying Mum applying thick swathes of makeup on her face for *The Sound of Music*.

She turned to me, screwed up her nose to make me laugh, then swatted me with the foundation puff. It made me sneeze and giggle at the same time. I got her back with the rouge brush and soon we looked like clowns who had been sent down the rubbish chute.

Her performance was only an hour later, but she didn't mind the mess we were in. She laughed as we washed our faces clean and was still laughing as she reapplied.

"Why would you give this to me now?" My voice is hoarse. "I'm meant to go onstage in less than an hour."

He frowns. "I thought it would inspire you. Your mum was an amazing actress, like you. I nearly forgot about it, but found it the other day under some old gym stuff. I thought you'd like it.

"Sorry," he adds, after a bit. "It was stupid of me. I should have been more sensitive."

I wipe my eyes with the back of my hand, grateful I am wearing waterproof mascara. "Thanks, Dad. It's sweet of you. But I'll look later, okay?" I close the album and drop it into my satchel.

We walk arm in arm to the theater. The sun's setting over St. Martha's chapel. The sky's streaked peach. A cloud of bats forms overhead then disappears.

"You know, Vin—" starts Dad, his voice uncertain. I look up at him. "Your mum—"

"Dad, can we, like *not* do this right now?" My heart batters my rib cage. I feel the emotions swell.

"Sure. Sure. I just want to say, she'd be so proud of you."

We're at the dressing room door. I bury my face against his chest to smother my feelings.

"Love you, Dad," I say. "And thanks for the album. It really was sweet." Our fingertips separate and I slip through the door.

*

I know I shouldn't, but I peek through the curtains. It's a full house. Fuller than full, with people sitting on the stairs. No wonder I couldn't get a ticket for Roo. Murwillumbah Community Theater shows are typically popular, with cast members inviting their family and friends. Throw in some 1920s glamour and you have a sellout.

It's such a bummer Roo's not here. I swear he's made it to most of my shows. Even to that one where I was a lamb whose only line was "Baaaa."

Lilah's front and center because, unlike Roo, she booked tickets the minute they went live. She's wearing a cute stripy suit I helped her buy from The Iconic. Freddie's next to her. He's not in a tank for a change. Instead, he wears a button-down and actual trousers. His hair is combed back. His face is fresh and open, looking around in wonder. Lilah seems tiny next to him.

I assess for signs he's into her, not just stringing her along. My heart would literally break in two pieces if he breaks hers. She's loved him for so long. But all I can see is that Freddie's his usual relaxed self, a casual arm slung over her shoulder. Her, fluttering like a Ulysses butterfly.

"Places!" says Samantha. Someone's given her a dab of rouge, which is shockingly incongruent with her hard-assed military style.

I slip into the theater wings. Nick Carraway strides onstage for his opening line. The curtains part.

CHAPTER 32

ROO: Arsenic in Kombucha

I sit in the lobby, my foot holding the door open just enough to watch the show. I can't hear everything. But I get the gist. Mostly, I get Vinnie. She takes over the stage like any good actress should. The only thing you ever want to watch.

I never read *Gatsby* at school. I had a knack for leaving class texts in my locker or losing them altogether. *Gatsby* was no different. We saw the Luhrmann movie, though. I watched it twice again with Vinnie—not because I'm studious, but because Vinnie can make me do anything.

"Can I help you?" An elderly man wearing a blue-striped cravat and a bright white T-shirt leans toward me. The glob of skin under his neck jiggles, as do his elbows. I swear I've never seen so much excess skin.

"I was told to keep an eye on things here," I say. Kinda true?

"Better close the door. Don't want any sound to travel, do we?" The gentleman pries my foot out of the doorjamb with his own. He's a deft little bugger.

The door squeezes shut and *Gatsby*'s gone. I'm going to miss Daisy's big finale.

I sit, arms crossed, doing my best to hear through the closed door. Their voices float in and out, unclear and indistinct. The old man eyes me like I'm a street rat and he's imagining the trap he's going to set for me tonight. I, meanwhile, have images of dripping arsenic into his kombucha, watching him keel over, and stepping over his body to catch the end of the play.

I don't have arsenic on hand so I resort to leaving the wilted flowers on the bar.

"Tell Daisy these are for her," I say. "From Roo."

I wander into the night, which is still and quiet compared to the bustling warmth of the theater.

CHAPTER 33

VINNIE: Better than Carey Mulligan

"There you are! Vin! You were so, so amazing!" Lilah squeezes me so hard it hurts. I laugh.

"You were great, Vin," says Freddie over her head. He kisses my cheek. I blush, feeling his stubble. Smelling his thick cologne.

I spot Dad smiling warmly through the crowd. He doesn't approach, no doubt giving me my usual length of rope and not wanting to crowd me.

I hear Molly before I see her. Her squeal cuts through the lobby chatter.

"We're going out to Jo's." She weaves her arm through mine. "We need to celebrate! Or do you guys have something organized?"

She looks across at Michael, the guy playing Nick Carraway, who is about a decade and a half older than me, with a toddler at home in bed. The rest of the cast is going out to a bar called Lindarella, which won't let us in because of the whole underage thing.

"I think we're good to go to Jo's," I say.

Dad kisses me good night and heads home. The five of us—me, Lilah, Freddie, Molly, and Jayde—walk in a line down Queen Street toward Jo's, which is the only place in town whose kitchen stays open after eight p.m.

The whole time, I scan the streets for Roo. I'm disappointed he didn't make it, since this was my best performance, I'm pretty sure.

Mental note to self: Send Roo a deprecating message. Promise to never be his friend ever again. Unless of course he apologizes sincerely.

We squeeze into the only empty booth. The hot waitress, Xi, sashays over to take our order.

"I love your new glasses," I tell her. "Too cute."

"Thanks!" She pushes them up her nose. Her bob is also great, but I told her that last time. I don't want to come across as insincere. "Do you guys want me to take your order or do you want to use the QR code?"

We order too much soda and too much ice cream. I should have something savory to settle my wired system. But I'm in the wrong restaurant.

"So, how was my take on Daisy?" I ask Freddie, the scholar. "Did you approve?"

"Hell, yeah. You were better than Carey Mulligan. Don't tell her I told you that."

I laugh. Lilah laughs harder and presses into his shoulder.

"I didn't know you two were a thing," says Molly, swiping her finger between Lilah and Freddie as if scribbling them together. She tips her head to one side. "But now I see it, it kinda makes sense!"

Lilah's hardcore blushing. Freddie's smiling, but he's hard to read. *Are* they a thing? He doesn't deny or object. But he also doesn't confirm. I know Lilah won't, either. She'll wait and wait until things between her and Freddie are contractually bound before she relaxes long enough to call him her boyfriend.

Thankfully, the sundaes steal the moment away from them and the conversation veers back to *Gatsby*. We dissect each role, turning it over and analyzing the actor's interpretation. We do the same to set design and costumes until Xi tells us it's closing time and she needs to clean our table.

Jayde and Molly grab an Uber home. Lilah's mum, Sadie, is picking her and me up. She'll drop me home on the way. Only Freddie is unaccounted for. I'm eager to see what he's going to do when Sadie arrives. Will he kiss Lilah? Arrange another date?

When Sadie pulls up in the dual cab truck, I climb in the back. Lilah and Freddie hover at the door.

"Any chance of a ride, Ms. Gatwiri?" he asks Sadie through her window.

"Sadie's fine," she says. "But sure! Jump in!" He slides into the middle seat so he's between Lilah and me. His thigh is warm through his cotton trousers. My spine prickles with that and the scent of his cologne. If I had to give it a name, I'd say Mango Spice. Post-show adrenaline must be heightening my senses.

Other than whatever the shizz is going on right now in the Freddie department, my body has behaved itself all night. No dizziness. No double vision. Shows have a tendency to exacerbate symptoms. But for whatever reason, my body is being an A+ student.

"How was *Gatsby*?" asks Sadie.

Lilah gives her the recap in excited, supportive tones. I barely listen because Freddie is stroking my bare knee with the side of his pinkie. The tingles in my spine accentuate, racing up and down, spreading through my body. While guilty thoughts needle, I let myself get caught in Freddie's rip.

"Vinnie? This is you." Sadie catches my eye in the mirror.

"Oh, sorry! Thanks so much, Sadie! Bye, Lilah. Love you!" I lean across Freddie (trying to forget about his body and failing miserably) to give her a kiss.

He pecks my cheek as I'm getting out.

"Call me," he says so softly I might have misheard him. But something tells me I didn't.

Upstairs in my room, I have a missed call from Roo and a Snap from Freddie. He must have sent it from the car.

Love heart emoji.

What am I going to do? I need to ignore this. Erase it somehow. This isn't part of the plan. Freddie is Lilah's manifestation, not mine.

After most opening nights, I can't stop replaying every line and scene hours after it's over, celebrating the good bits and trying to figure out where I could have had more inflection. More projection, or less.

But tonight, all I see is the love heart emoji imprinted on the back of my eyelids like a dangerous scar.

CHAPTER 34

ROO: A Wall of Petrochemicals

Vin doesn't call me back. She doesn't message about the flowers. I'm assuming Old Guy failed to tell her who they were from. If he gave them to her at all.

Mum's home when I get back. I can tell because when I open the door, I walk into a wall of petrochemicals.

"Far out! What is that?"

"Sorry, baby. It's turps. Terrible, isn't it? I need a studio."

She gets up to open the window. I wander over to her easel.

"Wow, Mum, it's really good!"

She laughs. "Just blocking in. Don't get too excited. A preschooler could do this."

"No, Mum. Your composition is . . . profound. Like the way you put the shaker here on its own. So lonely. And the mobile phone, standing erect and in command. I love it. You don't need Royal College guy."

"Ha. Well, you clearly have an underdeveloped appreciation for art, if you think that."

I go to my room to wait for Vinnie to call but also to keep searching for jobs.

I put in no keywords and no classification, just *Murwillumbah* into the search function to see what's out there. The only one I'm vaguely qualified for is dish pig at Myrtle's.

It's not the worst thought. Pavlović once bragged about his time as a dishy in a fancy restaurant. About how he worked his way up from the ground. He told me about the fancy meals he got at break. There's that. But more to the point, a dishy hides out back, elbow deep in warm water. It's not the kind of place Mum would likely venture.

I'm giddy with possibility as I compose an e-mail to apply. Before I send it, I read it twenty-five times. Run it through Grammarly then Google Docs. I bet I still manage to balls it somehow.

Under normal circumstances, an e-mail like this would promptly make its way to my Gmail trash can. Maybe it's Vinnie's Daisy or Mum's petrochemicals going to my head. I don't know. Whatever it is, I send the e-mail, my fingers crossed as it swooshes through cyberspace.

CHAPTER 35

VINNIE: Summer Stars

I can't find Lilah at school the next day, which is unusual because we've memorized each other's schedules, and there should be no way we can miss each other. I know she's at school, because her bag's in her locker.

I'm keen to debrief and see if Freddie contacted her. I want to know that the love heart was a mistake. That I am misinterpreting something. That, in fact, they spent hours on the phone last night.

Maybe that's why I can't find her. She's in sick bay, trying to catch up on sleep. Or maybe she and Freddie have dissolved into the back corners of school to mess around.

Imagining that makes me squirm. I push thoughts of the two of them away.

At lunch, I sit with Lu because I still can't find Lilah. She's not answering my messages. Probably because I can hear her phone pinging in her locker.

"Have you seen Lilah?" I ask Lu. "I haven't seen her all day."

"She's been with Ms. Montague."

"She has?" This is almost as bad as imagining Lilah and Freddie together. In some ways, worse. "Do you know why?"

"Something about Summer Stars, Lilah said. Aren't you involved?"

"Summer Stars? Oh yeah."

I want to show Lu I know what they're talking about. I'm the would-be, should-have-been Drama Captain after all. I should know everything about Summer Stars, the creative arts camp Ms. Montague runs by the lake every summer.

Lilah and I actually met at Summer Stars when we were seven and have been going every year since. Every week of the summer holidays, you do these fun workshops, like singing class, guitar lessons, and improv class with teachers who visit from all parts of the country. Then, in the last week of the summer holidays, you perform at the showcase for friends and family.

Because we're finally in Year Twelve next year, we get to be guardians, which means we are assistant coaches, helping little kids prepare for their performances and all that.

I don't know why Ms. Montague and Lilah are having private meetings about this. Is this a Drama Captain thing? I'm shining a bit less for Lilah right now. In fact, I'm cursing her for not telling me about the guardian meeting.

I try to absorb what Lu's saying about the koala hospital they're volunteering for, but I'm finding it really hard.

"I think I need to go to sick bay," I tell Lu. "Sorry to ditch you."

"That's okay. You do look a bit unwell. I was going to say."

I don't go to sick bay. Instead, I go to the Drama rooms, which are meant to be locked because there are no Drama periods today.

Lilah and Ms. Montague sit on the teacher's side of Ms. Montague's desk. I flame with jealousy, seeing them together as colleagues rather than as teacher and pupil.

Shine for her, I tell myself.

CHAPTER 36

ROO: The Finest Establishment

Sonia at Myrtle's replies:

From: sonia@myrtleslaundry.food
To: a_roo_awakening@gmail.com
Subject: Re: job application

Dear Roo,

Thank you for taking the time to apply for the job as dishwasher at Myrtle's Laundry.

As you know, we are a fine dining establishment and expect the very best for our customers. At all levels of business, we run a tight ship. Our chefs are trained in international Michelin Star restaurants. Our waitstaff and sommeliers have also worked at the finest establishments in the country and abroad.

In light of this, we take employment very seriously. And loyalty especially is one of our highest regarded values.

Please visit me at Myrtle's at 4 p.m. today, if possible, for an in-person interview.

Yours sincerely,

Sonia Harbringer
Manager, Myrtle's Laundry

I'm shaking as I read, unable to believe my application has been sort of successful. Myrtle's is a *much* better option than Macca's. Better than selling pills for Zinc and Adam. Better than working on my hands and knees for Pavlović.

My first thought is to tell Mum. But as I am opening up Messages to text her, I remember that she doesn't know I'm currently unemployed. She thinks I am down at Whitelaw's right now convincing an engaged couple they should take the deluxe package—the success of their marriage depends on it. So why on earth would I need a job at Myrtle's?

I text Vin instead. She knows about Whitelaw. Also, she's the kind of girl who'd appreciate the slickness of a place like Myrtle's. Maybe Sonia will give me a freebie every now and again and I can take Vin out for something special. She'll like that, I bet.

I close my eyes for a moment and let myself drift into a fantasy where the two of us sit on either side of the table, elbow to elbow, leaning over the tealight candle. Me, wiping food from her cheek. Her, lit up like a firefly. We wouldn't need to say anything because we know each other so well. Every corner and every secret.

The only secret she doesn't know is that in that moment, all I want to do is lean even closer and taste her lips, like it's the most normal thing in the world.

CHAPTER 37

VINNIE: Limp as Week-Old Lettuce

My phone beeps in my pocket. I check it. Roo's got a job interview at Myrtle's? Weird but cool. Anyway, I have something going on so I love-heart his message and slide my phone away.

"Sorry I missed the guardian meeting!" I say, approaching Ms. Montague's desk. "I didn't realize it was on."

"Oh, it wasn't a guardian meeting," says Ms. Montague. "You didn't miss anything, Vinnie. Actually, we were just about to talk about guardian stuff. Your timing is impeccable as always!"

"Thanks?" I'm confused.

"Sure. Take a seat."

I sit opposite them, on the student side of the desk. Lilah isn't making eye contact, which I am finding uncomfortable. Is she mad at me? Guilty? Even though I have more than ten years' training as an actor, I'm having trouble reading her motivation and emotion in this particular scene.

"So, Lilah and I were just discussing possible guardians for Summer Stars. I'm assuming you're keen, Vinnie?"

"Yes!" I muster enthusiasm. "Lilah and I have been desperate to be guardians forever, haven't we, Li?"

"Yeah," says Lilah. She still doesn't look up.

"Oh, Lilah won't have time to be a guardian. She's helping me directly this summer. But I love how enthusiastic you are, Vinnie. I knew we could count on you."

My stomach curls like a burning leaf. What is this *we* and *helping Ms. Montague directly*? I don't understand. I stare at

Lilah, trying to unlock something in her. But she's busy scribbling on her important-looking notepad.

"You can count on me," I say at last, doing my best to be professional. I'm trained for this. To put on a show.

"Great!" Ms. Montague stands and straightens her pants. "I need a coffee. Can I get you anything, Lilah? I still need you after lunch for a bit, if that's okay. I checked with Mr. Rolfe and he said he was happy for you to catch up with the Math lesson online later."

She grins at us both and strides out, leaving Lilah and me alone on either side of the desk, me looking at her and her looking away.

"Are you going to tell me what that was about?" I ask.

She's quiet, still scribbling.

"Lilah, please."

"I knew you'd be upset," she says.

"I'm upset because I don't understand what's happening. You know I can't be mad at you."

She finally looks up and holds my gaze. Her dark eyes quiver. She pushes aside a piece of hair that's dislodged from her tight bun.

"Are you sure you want me to tell you?" she says.

"Now I'm worried." But I need to know. "It's fine. I promise. Tell me."

"Ms. Montague approached me a few months ago," she says. "She told me she wants to mentor me, to help me reach my goals."

"Okay?" I say, confused. "To be a psychologist?"

"No," says Lilah. "To get into Juilliard."

I'm dead silent. Something ticks loudly in my brain.

"She thinks I have potential to really make it." She turns

away and crosses her arms. "Ms. Montague wants me to stop playing the supporting role. She says I need to step into a leadership role."

The ticking turns out to be an explosive and it goes off, raging through me. Is this what shining is meant to feel like? If so, I want out. I don't like it. Actually, I hate it.

I get up. Walk away from Lilah at the teacher's desk, my best friend, who's secretly been squirreling away nuts while I'm not looking. Taking what I thought was mine but clearly wasn't.

Just as I am about to exit, I turn back.

"Tell me you're not actually auditioning for Juilliard," I say.

"I might." She's as limp as week-old lettuce.

I make my exit, taking the hall in long strides, wishing the tears in my eyes didn't betray how I really feel.

CHAPTER 38

ROO: Dead on Time

I'm so darn tense as I walk up Murwillumbah Street toward Myrtle's. I've worn jeans, which I'm now regretting because sweat paints my legs.

Sweat's no doubt also making ink blots on the back of the only sorta-smart shirt I own, found crumpled at the bottom of the laundry hamper. I rinsed the stink out, blow-dried it with Mum's hair dryer, and even ironed it.

It's a pity it's blue and all anyone will notice are my sweat patches.

I check my watch. It's five minutes to four. I don't want to be early. Or late, obviously. I want to be dead on time so I make a good impression right from the start.

This is my first ever actual job interview. My one with Pavlović doesn't count. It basically involved him lurking around while I kicked a football in the park, like he was a pedophile or something. Then he came up to me and offered me a job. If I'd had options, I might have reported him rather than gone to work for him.

Damn it. I should have checked out interview tips on YouTube before I left. I am suddenly so mad at myself. I walk a block to kill the five minutes but also to calm down.

On my way back up the street, my stomach lurches as I see Zinc and Adam stride toward me. If I know anything about timing, I know that the three of us will meet out in front of Myrtle's incredibly clean glass door at exactly four p.m. All I can hope is that they have somewhere urgent to be. Maybe they'll spot someone cool across the road.

But no.

We meet at four p.m. smack bang in front of Myrtle's. I see the restaurant clearly and it can see me.

"Brother," says Zinc, dapping me up. "Long time no see."

It's been less than twenty-four hours, but I don't tell him that.

"You thought more about our offer?" he asks.

Not now. Really, not now. I steal a glance toward the restaurant and see a strong-looking woman wearing a pink blouse sitting at a table.

"Ah, I'm good for now, Zinc. But thanks, mate, for thinking of me. I just have to—"

"See? Told you he thinks he's too good for us," Zinc says to Adam. He pushes my shoulder. I step back to absorb the impact. It takes everything I have not to cry.

"I don't think that. It's just—look, I have somewhere to be."

"Oh yeah?" Zinc steps closer. Adam does too. The air between us stales. "Where you gotta be, Roo?"

I can't go inside the restaurant. Not now. It'll be leading sharks to blood. "Mum's in the hospital," I say and fast walk down Murwillumbah Street, my heart hammering, my ears ringing, my back dripping sweat. The rest of the street is mute and colorless.

CHAPTER 39

VINNIE: Smoothie Mustache

Where you at? I want to see you

I read Freddie's message over and over, my heart galloping. I write back before I can overthink it.

Heading home. You?

The message is in the ether before I can get it back.

He replies.

Freddie doesn't know where I live, which is a good thing. Wait—maybe he does. They dropped me off last night. Will he remember my street?

Dad's still at work so the house is empty. I need to text Freddie and tell him I have a contagious disease.

Should I invite Roo over? Once upon a million years ago, I would have texted Lilah and been like, *Get your butt here immediately SOS!!!* But that's not an option.

Dizziness creeps in. Literally, the last thing I need right now. Thinking is hard enough, what with Lilah's betrayal. What with me telling Freddie my whereabouts.

Text Freddie. Tell him he can't come. Text him now.

Instead, I find myself piling the ingredients of a banana smoothie into the nutribullet.

I pick up my phone to text Freddie that I'm literally about to throw up, which feels true, when there's a knock at the door.

I nearly drop the smoothie.

Another knock. I could hide? Pretend I'm not here. But my feet lock in and Freddie's face appears at the side panel; he's waving and smiling.

I exhale and walk to the door to unlock it.

"Hey, Freddie." I try to sound contagious. I've completely lost a gauge on my acting ability, though, so I have no idea if he'll buy it.

"Cute mustache." He swipes his thumb across my upper lip, smiling down at me. My upper lip tingles.

"You want to come in?" *Geez, amazing job, Vinnie Smith.*

"Happy to stand on your doorstep for the afternoon. It's a nice doorstep."

"Right." I muster a laugh. "Come in!"

The illness gig is clearly not working. Yet another sign that my acting career is in the toilet.

"Um, so . . . how was your day?" I ask.

"Gooood," he drawls, not looking away. "Because of you."

"Me?"

"Yeah. You're in my head, Vinnie."

"Okay," I manage. But that's all. I'm dumbstruck with how bad this all is. For me. For Freddie.

For Lilah.

Do I care about Lilah right now, though? I push her away.

"And you?" he asks.

"It was good!" I lie. It was literally the worst day in recent history and it's getting worse every second.

“I mean, did you think about me too?” He weaves his pinkie into mine and draws me closer. I could step back. I *should* step back. But I don’t. Instead, I remember his thumb dragging across my lip.

My whole body’s alight. No longer dizzy—it’s sharp and switched on.

I know it won’t take much.

He bends toward me, his breath warming my cheek. Our lips touch. I’m so lost, I don’t pull away. Nothing in me wants to. Not at all. I let myself melt toward him.

“I can’t,” I murmur, doing everything in my willpower to extract. We separate.

“Why?” he whispers into my hair. “You feel it. I can tell.”

“It’s not that, it’s . . . Lilah.”

“Lilah?” He looks puzzled. “What’s she got to do with this?” He gestures to the space between us.

“She likes you. Can’t you tell?”

He smirks a bit, his lip curving. “She does?”

What’s with guys and their broken sensitivity radar? “Duh. Of course. She’s liked you forever. You really can’t tell?”

He lifts a huge shoulder. “I guess? I mean, who wouldn’t want all this?”

“You’re not taking this seriously,” I say. “Lilah’s my best friend.” *Was* my best friend. “She’s had a mega crush on you forever. Then you took her to *Gatsby*!” The words are Play-Doh in my mouth. What best friend backstabs a person like she did today? Not just today—for months! Nothing feels real.

He laughs. “I went to see *you*, Vinnie.”

“Right.” I fall into the couch. He plunks next to me and nuzzles my neck. I use my hands to make a neck cast so he can’t woo me with his pheromones.

“Lilah’s cute and all. Believe me, I’m flattered. But I don’t like her like that. I like you. All of you. I want you so bad it hurts right here.” He hammers his chest.

“Even if I wanted you back—”

“Which you do,” he cuts in.

“Even if I wanted you, I can’t do that to Lilah.”

He slings an arm over my shoulder and puts his feet on the coffee table like he’s settling in for the evening. “Don’t my feelings count for anything?” he says after a while. “I’m human too, you know. Three-dimensional. Lilah will be okay, Vinnie. You can’t live your life trying to please everyone else.”

“I’m not trying to please anyone. I’m just trying not to hurt anyone. Specifically, Lilah.”

“The question is,” says Freddie, “would she do the same for you?”

The image of Lilah and Ms. Montague sitting teacher-side of the desk in the Drama room elbows its way into my head.

“Well?” prompts Freddie.

I lean my head on his shoulder and close my eyes, willing Lilah’s betrayal out of my brain. Because part of me knows Freddie is right. I wouldn’t have thought it until today—that in a dog-eat-dog world, Lilah might climb over me to get where she needs to be, even if it means sacrificing our friendship.

Freddie lifts my chin so our lips touch. I let him.

Dog-eat-dog.

Vinnie-eat-Freddie.

CHAPTER 40

ROO: How to Feel Like a Turnip

Mum's home, which is all I need right now.

"Roo!" She gets up from the easel when she sees me. "What's wrong, baby? Did something happen at work?"

"No, Mum," I mutter.

"You look like you've been scratched up. You've been crying?" She pulls me toward her. Her head rests against my shoulder and my sobs erupt into her hair.

I wish she hadn't hugged me. I don't want to cry.

"Sweetie, what is it?" She holds me at arm's length when the sobs fade. "Water?"

I nod, limp.

"Here." She puts a glass in my hand and guides me to the couch. We sit close. "You can tell me. Whatever it is. Is it Vinnie?" After a breath, "Aggie?"

I look up at her when she says her name. We've barely talked about her since the funeral. We both glance at the photo of the five of us over the mantel.

I shake my head. "No. It's not them."

We sit quietly, her holding my hand. "I'm sorry I never got you proper professional help for all that," she says.

"For what?"

"For the Aggie stuff. I really dropped the ball. I know that now."

"You didn't, Mum. What do you mean?"

"I mean, it was too much. For everyone. But especially for

you kids. Someone we love dies by suicide, and we just push it under the carpet? I really failed you, Roo. I was so deep in my own grief, I couldn't see my way out."

Now her eyes well up. I clasp her hand harder. "You didn't fail me. Not at all. I didn't need extra professional help. I had Mr. Whitelaw, remember?"

"I suppose. But were those sessions enough? Was he equipped for all that? I thought he was more of a career adviser back then."

"The sessions were fine, Mum." Whitelaw wasn't equipped for much other than being a douche. He had his head so far down a camera lens, he probably didn't listen to most of the stuff students told him. But we don't need to explore that right now. "What about you? Did you ever . . . get help or anything?" Mum's best friend of, like, twenty years killed herself. I suddenly feel awful that I haven't ensured she's had proper professional support until this moment. What a son.

"I did," she says quietly. "Still do, actually. Miri is great." She pauses and pushes her hair from her eyes. "Did I ever tell you . . ." She drifts off. "No, I suppose I didn't."

"Tell me what?"

I watch her struggling to find the words. Eventually, she says, "I didn't answer my phone that night."

I wait. There's more. There has to be. "Okay?"

"Aggie called me. Mike had gone out that night—a work thing, as you know. I saw her name flash up on the screen but I was so deep in my own self-pity, laid up watching some dumb thing on Disney—*Superman*?—willing my back to stop giving me hell. Anyway, I didn't answer. I should have answered. I could have stopped her. You know?"

I don't know. That's the thing, none of us do. I know from

Vin that Mike's racked with guilt because they were his sleeping pills. I know that Vin wishes she hadn't gone to Lilah's sleepover party.

And here's Mum two years later, cursed with the guilt of wallowing in Back Pain City instead of answering her best friend's call.

"Aggie knew how much you loved her. Don't blame yourself. Please."

She presses her forehead to mine. After a while, she says, "If it's not Aggie, or Vin, are you going to tell me what's broken your heart today?"

"I'm a bit of a failure." I pull away and slump against the couch. "That's all."

"Oh, Roo. You are not. You're anything *but* a failure! All those beautiful photos you're taking. Completing the diploma! And you already have a real-life job—something vocational. That's more than most kids your age can say."

"Yeah." I feel like a turnip.

So if she ever does find out the cold, hard truth, it won't just be learning her son's a liar. It'll also be coming to terms with the epic failure she somehow created.

CHAPTER 41

VINNIE: Freddie Interrupted

Freddie's the best kisser I've ever been with. Jez was sweet and all but a bit bitey and overeager. Then there was Harmony Lectern (yep, real name) from Summer Stars, who kissed me like I was a block of sandpaper. She was still getting used to her attraction to girls, so I should probably forgive her.

But Freddie? Freddie is swimming in oceans on hot nights. Huddling behind waterfalls. Clean night air. I want to do this for the rest of my life, take him upstairs and swim through him.

Thankfully, the garage door announces Dad's return with a squeal. The spell breaks. I rip us apart, conscious of the hole we've just torn through the universe.

"Nooo," he murmurs.

"You need to leave. Like, immediately."

"What? No. I'm staying. It's final."

"Please!" I beg. "You need to go. Right now. I can't explain any of this to Dad."

"You don't need to. Let us *be*, Vin."

He uses my shortened name like we've known each other forever. It's dangerously comfortable.

"We can't," I say, blood rising as I hear the car door close. I push his big chest with both hands, guiding him firmly toward the front door. "You can't, *can't* tell anyone about this."

He doesn't reply. Just looks at me, broken and hurt.

"Freddie, I'm sorry. It was a mistake. Please promise me you won't say anything to anyone?"

"Sure," he mumbles, letting me guide him out the front door. I don't know Freddie well enough to know what "sure" means, but I'm just going to have to trust that everything will be okay. That I haven't just broken my world entirely, whatever Lilah's done to me or not.

"Hey, there!" Dad enters the house by the side door. "To what do I owe the pleasure?" He winks at me and stretches out a hand for Freddie to shake, just as Freddie teeters on the top step.

I squeeze my eyes, trying to reset my vision that's decided it's a fine time to duplicate. If only I'd closed the door on Freddie. Now I'm going to have to lie, cover up, or do something drastic to erase all this.

"Freddie needs to be at practice," I say.

"No, I don't." Freddie's face snaps from hurt to please-the-parents. "Nice to meet you at last, Mr. Smith."

"Call me Mike. Lovely to meet you too, Freddie. School Captain, Freddie, I take it? Saw the announcement in the newsletter. Congratulations, my friend." They shake hands again. I feel myself sink into the floor.

"Thanks, Mike. Really appreciate your support. It was a bit of a surprise, if I'm honest."

"I'm sure it's very well deserved. I've been following your football career from afar. Vin tells me you aren't too shabby academically, either."

He grins over Dad's shoulder at me, enjoying the confirmation that I've spoken his name beyond our little fantasy.

"Ha! I do all right. I don't want to let my parents down, you know. They never got the chance to finish school. I don't want to waste all the opportunities I have."

Wow, he really knows how to charm the girl-he-likes's dad. Dad's honeycomb butter, melting into the plate. He keeps trying to catch my gaze as if to determine when exactly Freddie and I have set the wedding date.

"I have a lot of homework," I interject at the exact moment Dad says, "Come in for a bit, Freddie. What's your beverage of choice?"

Even if I did actually have homework, there's no escape now. I'm locked into this weird courtship. All I need is for Lilah to appear at the door. That would really set the afternoon dial to Perfect.

I scroll through my phone, playing the part of a detached teen, which is lost on Dad and Freddie, who by now only have eyes for each other. They sit on either side of the breakfast bar, perching on elbows. I'm starting to wonder who exactly Freddie came to see this afternoon.

Eventually, they remember I'm in the room. Dad takes a sip.

"How did you like Vinnie in the play, Mike?"

"Amazing, as always. Vin's a real star. A lot like her mum, really."

"Vinnie hasn't talked about her much. She was an actor?" He catches my gaze. I lower my head. Why now, of all moments, with all people, do we need to go there?

"Oh boy, yep," says Dad. "Acting. Singing. You name it. She could have been professional if she wanted to. But she was far more interested in doing it for fun. It was no surprise to either of us when little Vin took over the stage in the kindergarten nativity play. You've never seen a more convincing lamb in your life." He chuckles. Freddie smiles.

My vision is still split. I'm feeling dizzy now, too. I pour myself a glass of water. The only consolation is that Dad's too obsessed with Freddie to notice I'm not doing great, physically speaking.

"I really have to do homework," I say, heading toward the stairs.

"Wait, Vin. Tell Freddie a bit about *Cats*. Mum was amazing in that, wasn't she? I think that was one of my favorites. Which character was she again?"

"Grizabella," I say.

Dad glows. I absolutely do not. I thought we had an understanding that Mum is neatly filed away in a drawer we all know is there but that we don't have to excavate every five minutes. Especially not with the likes of Freddie.

"Get the album, Vin," says Dad, gesturing toward my room.

I groan. *No*, I say inside. But up I go. Maybe if I follow the commandments, I'll get through this game as quickly as possible, and it will all be over.

I take the stairs slowly, my legs wobbly and uncertain. When my knuckles grip the banister, they're white. I breathe deeply, trying to curb the swelling giddiness.

One step.

Two step.

In the quiet of my room, I lie on the floorboards, my back pressed into the cool wood. My eyes are shut so tight they ache. By now, everything aches.

I'm so lost in a jungle of pain, my world off-kilter, that I barely hear Lilah's voice downstairs. It takes moments for it to drift into my consciousness, forcing my eyes open. I stare into the blackness, wondering how on earth I'm going to get up from the floor, race downstairs, and stop what I know is about to be unleashed.

CHAPTER 42

ROO: Sneaker Gum

"Roo? Hang on, that's my son. I'll get him for you. Can I ask who's calling?"

I'm stepping out of the shower when I hear Mum in the corridor.

"Roo! A lady called Sonia is on the phone for you. She says it's about your interview at Myrtle's?"

Her eyes are wide as she hands me the phone. I towel my hands dry and reach for it through the steam.

Shit. Shit. Shit a brick.

I try to will Mum to leave, but she hovers in the bathroom doorway. I flick my wrist at her. Doesn't work.

"I just wanted to check in," says Sonia. "About your interview? I thought it must have been you at the door. But you disappeared."

"Ah yeah, sorry," I mumble.

"Look, Roo. If it's not for you, I understand. But I would have appreciated a phone call. Or you could have just popped your head in to let me know. I'm pretty busy, as you can imagine, and I don't love having my time wasted."

"Um, sorry. Yeah."

Mum's still there, like gum on the sole of your sneaker.

"The only reason I'm calling is that our guy's just called in sick and I desperately need someone tonight. Can you come in? Call it a trial, and if you really don't want to do it, then fine."

I stretch my neck. It's a second chance, but I know I'll have to answer Mum's questions.

"What time?" I ask.

"Six p.m. Wear black. And rubber-soled shoes. You'll be on your feet for five hours straight."

She hangs up.

I avoid Mum's persistent stare and squeeze past her to dress (alone) in my room. Even when my bedroom door's closed, I sense her hovering in the hall.

Eventually, I push open the door. Sure enough, she's there, eyes like comets.

"Myrtle's? Is that a good idea, Roo? With study and the studio? You know you need to relax a bit too. Go for runs with your mum. Listen to music. Be a teenager!"

"It's fine, Mum. It's just one night, helping at the restaurant. I promise. I'll do everything in my power to be a teenager after that."

She's relieved, gives me a shoulder squeeze, and ruffles my wet hair. I drip all over her, making her laugh.

CHAPTER 43

VINNIE: The Precipice

I've been on a precipice before. That time Roo and I stood on the lip of Marom Falls, gathering the guts to jump into the water hole below.

Another time, we climbed the fence at the Lennox Head cliffs. A forty-year-old man had taken his life there just a month before. While we were sitting in the long grass, looking for whales, three of the man's friends approached, each carrying bunches of dried flowers. They cried silently as they poked them through the wire. They told us we shouldn't sit on the wrong side of the fence because it was fatal. That we should always look after ourselves and make good choices. After they left, the flowers stood erect. A sentry looking out for people on the brink of dangerous decisions.

Now, I crawl along the precipice of my bedroom floor, push my door open with my head, and somehow make it down the hall, my world unraveling.

I use the banister to pull myself to standing, and blink a million times to still the swirling scene of Lilah in our doorway; Dad sipping soda; Freddie looking up the staircase at me, smiling.

"Come on in, Lilah!" says Dad, oblivious.

I clutch the banister and ease myself one stair at a time.

"I came to explain," says Lilah, "about Summer Stars. About Juilliard and all that."

I feel Freddie's eyes on me as I approach her.

“It’s okay,” I say.

“It’s clearly not okay.” She flashes hurt at me, then at Freddie, before disappearing into the night.

“Lilah!” I try to call. At that moment, my legs give way. By now, though, the whole world has crumbled.

Part Two

Falling Off the Map

CHAPTER 44

ROO: Cabbage on Black Jeans

It's my third night in a row at Myrtle's. I know I'm just a dishy, but I'm loving it. Sonia's great. So are the rest of the staff. I like Tarek, the head chef. He's the opposite of those angry chefs you see on TV. This guy's dimples and jokes for days. I tell him that a group of chefs is called "an arrogance of chefs." I also tell him that he wouldn't fit in with that crowd. That makes him laugh.

Meg, the maître d', reminds me of Vinnie. She's bubbly and warm and loves everyone. She even looks a bit like Vin, her honey bangs framing her face. Beautiful big eyes and lips. A second piercing on each lobe, like Vin.

The best part is post-work drinks and food, where the staff sit around the long table together, eating random stuff Tarek whips up for us, somehow still having energy to cook another round after the customers have gone.

It's after midnight, and we're still here, laughing and joking. They don't seem to mind that I'm seventeen, have cabbage on my black jeans, and blobs of mushroom sauce on my Crocs.

I spot the Corolla on the other side of the street and wonder how long Mum's been waiting there. I told her I'd get an Uber home or that someone from work would give me a lift. She didn't listen.

"See you guys." I give a round of high fives on my way out.

"Have a great night, Roo! See you tomorrow, yeah?" sings Sonia.

I jog across the road.

"I thought you'd be sleeping. You don't need to pick me up," I say through the window.

Mum looks cross. Elmer Fudd cross.

"Get in." I'm not too familiar with this particular tone.

I slide into the passenger seat, looking at her expectantly. Is this about me not being enough of a teenager?

She starts the car and we drive in silence through the dead streets of Murwillumbah. Mum's jaw is locked into a tight square. She gives me nothing.

"Are you going to tell me why you're so mad?" I say as we turn onto our street. "I don't have ESP, so feel free to spit it out anytime now."

She parks in our undercover garage, stops the car, but keeps staring straight ahead out the windshield.

"I dropped by Brad Whitelaw's studio this afternoon."

Uh-oh.

"Thought I'd just have a quiet word with him about your late nights at the restaurant. Make sure he understands why you might be a bit more tired than usual. That if it started eating into your work with him, I'd be happy to talk to you about quitting Myrtle's. That you don't want to jeopardize your opportunity at the studio."

I'm one part mad that Mum thought she'd do a bit of puppeteering of my life, and nine parts shitting myself that Whitelaw was not conveniently out at a photoshoot this afternoon.

She finally turns to me, and I see it's not just anger blazing in her eyes. It's hurt.

"Brad told me you never started there. That it was never a paid role with him. That he hasn't seen you for months. That TAFE is not even offering photography this year because of cutbacks. What the fuck, Roo?"

I flinch. She's never sworn at me before.

"Where's the money been coming from, before Myrtle's? Are you a drug dealer? A gigolo?"

"What? No, Mum! Nothing like that."

She pushes away a tear that's escaped down her cheek but maintains her set jaw. She waits for me to fill in the blanks.

"I've been working for Daniel Pavlović. He runs a taxi company."

"I know Daniel. He's a royal creep. And possibly a criminal," she says. "Why wouldn't you tell me any of this? Why work for Daniel, of all people?"

Because he's the only one who'd have me, before Sonia.

Because I could keep the fridge full and the Extra envelope fat.

"I don't work for him anymore. I have Myrtle's. It's great there!"

"Yeah, great. Washing dishes for a living. That is *not* why you left school." She's back to Elmer-Fudd-just-got-outwitted-by-Bugs, steam curling out her ears. "I gave you the option to leave and follow your dream. Pursue a good opportunity. But you've been lying to me this whole time. You need to go back and finish school. You'll be a year older than everyone else because you're going to have to start Year Eleven. But these are the consequences of your rather questionable actions."

I lean back against the seat and close my eyes. I can't face school. I won't. Other than being the stupidest kid there, school means I can't work at Myrtle's five days a week, which means I can't make enough money for the buffer, so Mum won't do her course. Not just that—she'll go back to taking every shift on offer. Next thing you know, she's out of work with an effed-up back and Rupert chucks us out of the apartment.

"It's a good thing I'm the age of consent and you can't tell me what to do," I say, getting out of the car.

"Roo!" she yells after me. "Roo, get back here! Now!"

"Keep it down, will you!" roars someone from an apartment above us. "People are trying to sleep!"

CHAPTER 45

VINNIE: It Only Takes Seconds to Turn to Ash

"Vin?" Dad calls through my door. "I have to get to work. Call if you need anything."

I don't reply. Just bury myself deeper in my duvet burrow. Because falling off the map feels like damp, sticky sheets and smells like stinking socks.

I hear him pad across the carpet toward me.

"Can I get you anything before I go?"

"No. I'll be okay. Thanks," I say from the burrow.

I've convinced him my collapse the other night was flu-related. Conveniently, the drama of the afternoon did bring my temperature up slightly, and I probably looked like crap. So when I dragged myself to bed to disappear forever under my blanket, he didn't question it.

I hear his footsteps disappear and the garage door squeal open.

My phone lies dead beside me. I can't bear charging it because I can't bear the cavity that is Lilah's silence.

Sunshine strikes through the curtain gap and lands on the vision board that hangs on my lemon-colored wall. Staring at it, all lit up like a freaking celestial artifact, causes a huge wave of energy to power through me. All that naive stupidity. That sparkle-pen fuckery and bubble writing. Who the hell hangs their future on lists and hand-drawn words like *BELIEVE* and *SHINE*? How ridiculous.

Yanking my bathrobe over the clothes I've worn for days, I lug the bugger to the garden, bits flying off as I charge down the stairs. I grab the barbecue lighter from the cutlery drawer on my way and chuck the vision board into the fire pit.

Ignite.

The corners of magazine cutouts turn black and dissolve.

It's funny how all those conversations took literal weeks from our lives but only seconds to turn to ash.

The board itself takes a while longer to catch alight. When it finally does, I stare into the flames for an indistinct period of time. Gilda, from up the road, walks past and waves but hurries away when she sees what must be a crazed look in my eyes.

With the board gone, there's officially nothing.

No New York.

No Juilliard.

No Saint Bernards called Lollipop and whatever.

No Lilah.

There was no Drama Captain anyway. Burning the board is purely metaphorical. Our vision turned to ash days ago and laughed in our stupid faces as it floated into the atmosphere.

My future is with MS, and I already have a map for this, courtesy of Mum.

Start at diagnosis.

Track east toward escalating symptoms.

Track south toward blurred vision and continuous loss of feeling. (Throw in a few major falls for fun.)

Follow the landmarks down the crevice of depression, months of sleeplessness, and chronic pain toward that night when it all gets too much.

The fire has at last awakened my appetite. I need to eat a small house. Unfortunately, Dad's not been to the supermarket for a while, so I am looking at half a block of cheese and a limp carrot to fill the void.

I eat it all. It does a lousy job, but I'm not expecting much at this stage.

The afternoon passes in a haze of Netflix shows I don't care about. The only feeling in me is cheese-induced nausea.

I wander around the house in a nihilistic funk. How do people do life without a vision board and a best friend?

Dad's working late so I figure there's only one way through the meaningless terrain, and it starts with picking up socks and underwear from my bedroom floor, washing sheets, and folding clothes. At last, I get to my desk, grouping pens in order of sparkliness, putting them in their respective pen holders. I even give the desk a Spray 'N Wipe. I have to admit, I feel somewhat better.

I sit at my disinfected desk and, at last, charge and turn on my phone. There are no messages from Lilah. Just a bunch of random quips from Roo commenting on the war in Ukraine, on floods in Victoria, and the overall effed-up state of the climate. Then there's:

Vinnie, are you okay? Just busy, right?

Followed by a black-and-white photo of a dandelion puff growing out from a crack in the pavement. It glows in sunlight. He's taken it from earth level, making the dandelion appear as tall as the buildings behind it. I can't help smiling for the first time in days.

I open Roo's other photos that I AirDropped to my phone last week and study each a hundred times—even the one of Mum's calf on the rock.

Roo is so good at this. He makes manifestation irrelevant because the world exists right here, in a single image. No future required.

CHAPTER 46

ROO: Twenty Percent Gone

I don't care what Mum says. I'm going to work. I stuff my feet into Crocs, which are still tacky from yesterday's shift.

"You know what I call that?" She nods toward my Crocs. We're currently at the tail end of fight number twelve since the other night. "Lack of self-respect."

"I take it you mean it lacks respect to wear Crocs?"

She lifts an eyebrow and I grab the car keys.

"No you don't. I need the car," she says.

"Then can you drive me?" I ask. "Please?"

"No." She puts her hands on her hips and juts her chin in an angry way.

"Fine. I'll take an Uber."

"Which is about twenty percent of what you're earning tonight. Smart, Roo. Really smart."

She knows any reference to my intelligence or lack thereof will inflict a scorpion-like sting.

"Thanks for that, Ma." For the first time in my life, I slam the door on her.

I'm a jerk, I know. No one should treat their mum the way I'm treating her. But she crossed a serious line. If I had to choose a moment to be an utter testicle, it's now.

Mum's right about the whole twenty percent of lost income, however. I curse the fact that Vin doesn't have access to a working vehicle, otherwise I'd grab a lift from her. Not that she's bothered answering her phone.

I wonder what's up with her. I put it down to Year Eleven exam stress. Post-*Gatsby* blues. Maybe she's ruminating about the whole Lilah being Drama Captain thing. I text her a photo of my Crocs, hoping they'll cheer her up, whatever her state of mind.

She replies with a smiley-face emoji, which for once in its stupid existence actually makes me smile. I'm glad she's alive.

I boycott Uber and instead speed walk up the street. Google Maps assures me that if I walk as fast as Crocs will allow me to, I should make it in time.

But between a blocked road and blisters, I'm fifteen minutes late. The last thing I need right now is to get fired.

Sonia not so subtly glances at her watch when I push open the glass door. She's standing at the reception with Meg, looking at tonight's reservations.

"Sorry," I mumble. "Transportation issues."

She furrows her brow. Meg smiles in consolation.

"Roo, remember what I said about maintaining utmost professionalism? We open in ten minutes, and that kitchen needs to be fully prepped. That includes you, my friend."

"Yep. Sorry." I lower my head.

"Take it as a warning. Also, this—" She gestures to my sweatiness.

"Sorry," I mumble again and slink out the back to the kitchen.

"Roo!" Tarek shoots me a giant grin. "Come try this, buddy!" He slides a small plate of something pastry-ish toward me. I hesitate. "It's vegetarian," he adds. "Promise!"

I take a morsel. Butter pastry melts on my tongue; flavors seep into me. My failure to turn up to work on time drips away and all that exists is Tarek's hazelnut-and-honey pastry that's beyond doing my head in.

"You're a genius," I say.

"I know. Just needed to hear it aloud." He smiles. "Finish it! Go on."

I can never lose this job, I decide. Next time, I will take an Uber, even if it means I'm only on $15 an hour instead of $18. Next time, I will do whatever it takes to keep this job. Mum's just going to have to suck on the fact that her anonymous donor had sperm fit for a dish pig. It mightn't be her ideal, but if my dish piggery means we have enough money and I get to sample Tarek's creations every so often, then so be it.

*

A few days later, I'm checking the roster over and over. Refreshing the browser. Checking again.

Saturday: Amira

Sunday: Amira

Tuesday: Ralph.

Wednesday: Ralph.

Thursday: Amira.

Friday: Ralph

I don't flipping get it. I was on this roster, I swear. Three whole times. Now, I'm a ghost.

I pick up my phone to call Sonia. Put it down again.

She must be mad about me being late and sweaty. I am so unbelievably pissed at myself for once again letting myself down. My dreams of being a dishy for the rest of my life sail out the window on a whimsical cloud.

"Any socks? Undies?" Mum appears at my door. "I'm just putting on the washing."

I turn to face her, hoping my expression doesn't reveal the fact that I've effed everything up again.

"Nope. I have enough clean stuff. So we're talking to each other again?"

"Of course. Roo, we can be mad at each other, disagree occasionally, then move on. That's what adults do."

"So you do think I'm an adult?"

She rolls her eyes. "Sure. Until five seconds ago I did."

"Adults tend to make their own decisions in life, yeah?"

She sighs and sits on the bed, perching the laundry basket on her lap. I roll the computer chair closer.

"Of course they do. But, Roo, can't you see why I hoped there'd be more for you than washing dishes?"

"You know Myrtle's is award-winning."

She sighs. "You don't get it, do you?" She presses her palm against my knee. "Forgive me, but I was really excited you'd found something you loved. Photography, I mean."

"Who's to say I don't love washing dishes?" I lift the side of my mouth.

She chuckles softly. "If it's really your dream, then I support you. Do you need a lift to work tonight?"

Man, she's too nice to me. It's a pity I'm such a dunce. I glance at the roster that was open on my computer, but has thankfully disappeared behind my screen saver.

"Nah," I say. "Should be good."

That's if you consider it *good* killing time on the streets of Murwillumbah as you contemplate what a fuckup you are.

When Mum leaves, I refresh the browser again. I try Sonia. Reach her voicemail. Hang up.

I don't need confirmation of my fuckuppery.

CHAPTER 47

VINNIE: Metallic Rainbow Thumbtacks

I'm rewatching *Paddington 2* for the eleventh time this week when Roo's face appears at the living room window. He taps the glass.

Even though Paddington is about to wash windows in the cutest way possible, I get up and let him in.

"What are you doing here, stalker?"

It's so good to see him. I fall against him. He wraps his arms around me. Suddenly, I'm wondering why I didn't order his butt over here sooner. All this time I've been fermenting, I could have been fermenting in Roo's comforting presence.

"No offense, Roo, but you look like your grandma just died."

"That's harsh, Vin." He grins, though. "You know I'm still mourning Gran's death from, like, ten years ago. Sensitive much. You're not looking too spectacular yourself."

I contort my face in mock horror and clutch the lapels of my robe, which by now probably smell like the back of someone's fridge. "How dare you!" I gasp.

I drag him inside by the sleeve and onto the couch, lean against him, and press play. We watch wordlessly. When *Paddington 2* finishes, I click through to *The Greatest Showman*.

He manages to sit through the opening song, but before long yanks the remote from me and switches off the TV.

"I've endured Hugh Grant. I will not endure Hugh Jackman. Enough is enough."

"Then are you going to tell me what's going on?"

He sighs. "Let's just say, work is a bit slow."

"Myrtle's? I can totally see you swanning around with plates." I mime a classy waiter, my elbows bent, my fake plates balanced tentatively, my lips pursed in concentration.

"Actually, I'm more of the dishwashing variety." He mimes now, elbows deep in imaginary water, his face grimacing. I laugh.

"And it's a bit slow? The dishwashing variety?"

"Yeah." He sighs again.

Paddington has buoyed me. So has Roo's arrival. I'm feeling perky when I say, "We should go on holiday. Get out of here. Don't you reckon?"

"Yeah. Good idea," he says. "Like, if we had money. And you didn't have to go to school."

"I don't have to go to school. I haven't been all week. They won't miss me."

He rolls his eyes. Then his expression flattens. "Wait. You're serious?"

"Yes!" I say, punching the cushion on my lap. "Dead serious!" Suddenly, it's all I can think about—being in a faraway land with Roo. No Freddie. No Lilah. No Ms. Montague. Hey, even my symptoms might decide to stay home.

"Actually, I think I have a really good idea . . ." The thought forms slowly, then crystallizes. Next thing, I'm printing photos and pinning them on Dad's underused corkboard with metallic rainbow thumbtacks. Roo sits on the couch—arms crossed, legs crossed, one eyebrow raised skeptically.

CHAPTER 48

ROO: That Old Camp Feeling

Vinnie's cheeks are pink. Her eyes bright. She looks so beautiful when she's charged like this.

"Okay, so we're going to go to as many landmarks as we can in a week. Great Barrier Reef. The Daintree Rainforest. Uluru. You're going to take photos"—she taps the one I took of her at Crystal Shower Falls—"Exhibit A. Then, when we're back, I'll get them printed, framed, all that, and we'll rent the Citadel. I'll get everyone who's anyone to come check it out. Sell prints of your work. Tell them you're for hire. We can call it 'Lensibility'—ha. Well, we can work on that. It'll be the beginning of your photography career. Who needs Brad Whitelaw, anyway?"

The thought of a solo exhibition at the Citadel sends bile shooting up the back of my throat. Still, I can't bring myself to stop her. She looks so happy, bouncing around her living room in socks, waving her dad's ruler as she coordinates my sunny future.

The best thing about being a loser is that I get to give Vin a purpose.

"Ah, first problem—money," I say. "You realize that flying to the Great Barrier Reef is going to cost, like, a thousand dollars or something ridiculous. I don't have that kind of money. And there's no way you're paying my fare."

"Yeah, yeah. Okay. It doesn't have to be the Great Barrier Reef. We can go local. Like, oh, I know—we could go to all those places we used to go as kids." She taps the photos again.

"Yes! We can get back that old camp feeling . . ." She trails off.

"Smoke in eyes. Damp socks. That kind of thing?" I say, trying to make her smile. But she's disappearing.

I think I know where she's going, which makes me wonder if Vin might be onto something. If we can borrow a car from someone, we could revisit all the places we went when Aggie was still alive. They're all drivable. We could sleep in the car, if we had to. I don't want to do an exhibition. But I do want to drive places with Vin. Especially if it means she might talk about her mum for once. It can't be good for Vinnie, keeping that all bottled up inside her.

"You know what?" I smile genuinely now. "I think this idea is awesome. I can ask Mum if we can borrow the Corolla. We can fish out the old camp gear. Yeah. I'm keen." I grab both her hands.

"Great!" Her smile broadens. "You take photos. I organize the show. We get a week off life."

"Sounds good to me."

That night, I think of the two of us traveling around Northern New South Wales in Mum's Corolla. We'd have to use Mike's two-person tent because Mum sold ours on Marketplace. My cheeks are warm, imagining my body alongside Vin's, the stars above us, the camp feeling flickering.

CHAPTER 49

VINNIE: End of Days Bolognese

It's been a bunch of hours, and I haven't once thought about Lilah, Freddie, my untrustworthy body, or my cesspit of a future. That's because I have a project. It's called Roo, and it's got his cute face on the label. I have a spreadsheet, a PowerPoint, and several pages of To Do items crossed off in my notebook.

Tonight's task is twofold: arrange transportation and convince Dad that this is an awesome idea. He's usually accommodating, especially when I make him Bolognese. I use the End of Days Bolognese recipe from my favorite YouTube channel.

But he's worried I'm going to be missing school at a critical time. I've prepared for this.

"Roo's in a bad place," I say. "I can't wait eight weeks until the end of term. It might be too late."

His eyebrows knit together. He loves Roo—always has. He knows Roo has a tendency to be somber. As a high school teacher, he's seen how close kids our age get to the precipice.

With Mum suiciding, with Roo dropping out of school, stuff not working out with TAFE and Mr. Whitelaw, Roo's a candidate for some really unfortunate decisions as far as Dad's concerned.

He pushes his glasses up his nose and smiles sadly.

"Roo's lucky to have you as a friend," he says. "Look, I'll help you catch up on your studies over the summer. And I'll call your teachers in the morning. You go be with Roo. I trust your instincts on this one."

"One more thing," I say, trying not to beam too hard.

He quirks an eyebrow and wipes sauce from the corner of his mouth.

"I need Joy."

"The Kombi?"

"Yep."

"Well, she hasn't been on the road since Tingha all those years ago. Who knows what state she's in."

"I'll get her checked out. Actually, I've already booked her in."

He smiles and nods.

"I've also renewed the insurance," I add. "Under your name. Hope you don't mind."

He pats my hand. "I don't mind, Vin. There's nothing to mind about helping a friend. I'm just glad you're well again."

I smile back. "Thanks, Dad. You're the best."

We leave the dishes until after a French movie on Netflix. Dad's handing me a plate to dry and put away when he asks, "Just one thought, Vin. About the trip. How are you planning to pay for all this?"

"I have money," I say.

"Mum's inheritance, you mean? I thought that was for New York." He looks concerned.

"It is. But I have enough."

He pushes his palm across his beard, making it wet with dishwashing water. "Look, I'll pay for the Kombi. I should have done that ages ago. And if you run short at all—" He dries his hands on his jeans and pulls out his wallet. He hands me four fifties.

"Dad, you don't have to."

"I know. But I want to. For Roo."

"For Roo," I say, taking the money.

CHAPTER 50

ROO: Respectfully Surprised

Mum finishes her shift at eleven that night. It's her seventh day working in a row, every shift twelve hours long. You're not meant to do that, but it's been a long time since Mum followed a Work Health and Safety recommendation.

At the door, she takes off her boots. When she stands, she winces and presses her palm to her back. To think I had actually convinced myself that tonight was the night to tell her about our road trip. As if Vin and I will be doing any road-tripping. I need to get my butt back out there and find whatever job I can because I can't bear seeing Mum like this.

The next morning, I'm woken by Vin launching at me. She smells like caramel. I try not to be too much of a weirdo, sniffing her hair.

"Rise and shine, sugar brains. I have a surprise for you."

Only because it's Vinnie asking, I get up as far as my elbows, reach for my specs, and run my tongue over my furry teeth.

"No. I mean *up* up. Like, dressed and everything. Pack your bags. Your carriage awaits."

"You lost me at carriage."

"Joy!" She steers my chin so I face the window. Sure enough, Aggie's turquoise Kombi van is parked on the street. I haven't seen her for years.

"That thing still works?"

"That *thing* is our home for the next week. Pay some respect." She tsks in mock despair.

"Sorry. Respectfully, I am surprised."

"She's been to Charley Barker's and everything. You should hear her purr." She rolls her *r*'s against my ear. I shiver.

Okay, sure, I was excited about this crazy idea for a minute. That was before I realized I can't leave Mum. I can't not look for work. Holidaying with Vin for a whole ridiculous week is a beautiful fantasy.

"That's great and everything. But I have zero money. Sorry, Vin. I need to find a job."

She narrows her eyes. "This trip *is* your job! Remember how I am going to help you sell your work? I've put a deposit on the Citadel and everything. You can't back out now. I won't let you."

"Gah! I told you, Vin. I haven't got cash. I need a job." I'm trying hard to ignore her disappointed face, as cute as it is. "Tell me you can get your deposit back."

"It's nonrefundable!" Sunshine beams out of her eye sockets. I let my head bang against the wall and squeeze my eyes.

"Oh, hi, Vin!" Mum appears at the door, her hair up in a scraggly ponytail. She nurses a teacup. She has gray smudges under her eyes and leans forward slightly, which means her back is giving her grief. "What are we talking about?"

I raise my eyebrows at Vinnie, to let her know I haven't told Mum the Plan. Though *plan* sounds somewhat sensible.

"I'm taking Roo on the road, Carla. To remind him what an awesome photographer he is. We're revisiting old haunts. And I am putting together a show of his work."

I shake my head.

"It's fine, Mum. I'm obviously not going," I intercept. "I can't, with Myrtle's and everything."

"Myrtle's? *Pfft*," says Mum. "A show, on the other hand? I'm curious." She makes herself right at home and perches on my desk.

Vin stands, in performance mode. "It's going to be a showcase of Roo's work at the Citadel. Well, mainly photos Roo takes on our trip. We'll use the exhibition as a career-launch kind of thing. Sell some work. Get some clients. Brad Whitelaw, eat your heart out."

"Oh, I like this." Mum smiles at both of us in turn.

"Yeah, except Vin and I have no money, so it's less a career launch and more a really bad idea."

"I have money," says Vin.

"Please don't tell me you mean your New York money."

"I mean my New York money." She grins like an alpaca.

"You guys up for breakfast?" says Mum, clearly done with our pipe dream. "I bought fresh strawberries from the supermarket this morning."

Finally, an adult is in charge.

CHAPTER 51

VINNIE: Squished Together in a Laundry Room

When Roo's busy on his phone after breakfast, Carla drags me into their tiny laundry room.

Don't get me wrong. I've always loved Carla. She reminds me a bit of Zooey Deschanel, with her bright turquoise eyes. But I'm wondering why we're sharing one square yard of floor space.

"Listen," she whispers, "you can't tell Roo, but here—" She gives me an envelope.

"What's this?"

"Twenty-five hundred. For your trip. For the show. Will it be enough?"

"Oh, Carla, I couldn't."

She shushes me with her hand. "Roo *cannot* know. But please. You have to take it."

I study the envelope. Peer inside. It's cash. Lots of it.

"I have money, Carla. I haven't told Roo, but I don't know if I really want to go to New York anymore and, if I do, I'll figure it out. This is more important right now."

Her faces pinches. "Well, that's sweet, Vin. It really is. Though I know your mum would be turning in her grave if she could hear you doubting your New York dreams." She must catch my tense expression because she grabs my hand and squeezes it. "Look, I feel bad, okay. I've let Roo down. If I knew he was working for that . . . *ugh*. Anyway, please take the money. I'll sleep much better if I know Roo's doing something worthwhile, you know? Then you've still got your money if you change your mind about New York."

"Okay, okay." I squeeze back. "Only if you're sure?"

"Trust me." And I do. I tuck the envelope into the waistband of my jeans and pull down my top.

"I won't tell him. I promise."

"I love you, sweetie. I really, really love you. Like a daughter." She hugs me so hard my chest squeezes.

"I love you too," I say, when she finally lets me go.

"Have you packed?" I ask Roo. He's still on his phone at the kitchen table.

"What? No."

"You better. We leave in an hour." I wink at Carla.

"You'll need this," she says, throwing me a can of mosquito repellent. "Oh, and sunscreen. Don't forget towels! We always used to forget towels."

Roo shakes his head. "The money, though—"

"Always with the money! What did I say about being a teenager, Roo?" says Carla.

He sighs.

"I promise you, I have enough. Dad gave me a bit. I have savings! Your mum is right, Roo. You need to relaaaaax." I massage his shoulders. When he sighs again, it's more resigned. I dip my head over his shoulders to inspect his expression. There's a definite upward curve to his lips, which I take as a good sign.

Carla must have seen it too. "Roo can never say no to you, Vinnie Smith."

CHAPTER 52

ROO: Possible Anythings

Mum's right. I can't say no to Vinnie Smith.

When we return, I'll find a decent job or get my job back at Myrtle's—both, even. I'll work extra shifts and pay Vinnie back my share. I don't know how yet, but let's just believe for a tiny moment that the universe will provide. Meanwhile, I gaze at Vinnie as she squints down at the highway stretching in front of us, her nose wrinkled, freckled, and adorable.

"Oh crap, we forgot the towels," I say, an hour out of Murwillumbah. Vinnie laughs from the driver's seat.

"Don't worry. We can use toilet paper."

"That sounds like a terrible idea."

Joy's as slow as her age predicts, and her exhaust pipe has a habit of drowning out human conversation.

"Pass me a Skittle," demands Vin, opening her mouth in a perfect O.

I throw one at her when she turns briefly before swinging back to face the road. It bounces off her cheek and lands in her lap. She laughs. "Again!"

This time, it misses her completely and hits the window before sliding into the never never of Joy's underbelly.

"You are so bad at this," she says. "If your throwing continues in this atrocious manner, I'm going to have to leave you on the side of the road."

I chuckle. "Then who will direct you? You'll end up driving to Brisbane. Uluru, possibly. Kakadu."

“Are you implying I have a bad sense of direction?” She shoots me a dark look.

“Well . . .” I smile. “Let’s just say you have a lot of strengths, Vinnie Smith, and I am not sure navigation is one of them.”

She pushes out her bottom lip, faking sadness.

“You’re in so much trouble,” she says. “I’m taking you across the country in a Kombi. Anything is possible.”

I can’t help it. My stomach burns thinking about all the possible anythings.

Even though I’m not on the work schedule for the coming days, I texted Sonia to let her know I’m away. She replied to say,

Thanks for letting me know. Stay well.

I’m hoping this is a sign all will be okay and I’ll have shifts when I get back. I stash that in the pile of possibilities.

I’m conscious that our bank account is going to take a hit with me not earning. But Mum’s promised me it’s under control. She’s done the math, and we are going to easily pay our bills, she says. When I asked her if she’d already paid for the course, she nodded reassuringly.

I just need to tuck my guilt into my pocket and focus on being here with Vinnie in the Kombi. With all her theater stuff, school, her billions of friends, it’s surreal to think it’s just the two of us for a whole week. Just us and the world.

I’m scared to think too much about having Vinnie to myself in case I jinx it. Next thing I know, she’ll get a text from Lilah telling her about some party, and she’ll do a U-ey, driving eighty miles per hour to get back for it.

“Joy’s holding up okay,” I say. “Sounding pretty healthy.”

“Ha. You mean that sarcastically. Unless you think it’s

healthy to sound like an ninety-year-old with emphysema. I'm still marveling at the fact that the mechanic reckons she's in tip-top condition. If this is tip-top by his standards, I'm curious what he thinks about a car in actual good condition. He reckons Joy's worth a bit, everyone loving vintage these days."

"So, if we run out of money for canned spaghetti, we should sell Joy to feed ourselves?"

She smiles. "Imagine how much canned spaghetti you can buy with one 1960s Kombi in tip-top condition."

Farms become rainforests and windier roads, which cause slight motion sickness, for me anyway. We sing to Vin's Taylor Swift playlist. Well, she sings, and I watch her singing. Occasionally, I mouth some words to appear festive.

CHAPTER 53

ROO: One Soup and a Sandwich

After a couple of hours driving, we roll into a little town called Woodenbong, halfway up the Great Dividing Range. Vinnie pulls into a gas station to fill up, then we look for somewhere to have lunch.

Unless you want a cold meat pie from the gas station, there's just one option—Jack's Shack—a brick-and-tile house with red gingham curtains, perched on the main road. The doorbell tinkles when we enter. We're the only customers in a café that could fit the whole of Woodenbong's population, judging by the number of empty tables.

"Should have booked," quips Vinnie.

"Yeah. Pity we're going to miss out."

We pick a table under the window. The tablecloth matches the curtains and is protected in clear plastic. God save the gingham.

"Do we order at the counter?" I ask, just as a large guy in a small undershirt and low-slung jeans approaches. He walks slowly on account of his stomach and the vast number of empty chairs he has to prop aside as he passes.

"Hi, guys!" he says, grinning and whipping out a notepad. "Welcome to Jack's! What can I get you?"

"Is there a menu at all?" asks Vinnie.

"All up here, lass." He taps his head. "We have pumpkin soup or Devonshire tea. Or I can make you a toasted sandwich if you want. Baked beans too, most likely. But I better check the storage before I promise beans."

I imagine the guy on his hands and knees, peering into a cupboard, looking for beans. I love that this is a café that promises baked beans the way another café might promise tiramisu.

Vin raises her eyebrows at me. "What are you going to have, Roo?"

"Ah, soup?"

"Two soups, please," says Vinnie.

"I can probably just get one out of the pot. How about one soup and a sandwich?"

"Okay?" She catches my eye. I nod.

"That's fine. Thanks, mate," I say. All this talk about one soup and a sandwich has my stomach growling.

"Are you Jack?" asks Vinnie. "Like, from the shack?"

He beams down at us, something green caught between his narrow teeth. "Sure am!" He sweeps his arms wide, his notepad flapping open. "Do you guys like dolls, by any chance?"

I am pretty sure I misheard him.

"Dolls?" I repeat.

"Dolls?" asks Vinnie.

"Yeah, you know—*dolls*."

Vinnie smiles so hard her cheeks must ache. She's loving this. I, meanwhile, am wading through a Dalí painting.

"We *love* dolls!" she says, eyes flashing. "Don't we, Roo?"

I nod. Sure—I love dolls. For Vinnie, for Jack, anything. Also, I'm curious.

Jack shuffles off, hitching his jeans over his butt crack. He disappears for ages. I can't bring myself to mock him or laugh or anything. We just stare at each other, the heft of curiosity between us.

It takes a while, but here he comes, the same chair dance, this time carrying an armful of plastic dolls dressed in what looks to be a thrift store full of lace and, of course, gingham.

I don't know the collective noun for dolls, but if I did, I would use it when describing this scene.

CHAPTER 54

VINNIE: An Armful of Dolls

"Wow," I say. I nod at Roo, prompting him to say something. We can't just stare open-mouthed at Jack all afternoon. That would be rude.

"Yeah. Wow," says Roo at last.

"Are these . . . yours?" I ask. I was never much into dolls. More into puzzles, and imitating fictional characters. Mum and I used to do the Evening Show with Garth Welding, which was basically the two of us set up in front of Dad, doing skits of Chewbacca and Han Solo going to school. There was never time for dolls.

Jack's dolls have a vintage quality to them. He beams at us proudly. "Made each and every one. Well, dressed 'em anyway. Check this out." He shoves a pale-skinned doll toward my nose, and I do my best to stuff away surprised laughter as I inspect the fine hand stitching on the seams. There's ruby ribbon woven into the white hem. The doll is vanilla scented.

"That's very impressive, Jack," I say. "What got you into dolls?"

I glance at Roo, who's looking too stunned to talk. This is where ten years of improv comes in handy. Where Roo's frozen, I couldn't wish for a more juicy setup.

"Always have been, always will be. Actually, it was my sister, Margie, if I'm honest. She and I spent a good many years creating doll frocks, setting up doll parties, hosting doll swaps—things like that. Then she died of a heart attack."

"Oh," Roo and I say together. I was just getting attached to Margie. I feel bereft.

"Was she very young?" I ask softly.

"Not so young. Fifty?"

That puts the time stamp on this doll caper as quite recent. Jack can't be much past fifty himself.

"Sorry to hear about your sister," says Roo.

"Thanks, mate."

Even though we only met Jack a moment ago, I instinctively pat his hand.

Minutes ago, it was laughter bubbling inside me, fighting to explode. Not anymore. Not with Margie dying and Jack with his armful of dolls in his near-empty café.

I have a thought then. Something to take away the sadness.

"Roo, get your camera from the car. I have an idea."

It takes him a moment to stir, but eventually he gets up and fetches his SLR. I help Jack set the dolls in sitting positions on the table next to us. I'm not an expert. But I'd say the sun streaming in from the street-side window is perfect lighting.

"We need food. Tiny food, ideally. Do you have anything?" I ask Jack.

He glows. "Give me a sec." This time, when he shuffles through the restaurant, it's urgent. He returns with a Tupperware container full of miniature plates and cutlery.

Roo hangs back, letting me set the stage for Mercy and Tamara to host their first ever tea party at Jack's Shack. They invite Melissa, Monique, and Melanie.

He serves his dolls Devonshire tea, aka broken-off bits of scone and small dollops of homemade jam and cream. Filling tiny teacups with real tea, though, is practically impossible; Jack's teapot collection is nowhere near as good as his doll collection.

"You're on, Roo," I say, stepping back and dusting my hands.

He steps forward and follows my direction. Eventually, I keep quiet because I know every artist needs space to do their best work.

We're so caught up with the doll photo shoot, I totally forget about pumpkin soup and toasted sandwiches until the fire alarm goes off. Seconds later, smoke billows from the kitchen.

"Darn it!" Jack lumbers as fast as he can to the kitchen to unplug the sandwich maker and toss a blackened something into the bin.

"This is literally the best and the weirdest day of my life," Roo whispers.

"Anything to make you this happy." I grin at him and thread one arm through his. I lean against him. We only have a week of this. But in Jack's Shack, with Melanie, Melissa, Mercy, Monique, and Tamara, I feel something that I wish could last indefinitely.

CHAPTER 55

ROO: By the Fluorescent Penis

We make it to Tenterfield just before sunset. We're camping at the showground, which is only $14 a night, just a small chip out of Vin's New York fund. Not that it *is* the New York fund we're using. When the trip's over, I'll find a decent job and work extra hours to pay her back every cent we spend.

The end of the day flickers through the campsite. It's just us and a couple from Bourke in a Jayco. Vin talked to them for nearly an hour about their entire family history. She even had them show her pictures of their son's wedding in Rajasthan.

Vin and I eat Domino's under the bridge, leaning against graffiti about fucking the system and a giant pink penis. It's comforting that 125 miles later, all you need is a spray-painted penis to feel at home. That and Vinnie Smith.

An ant crawls up my arm. I don't flick it away. Instead, I let it walk from my arm over to Vinnie's and back again. We watch it crisscross us, tying us together.

"So, what's this all about, Vin?" I ask.

"The ant? Life. It's simple."

"No. You know what I mean. This trip. You've never made us go on holiday with such urgency before. Look, I get I'm a blast and all. But why now, specifically?"

"Fluoro penises?"

I smile and take a chunk of cheese between my teeth.

"Is this the Drama Captain stuff?" I want to ask about Freddie Sinclair and her hot cheeks as his arm draped over her at Jo's.

But I can't bring myself to. I don't want him casting a giant-shouldered shadow over what promises to be the best week of my life.

She sighs and leans against the penis.

"Not really," she says. Then she tells me about Lilah back-stabbing her and Ms. Montague cutting her out of the Summer Stars stuff.

"That's really rough, Vin," I say. Our knees rest against each other, mine in jeans, hers bare. I let the gentle current of that wash through me.

"Yeah. But you know, you're the best distraction I can think of."

"Your knack for giving compliments astounds me."

"You know what I mean. You always have a way of making me feel better. I dunno." That's the thing—I do know exactly what she means.

An image pops into my head: the two of us sitting together on her front step at her mum's wake, her holding an egg salad sandwich, me a can of lemonade. Us saying how sad things were but that was all. The rest of the time, we didn't say much, but somehow, I knew it was the best we could have done with the afternoon.

The ant disappears and reappears on the ripped knee of my jeans. I wonder if it's the same ant or the ant's buddy.

"I do my best," I say. "To make you feel better, I mean."

"Thanks."

We're quiet, watching the ant. Then she says, "It's actually not really for me, though—this trip. I know I can be selfish and bratty. But I really do want you to do this exhibition."

"You're not selfish and bratty."

She punches me softly. "Not much, you mean. Anyway. I

want you to be proud of yourself. You just had to look at Jack's face today! You made that happen!"

"*You* made that happen."

"We made that happen." She laughs then turns serious. "But, Roo, if things are this corny between us, I'm sending you home and completing the trip with this little guy." She lifts the ant to my nose. "He might not take photos. But I bet you anything he doesn't have a corny bone in his body."

"Do ants even have bones?"

"Okay." She laughs again. "You're not corny. You're allowed to stay on board. Sorry, little guy." She lowers the ant to the ground. It scurries around us for a while, like it thought she was serious and is trying to get her to give it a second chance.

"I'm getting eaten." I stand, brushing myself off. "Mozzies love me."

"Course they do."

It feels normal when she takes my hand and we walk like that all the way back to the showgrounds, back to Joy. Bertha and Jim from Bourke offer us a cigarette, which we accept even though neither of us smoke. I don't know why. Maybe it's something to do with the pile of possibilities.

CHAPTER 56

VINNIE: A Mosquito Net Between Him and the World

"You take the van," I say after we've brushed our teeth.

"No way. You have the van. I'll sleep out here."

We don't have a full tent—just the inside structure. The waterproof layer is missing. Also, the camp mattress is as thin as a pancake. Did we ever actually sleep on this? I swear it's four inches thinner than it used to be.

"I won't let you."

He smirks. "Well, I won't let *you*."

"We'll flip a coin," I say. "I'm heads."

It's tails, so Roo makes me sleep in the Kombi. He takes the pancake.

"Night," I call from the van, feeling guilty about him being out there with nothing but a mosquito net between him and the world.

"Night," he calls back. "Thanks for all this."

"You're welcome."

It's only the beginning, but I feel really good about my decision to steal Roo away from civilization. He took photos of the sunset tonight over the skate park. I made silhouettes with my body. Of course, they were amazing. Not the silhouettes. The photos.

A mosquito drones in the van for ages. The photo bunting strung up in the roof cavity swings in the breeze. I've switched off the fairy lights so I can't make out the exact shapes. By now, though, I've looked at these photos so much I know which one is which.

I pull down the one of Mum on the rocks in Lennox. I hadn't realized it before, but she looks a bit like she's sacrificing herself to the ocean. It's eerie and scary, but a powerful image. I peg it back on the string and watch it flap with the others.

The air is so thick, it's hard to sleep. I'm finally nodding off when I hear clunks of rain on the roof. Roo's out there without a waterproof cover.

"Roo?" I call. "You still awake?"

He doesn't reply. I poke my head out the back and hear him snoring softly. I should poke him awake and drag him into the van.

The drops are heavy and slow, then they stop. I kneel there, watching him for a while, waiting to see if the rain is going to get worse.

His chest lifts up and down. Soft curls frame his face. He looks so peaceful, his glasses folded next to his pillow. It's weird to think how well I know this face; but out here in the moonlight, I'm relearning the shape of his jaw, the curve of his nose, the arch of his brow. I get a sudden craving to lie beside him and rest my palm against his cheek.

Wow. He's your best friend, Vinnie. What are you doing?

The clouds drift and stars shine through. Fairly confident Roo isn't going to be rained on, I slide back into the van and let sleep take possession.

I wake with the sun in my eyes and what feels like a slab of concrete on my chest. I'm that tired, you'd think I hadn't slept. My vision isn't great either. I blink, trying to shake the dodgy optics. Here I was planning to be healthy but the universe laughs in the face of my so-called plans.

I hate my body right now, especially when I think about everything I want to get done today. I can't waste time being ill.

I indulge my symptoms for five, maybe ten minutes. Finally, I've had enough of myself and leverage upright. I misjudge the space and smash my head against the roof of the van, which results in a blasting headache. Exactly what I need.

I find Roo drinking coffee with Bertha and Jim under their annex. Bertha's smoking. Roo isn't. Steam rises from his cup.

"Morning!" I say, as sunshiney as can be.

Jim says, "You kids off to Girraween, I hear."

"That's the plan. I might have to steal Roo from you soon and get this party started."

"Ahh." Bertha takes a long drag and squints at me over the end of her ciggie. "Love a good romance. Makes me nostalgic." She grins at Jim, exposing damaged teeth. He pats her knee. Roo and I also exchange a small smile. It's funny to think of the two of us as "a good romance."

Could we ever, you know, kiss? Last night, I wanted to cradle his face. This morning, I try to imagine what his kiss tastes like. Berries? Salt?

Darn it, Vinnie.

We buy seeded rolls and a jar of peanut butter from Coles before hauling Joy toward Bald Rock in Girraween National Park. I'm still dead tired and my vision isn't great, so I get Roo to drive.

Fire's been through the park since our last trip a few years ago. Tree trunks are blackened. Lime-colored baby leaves spring from bark. Forests like these are made to burn.

Joy coughs as Roo pulls over on the side of the road.

"The car park is ahead, according to the map," I say.

"I just have to do something." I'm expecting him to go pee and am about to chastise him for not going back at the campsite. But he reaches for the SLR behind the passenger seat. He wanders into the scrub, pointing his lens through the trees. I feel calm watching him.

"Can I see?" I lean across the gearshift when he climbs back into the van. He flicks through. My favorite is one of tiny stars dancing between leaves on a stream of sunlight. They are not really stars. They're insects.

"I like this one."

"Me too." I like that he can be happy with his work. If I can keep my symptoms under control on this trip, I know I can help Roo see himself the way I see him.

From the parking lot, we head up the track. When we reach the stone face, I inhale, registering its steepness.

"Race you," says Roo.

"No way! We can't run. Impossible!" *For more reasons than he can imagine.*

"Speak for yourself!" He charges ahead. I shouldn't push myself. I'm peeling the sticky seal off my next MS symptom if I do. But Roo's set an irresistible challenge.

When I nearly die after about fifty yards, it's nothing to do with MS—just general lack of fitness, and these days Roo's way more muscly than me. I have no chance of catching up. I focus on my breath and my footing, conscious not to spill my brains against granite. That would be unfortunate. When he collapses, I catch up, panting hard between laughter.

"I swear this was easier when we were kids," he wheezes.

"It really was." I sink next to him. We stare up at the sky and use our arms to block the sun. I could sleep here, with the morning rock cooling my back, Roo's warmth next to me, and the sun in my eyes. Just as I feel myself sinking into another plane, he pulls me up.

We get higher and look over the tablelands toward the east. We can see the ocean from here, ridged by the caldera—the lip of the volcano that erupted thousands of years ago.

I'm pretty sure this was the spot Roo took the photo of Mum and her calf muscle. All that wasted strength.

I glance at him. I could ask. Bring Mum up in casual conversation. No big deal. But he lifts the camera and lines up the next shot.

CHAPTER 57

ROO: Daisy in the Rock

It's weird being here again, just with Vinnie. Last time we were here, we were a complete set: me, Vin, Mike, Aggie, and Mum.

We already knew about Aggie's diagnosis when we camped in Tenterfield for Mike's fortieth birthday. Vin and I used to research MS on Mum's phone when the parents weren't looking. We probably knew more than we should have.

We didn't know then that Aggie sometimes thought about dying. To us, multiple sclerosis was something you lived with. We didn't often see how much it affected her. Sometimes she complained about seeing double. She'd get tired a lot. Like, really tired. Once, she pulled out of a camp trip the day of, which was weird at the time, especially as it was always Aggie planning the camping adventures. But if anyone could cope, it was her. That's what I thought, anyway.

It was Aggie who planned the climb up Bald Rock to watch the sunrise for Mike's fortieth. The rock was slippery with condensation. We used headlamps to light the way. Vin and I wore matching beanies. We exhaled fog into the air.

There was no sunrise that morning because there were so many clouds. The parents drank champagne from plastic cups, and Vin and I had apple juice. We cheersed Mike and later sat on the rock weaving flower crowns while Mike came up with forty things he loved about life. I remember sherbet and Care Bears were on the list.

Now, Vin and I sit back-to-back, looking out at the world.

"Are you going to take my photo?" She wipes peanut butter from the corner of her mouth.

I draw back and snap one. Then another. First, it's her with the view behind her. I zoom in and take one of just her.

I show her the photo on the viewfinder. "Do you think I'm fulfilling my potential?"

She shrugs. "I think you're *finding* your potential. There's a difference, don't you reckon?"

"Have *you* found your potential?"

"Maybe." She turns to face the horizon.

"You mean, you're waiting to get to New York? You'll find it there, you think?"

The thought of not sharing a continent with Vin is devastating. Knowing me, I'll follow her, even though I said I wouldn't. Even though I don't have a job and have pretty much no money. I just can't imagine a time or place without Vin in it, helping me find my potential, or whatever her latest project is.

She swipes the viewfinder and smiles, landing on a photo of Jack holding his dolls. She stretches her fingers apart to zoom in.

"He was really passionate, wasn't he?" she says.

"Yeah, he was. I envy you guys," I admit.

"Who?"

"You and Jack. You and Lilah. Even Freddie. You all know so much about yourselves and what you love. It must be nice."

"You mean Skittles?"

"You know what I mean. Your acting. All that."

"You know too, Roo." She puts her hand over mine. On one side is the cool rock. On the other side is Vin.

She lifts her hand too soon and plucks a flower that's somehow grown from the rock. I'm sure there's soil somewhere there.

From here, it looks like it's just a daisy in the rock. An impossible situation.

She plucks green foliage and a purple flower that grows on a vine. She weaves them together, just like we did for Mike all those years back. I get into it, helping her find more. We shouldn't pick flowers from the "place of flowers" because it's a national park. Still. I smile as she lays the crown on my head.

"Don't move." She takes my camera and points the lens at me.

"Careful," I murmur, conscious not to move my mouth, as per instruction.

She clicks. I hear and see the shutter curl on itself like an armadillo. I almost never get my photo taken so I don't get to see that often.

"Nice." She gazes at the viewfinder, proud of herself. She shows me. It's not bad. Trust Vinnie to take zero interest in photography theory, yet somehow manage to have me front lit and in perfect focus.

On our way down the rock, Vinnie drops back. While I wait, I see her stop every few footsteps. She looks like an elderly person, scared of breaking a hip. At some point, she reaches for a thin tree to steady herself but misses and lands on the rock. She yelps.

"You okay?" I rush back to help her up.

She nods but doesn't move straightaway, blinking as if to wring out the pain. I offer my hand.

We hear singing. A family round the boulder. Two boys and a girl on her dad's shoulders, all of them belting their hearts out. It's super cute. Vinnie smiles encouragingly. Seeing us, they stop.

"'Do-Re-Mi,'" she says. "*The Sound of Music*. Keep going! It's magnificent!"

They look embarrassed. Then Vinnie does the unthinkable and starts singing solo. She's got an amazing voice, especially when it bounces off the rock amphitheater we're standing within.

"You're a really good singer!" says one of the boys, who I am guessing is about eleven. He gawks at Vinnie like she's the actual Julie Andrews. She may as well be.

"I'm pretty well trained," says Vinnie. "But you—you're a *really* good singer." The boy nearly blows up with pride.

"Am I a really good singer?" asks the girl on her dad's shoulders.

"Oh my goodness, you're amazing!"

"What about William?" The girl points to the teenage boy standing just behind his dad. Since we arrived, his singing has been minimal.

Vinnie looks serious. "I thought William had great pitch," she says.

The teenager nods appreciatively. I notice a smile creep onto his face, and I understand him completely. Being seen by Vinnie Smith—heard and recognized—feels really good.

"Stand over here," she commands the family, ushering them to huddle next to the rock. "You'll get better acoustics. Yeah, that's it. Do you guys know 'My Favorite Things,' by the way?"

The girl nods like crazy. She slides off her dad's shoulders and grabs Vinnie's hand. Even the dad looks stoked.

All of them, including the dad and Vinnie, sing. Vin waves at me. Eventually, I get it. She wants me to take photos. She subtly steps aside, letting go of the girl's hand as I snap a few.

"This okay?" I mouth to the dad, who gives me a thumbs-up.

When they're done, I show them.

"Can you e-mail this one to me? It's really nice," says the dad.

“Sure,” I say.

He fishes in his backpack and retrieves a pen. “Ah, I don’t have anything . . .”

“Just write it on my arm.” Vinnie holds out her forearm.

We talk for a bit about the morning and the view. The younger boy gets bored and scoots ahead.

“Better catch up before he ends up in Stanthorpe,” says the dad, who we know from the e-mail address is Paul. He salutes us and they disappear around a boulder.

CHAPTER 58

VINNIE: Upper-Class Underwear

By eleven o'clock, the day's fry-pan hot. My T-shirt is soaked. We've made it back to the parking lot without incident, unless you count me nearly splitting my skull when I slipped. Luckily, Roo thinks I am just a klutz. He hasn't noticed I'm suppressing a likely autoimmune disease. The double vision has subsided, and though I feel dog tired and achy in the tailbone department, I know I can get through the rest of the day.

I grab Roo's phone, which still has battery and just one bar of reception. I know I should charge mine so I can text Dad to let him know we haven't been murdered. But charging my phone means seeing whether Lilah's contacted me or not. I don't want to know. I also don't want to have the opportunity to message her because, before I know it, I'll be apologizing and I don't think I should.

She started all this. *She* betrayed me.

Potentially hearing from Freddie is another good reason to pretend I don't have a phone.

Solution: I use Roo's phone to text Dad. He immediately replies with a love heart and a thumbs-up, which probably means he's in class or a meeting so can't message properly.

Roo peels an orange while I look up swimming holes nearby. I remember us all going to a waterfall years back, and we definitely swam there. At last, I see it on the map.

"Do you know what you call a group of oranges?" he asks.

"A band?"

He shakes his head. "A pocket of oranges."

"That's so cute. Now if you're done, let's find this waterfall."

He drives. I direct. We get lost twice. Eventually, we park, walk a couple miles, watch the falls cascade below, then amble over the rocks to the water hole.

I start to undress, kicking off my sneakers and pulling off my T-shirt. Roo stands nearby, fully clothed, looking awkward. He turns away slightly, but I can tell he still sees me.

"I didn't bring a swimsuit," he says.

I laugh. "Neither did I. Who cares? Go in your undies."

I'm down to my bra and knickers, cursing myself for wearing Kmart underwear, which are ripped at the seam and discolored from going in the washing machine with my new jeans.

I'm in the water before I can overthink it.

"Gah!" I cry out as the water bites my skin. It's vicious. Roo laughs.

"Cold?" he says.

"Bloody cold! Well? Get in!"

He still has his sneakers on.

"I'm good," he says.

"Wuss." I breaststroke away, and with every lap I feel less like my butt is Antarctica. Actually, the cold sting is superficial because my body quickly warms up. I'm almost high with gratitude that my symptoms have lifted and I get to experience all this.

I tread water in the middle. Roo's taking photos of the view. He turns and snaps one of me in the water hole. I poke out my tongue, probably too late.

"If you don't come in, I'm going to delete your memory card," I say. "Also, you'll regret it. This is amazing. You're missing out on life right now."

He frowns. "I thought it was you who wanted me to take photos for the exhibition. If you delete my memory card, you'll put a dent in my potential and have nothing for your show."

"*Your* show, you mean. Anyway, I *more* want you to get in the water hole. This is your true potential. Come on! I promise not to judge you by your raggedy undies."

"My undies are not raggedy. They're upper-class."

I laugh but turn around so as not to embarrass him. I hear a splash.

When I turn, he's gasping.

"Roo!" I freestyle over.

"You forgot how bad I am at swimming. I forgot too."

"Doggy-paddle. It'll warm you up."

He paddles his hands. His leg rubs against mine. Electricity shoots up my spine. That was unexpected. I paddle next to him, our skin touching intermittently and electricity turning on the central heating in my gut.

I decide the torture session is over and lifesaver swim him back to the rock. He's all slimy and slippery as I pull him out of the water. He swears when he slips back. I strengthen my grip and tense my back leg so he doesn't pull me in with him.

We're an awkward jumble of limbs, but finally he's out. Only I stumble back on the rock and land smack on my butt again.

I cry out in pain. "Hurts so much." My eyes water.

"I'm so sorry, Vin. I'm useless." He holds me at the waist and lets me swing my arm over his shoulder. We stumble over the rocks until we get to our pile of clothes. Because we have no towels, we air-dry in a patch of sun, our flesh goose bumpy. He wraps his T-shirt over my shoulders and pulls me to him, warming me against his damp, goosey skin. I tingle where our bodies meet.

Somewhere between now and our last swim in this water hole, Roo picked up a new and improved physique. Not thick and solid, like Freddie's. Sinewy, like a strong vine that can carry you between canopies.

CHAPTER 59

ROO: The Great-great-great-Cousin of a Bushranger

"It's not a very good idea," I say as we huddle in Thunderbolt's Hideout. It's a cave made from rocks. The notorious outlaw, Thunderbolt, supposedly hid out here, horses and all. Vin's decided we're sleeping here.

"Where's your sense of adventure?" she probes, opening the backpack and pulling out a box of matches. "We have fire. We have lentils. The world is good, my friend."

"There's also a perfectly adequate campsite a little way from here. Less likely to get murdered there. They even have a toilet."

She shrugs and scampers around, collecting twigs. She makes a stick tepee, strikes the match, and immediately the flames catch.

"We need to find something bigger." She looks at me, but I'm taking no part in this madness. I'm happy to follow Vinnie to the world's end but would rather sleep in actual civilization.

Also, snakes.

Sensing my lack of action, Vin continues gathering firewood.

She sits on her haunches, watching the flames, her face lit up. Even when she makes me crazy with her bizarre plans, I still love her, I realize.

I love her.

"The fire will keep away the mozzies," she says.

"And the brown snakes?"

"Obviously. Have you ever met a snake who likes fire?"

"Not lately."

We eat cold lentils out of the can. Later, we play tic-tac-toe in the sand. I try not to be a big scaredy wuss and do my best to be fun and everything Vinnie loves in a person. Because if I am honest with myself, there's only one thing I really want in life. Her. Being here alone with her on the edge of civilization, I can almost convince myself it's possible.

"Did you know I'm related to Thunderbolt?" she says, scraping out the last of her lentils with the bent fork we're sharing.

"What? No. How?"

"He's, like, my great-great-great-cousin or something. My great-great-granddad was his cousin. Something like that."

"Wow. That's pretty cool."

"Yeah. Apparently, when my great-great-granddad died, he left behind his wife and eight children. About fifteen months later, his wife had another baby. Folks in town thought it was Thunderbolt's baby."

"Scandal," I say. "Sounds like he didn't respect his cousin much."

"Yeah. Totally. Though things were different back then. I guess you loved whoever you could. Anyway, the baby and the mum both died in childbirth."

"Oh no. What did Thunderbolt do? Did he raise the kids out of guilt?"

She shrugs. "I don't think so. He probably was too busy with his bushranger responsibilities. I think the oldest girl looked after the younger kids. Or some of them got farmed out to other families. I am never good at remembering historical details."

"Well, that's pretty cool. Not many people can say they're basically Thunderbolt's relative."

"Basically," she says, the last lentil teetering on the fork.

We talk for hours about our weird relatives. Somehow, we manage to leave out Aggie. Talking about Aggie doesn't feel like it would be funny or weird. Just sad.

I wonder, as we lie together on the thin mattress (which is barely enough for one, let alone two), when we will be able to talk about her. I keep looking at Vinnie, waiting for a sign that she's ready, but I don't know yet what the sign looks like.

Later, when I'm sure she's asleep, I mouth, "Love you, Vin."

"Hm?" she mumbles, turning slightly.

I stiffen, worried she's heard me and whisper, "Shhh, nothing. Go back to sleep."

Her sleeping sounds assure me she's dead to the world.

When I wake in the night, Vinnie's not here.

"Vin?" I call through the cave. All I hear is my own voice bouncing back. "Vinnie!"

We stupidly left the flashlight in the van, so the only light I have is from embers and the moonlight that glides between rocks. I listen for her because I can't see her. My heart is doing a heck of a job of drowning out every sound, though. "Vinnie!" I yell.

"Here," she murmurs.

I stumble, using the stone wall to guide me. I see the shape of her body, hunched.

"You okay?"

She doesn't reply. I press my hand against her back and stroke it. She's trembling. Is she crying?

She's wobbly when she stands and leans against me.

"I'm fine," she whispers, her voice croaky.

I steer her back into our cave, where she curls on the mat. I lie behind her, a tiny space between us.

"Wiggle closer," she says. "Keep me warm."

"Okay."

I spoon her body.

To keep her safe.

"This okay?" I whisper into her hair.

"Of course."

Soon, I feel her drift into sleep, sinking into me like she completely trusts me. I lie with eyes wide open, thinking about nothing but her. Imagining a parallel universe where she and I can do this every night. Telling my body to keep it cool.

This isn't about me, though. Something's going on for Vin. Her skin's cold yet clammy. Goosey and trembling. Her breathing's shallow.

First light breaks and the magpies sing. A kookaburra laughs its head off. Vinnie sleeps in my arms.

CHAPTER 60

VINNIE: The Head of a Goat

I peel myself from Roo. His warmth lingers on my skin. I study him, dappled in shadows. His nose scrunches then twitches, like a puppy dreaming about chasing rabbits. *What are you dreaming about, Roo?*

I'm so absorbed by him, I almost forget to do my usual body scan, assessing for symptoms. Last night's bout of dizziness has eased, thank goodness. My vision's clear. Apart from a sore tailbone, I feel okay. Tired, sure. But fine.

The twitching stops. Roo cracks an eye.

"How are you feeling?" he asks.

"Great! Up and at 'em, sleepyhead. Didn't I tell you camping out here would be the best?"

"The best," he deadpans, creaking into sitting position. He's rumpled, a twig caught in his messy hair. He fumbles around for his glasses, which I hand to him.

"Bakery?" I suggest. "I could eat a horse."

"I'll settle for a croissant."

I sit opposite him at the Tenterfield Bakery, my palms absorbing the warmth of my hot chocolate. Roo's on his second croissant, flicking crumbs from his shirt as he wolfs it down.

"Can I borrow your phone?" I ask.

I text Dad, then do a quick Google search for Ruby's Crystals, the little shop I scouted online before we left.

Ruby, Mum, and Carla were best friends at college. Ruby and Mum did a year in New York together and when they came back to Australia, they moved into Carla's place. A few years later, Mum and Carla moved north to have Roo and me. Ruby moved to Tingha to look after her elderly dad.

Judging by Ruby's active Facebook page, I've ascertained she still lives there, and the shop has a five-star Drop On By! vibe. I call the number listed.

"Ruby's!" she answers in a voice ragged from smoking.

"Hi, Ruby! This is Vinnie. Aggie's daughter—"

She cuts me off with an abrasive cough. "Holy crap! Vinnie! I was just thinking about you guys the other day. How are you, sweetheart?"

"Good. Good! Actually, Roo—do you remember Roo? He and I are doing a little road trip. We're in Tenterfield now—"

She cuts in again. "Say no more. I'm making up the spare beds now. Cute you guys ended up together."

I don't correct her. Just smile and nod at Roo, who looks like he is piecing it together from my side of the conversation. She gives me instructions to find her place. Even though I have Google Maps on Roo's phone, I write them on a napkin.

We sing to a random country-and-western playlist I download on Spotify, making up lyrics, which are only vaguely less cheesy than the real ones. We reach Ruby's by lunchtime. She bursts out of her shop, eyes bright, graying hair cropped close to her skull. She's shorter than I remember, and skinnier. Her sharp collarbone digs into me when she hugs me.

"Cop a look at you guys." She crosses her arms. "Well I never. Aggie would be proud of you, Vinnie. And you, Roo—phew!" She whistles through yellowed teeth. "Bloody hell. You turned out well, didn't you! Thank goodness you guys got in touch. I've been meanin' to call Carla for months. Now I have no excuse."

She bustles through the shop and through a beaded door that hangs at the back. I glance at Roo. Should we follow her? He shrugs.

When she doesn't come back, we duck through the purple plastic beads and enter a cavern of hanging plants and ceramic sculptures. It stinks of tobacco. Despite that, Ruby's home behind the crystal shop is cozy and inviting. I've never been here before because her dad was so sick last time we were in the region.

She's filling the kettle, a streak of sunlight yellowing her hair. Because of the smoking, she looks decades older than Carla. Way older than Mum would have looked at this age. The thought makes my throat constrict.

We sit around her laminate table. Ruby lights a cigarette but thinks better of it and stamps it out in a bowl that has the head of a goat and a mound of stubs in its buttocks.

"How's Carla anyway?" she asks Roo. "Her back better?"

"Yeah. It's okay. She still works too much. Oh, but she's getting back into painting. Doing a fancy course and everything."

"That's great news! She's darn talented, that mum of yours. Could have made it in the art scene, I reckon. But she had to go and have you." She chortles, which brings on a sticky cough.

A wave of guilt passes through me, thinking about Carla giving me her money for the course. I'm going to pay her back. That's a definite.

"All right. Tell me everything about you two." Ruby leans back and crosses an ankle over her knee, her hands knotted in her lap. Her feet are bare and cracked. "How'd you end up together?"

I shoot out a laugh because what else can I say? *We're not together, but I have thought about kissing him*. Roo looks uncomfortable.

“Oh, we’re just friends,” I say. “That’s it!”

His cheeks pinken. He lowers his eyes, but he’s smiling.

“Yeah, great friends,” he says.

“Best friends!” I add enthusiastically.

I feel his leg next to mine under the table and think about our bodies entangled in the water hole. How he curved around me last night in the hideout. Every nerve springs to attention.

I’m so aware of him, as Ruby quizzes Roo about photography. I hardly say a word—just smile and nod feverishly, hoping they can’t hear my thoughts.

CHAPTER 61

ROO: Celestial Dust Goddess

"So what brings you out here anyway?" asks Ruby.

"It's all Vinnie's idea." I speak for her because she's gone quiet. Maybe it's to do with last night. She hasn't said a word about what was going on. "She's making me take photos so she can pimp me out." I shoot her a sardonic grin to show I mean well.

"Making you? Pah! You love it." She blows me a kiss, then suddenly looks coy, which isn't like Vinnie.

Ruby grins. "Like your mum, hey, Vinnie. Aggie was a fixer too. Failed with me. Obviously."

I glance at Vin, wondering if she's ready for Aggie-talk.

Ruby crosses her arms on the table. "Yep, did her best with Carla too. Wanted Carla to do more painting, get gallery representation, all that. I remember the two of them trekking around the city, Aggie with a big satchel over her shoulder and fake glasses to make her look impressive. She pretended to be Carla's agent. Went to every gallery in Sydney, just about. Made out that Carla was some sort of wunderkind, and if they didn't represent her, they'd be sorry. Ha! She had some guts, that Aggie, I'll give her that."

Vinnie nods. I try to read her thoughts. Her mouth is stitched tight.

"She had guts, didn't she? Even her choice to die took a truckload of courage, if you ask me."

Okay. It's enough. *Please stop*, I think. Vinnie lowers her eyes. I squeeze her hand under the table.

"Not courage," she whispers. I barely hear her. I only know

she's talking because her mouth is no longer pinched into a straight line.

We only ever talked about Aggie's suicide once, the day after it happened. It was bleak weather—storming. Trees down. Aggie dead. Mum was downstairs in Vin's kitchen with Mike. Vinnie and I were in the bathroom, sitting on the edge of the tub. While rain hammered the window and wind shook the walls, she was motionless.

She recited Aggie's death like stage direction. Mike blamed himself, she said, for leaving out the pills. She blamed herself for going to Lilah's. Was there a note? I asked. No. No note. No one will ever know what Aggie was thinking. Vin told me she felt guilty that she hadn't cried yet.

I was so lost in: *Crap, what do I say? Have I said enough?* But should have asked: "How are you feeling?"

I didn't know that those five minutes on the edge of the tub would be my only opportunity. Since then, stirring Aggie's name into conversation means Vin changes the topic so fast, you get whiplash.

Now, she stands and leaves via the beaded curtain. There's a light chinkle as the plastic beads fall back into place.

"Did I say something wrong?" asks Ruby. I don't understand why she's confused. Isn't it obvious?

"Er, it's tricky for Vin, all that stuff about her mum," I say.

Ruby narrows her eyes and frowns. She picks up the cigarette she stubbed out earlier and relights it. She sits back and blows smoke toward the ceiling.

"Must have been awful for Vin and Mike. I guess I found a way to make sense of it in my head. Don't have my own kids, so never stopped to think what Vinnie makes of it all. Hell, I'm sorry."

I don't say anything, though I'm relieved she feels bad. I push back my chair.

"I'm going to check on her," I say.

Vinnie's not in the shop. I find her around the back in the garden, which is less a garden and more a patch of sand, with crystals forming mandala patterns among stubby plants and shards of grass.

She sits on a white block of granite, drawing in the sand with her foot. Her cheeks are damp.

"You okay?" She doesn't reply. "Ruby's sorry," I add. "She told me she was."

"Do you think she's right?" she asks eventually, pushing away tears but not looking up.

"About—?"

"About Mum being brave. Is it brave to take your own life?"

My heart hammers. This is it. This is Vin and I talking openly about Aggie. I can't mess this up. I need to tread carefully.

"Ah . . . um—" I start.

Her shoulders hunch and she turns away from me. *Good one, Roo. You handled that with a lot of grace. What the hell, man?*

I scrabble for words. What do I want to say? I can't bring Aggie back. I can't make things better.

"It's okay to hurt, Vin. No one denies you that" is all I manage. She's quiet but turns back and leans against me, so maybe it was an okay thing to say after all.

Ruby appears before we can pick up any more pieces; the sun filtering through her sundress, dust billowing around her with each step. She carries two glasses, which she hands to us. Tiny bubbles stream upward.

"A glass of champas on the house. An apology for being a blockhead," she says.

Vinnie smiles a bit. We clink glasses and take a sip. The bubbles itch the back of my nose. I've never had champagne before and swear I am drunk after the first sip.

Ruby takes us through her crystal garden and tells us what's what and what stones help which ailments. I retain nothing. Vinnie, however, looks like she's taking serious notes. She asks questions like, "So is this one of the crystals you charge with the full moon?" All seems to be forgiven.

I ask Ruby if I can take her photo. She's pretty extraordinary, out here in her garden, a celestial dust goddess bathed in afternoon sun. She says she can't remember the last time someone took her photo. I tell her not to pose. Just to keep talking to Vin, which she does. She doesn't mention Aggie again. While I'm happy for Vinnie, I'm also sad because I think if we can't talk about Aggie with one of her mum's oldest friends, when can we?

CHAPTER 62

VINNIE: Emu in the Sky

"Vinnie was an amazing Daisy," Roo tells Ruby that night as we eat at a picnic table under the stars. She's been drilling me about all the plays I've ever been in and seems particularly excited about *Gatsby*, which is her favorite Luhrmann film.

I'm proud of myself for maintaining an MS-free zone, despite having had a sip of champagne and all the emotion brought on by thinking about Mum. Tonight, I'm basically a normal human teenager. As long as you don't count the way I am thinking about my best friend, Roo, imagining his warmth, his smell, his hands on me . . . *Stop, Vinnie Smith. Just stop, will you? Sheesh.*

"Love Daisy," says Ruby. "Carey Mulligan all the way, right?"

"Vinnie Smith, more like it," says Roo, smiling at me.

"You didn't even see me," I say to Roo. "You can't just assume I was good."

"Other than assuming you're good at everything, which I do, I did actually see you perform. Your brilliance is verified."

"When? I couldn't get you tickets. You weren't there." I'd looked for him, hoping he'd snuck in.

"I watched from the lobby on opening night. I left you flowers with the old guy."

"What the—?" I stare at him. Flickering candlelight makes funny shapes across his beautiful face. "What flowers? What old guy?"

"The one who mans the lobby. Told me to fob off. Cravat Guy?"

"Oh no! Gerard? Ha, that's hilarious. Yes, he's a bit of a tyrant. But a sweet one! Since he retired he's put one hundred percent of his energy into community theater. It's pretty cute."

"Cute and hostile like a nasty turtle. He stole your chrysanthemums and made you think I was a bad friend."

"I never thought that. I'm so sorry about Gerard." Roo was there. Roo is always there. I'm heating up in places I didn't even know existed.

"Speaking of *Gatsby*, I have a surprise for you guys," says Ruby, taking our plates and stacking them precariously. "Wait here."

Roo and I sit quietly. I'm trying not to look at him while hoping desperately he's looking at me, and urgently wanting to look at him. Hold his face in mine. Kiss his lips . . . *Oh, come on, Vinnie Smith! Get your act together! This is your* best friend.

When I steal a glance, his eyes are closed and his legs are crossed at the ankles. He smiles into the night. I wonder what he's thinking about.

Ruby returns with a white sheet bundled under her arm. She strings it up between the washing line and the gutter, then chucks us each a pillow. She demands we study the stars while she sets up the projector. Roo points out the emu in the sky. It's made from the dark space between the stars. Now that I've seen it I feel ridiculous that I have never seen it before.

Ruby only has one DVD that still works, so we watch Luhrmann's *Romeo + Juliet*, the screen flapping and distorting Leonardo's and Claire's faces. The laptop dies at the beginning of Act Two.

"Bugger!" says Ruby.

"Vin should do the monologue," says Roo. "We can't finish the night not knowing what happens."

I roll my eyes. "Everyone knows what happens at the end of *Romeo and Juliet*."

I can tell they both want me to do it. I don't know, though, if I can. My jaw is locked. I'm scared that being Juliet out here under the stars will be me declaring my undying love for Roo. And that will be awkward.

"Vinnie! Vinnie!" they chant.

I breathe deeply to rally, then stand in front of the billowing sheet. I can do this. I can pretend this is all a big performance. It's what I do best.

Roo pushes himself up from the cushion. "I guess I'd better be your Romeo."

Dang it.

Yet somehow, we manage to finish the whole play—Roo reading lines from his phone, me acting like cardboard. Ruby certainly doesn't seem to mind. She descends into applause.

"This is the best night I've ever had!" she roars. The end of her cigarette glows.

*

Roo and I lie on either side of the room in the dark. He's asleep. His breath is a breeze across the desert, cooling and comforting. I want to say his name, but I don't want to wake him.

My body pulses, remembering the sensation of being curled against him in Thunderbolt's cave. Grateful that Roo's oblivious.

It's weird. I've known him my whole life, but all of a sudden, it's like we've never met and I'm desperate to know everything about him. Every particle. Every thought. I want him wrapped around me and I want to sink into him because . . . I *like* him.

Like, in a way friends shouldn't.

In the privacy of the dark, I allow myself to imagine our

limbs coiled together. His cheek against my back. No space between us.

What am I doing? This is *Roo*, who I've known forever! How would he feel finding out his best friend is into him? Won't he be weirded out?

If only I could control this feeling surging through me, cloaking me, and hemming me in.

I groan audibly because no one knows better than me that bodies do whatever the hell they want sometimes.

CHAPTER 63

ROO: Monkey Just Ate Bum Fluff

Ruby is at the guest room door, nursing coffee.

"Rise and shine, bright sparks," she coos.

From the single bed at the other side of the room, Vinnie groans. I sit up and adjust my pajamas so they cover my bare stomach.

Ruby laughed when Vin asked her to come to Green Valley with us last night. "And what, ride a roller coaster or something?"

"Why not?" Vin had said. "You'd be hanging out with us an extra day."

Judging by her wide smile, I got the impression Ruby loved our company. She told us that since her dad passed away, she's lived alone. Online orders keep her busy, but the shop barely has customers. Yesterday, the only visitor wasn't looking for crystals. He wanted directions to Inverell because he'd run out of phone juice.

Ruby rides shotgun. Vin's asked me to drive again. I try to catch her eye in the rearview, but her head lolls against the backrest, her eyes closed. We pass eucalyptus forests and paddocks where sheep look like rocks.

Joy is having a hard morning and can't even hit forty miles an hour. I let her sit at thirty-five. When we turn off the tar and shudder down the dusty track, I get a knot of familiarity in my stomach.

There it is: Green Valley Farm. Like lots of places you visited as a kid, it's shrunk. We're the first to arrive so are greeted warmly at the gate.

We drink scalding coffee under the peppercorn tree. My tongue is burned raw. While Ruby and Vin make observations about the quaint park, I get an insane urge to be twelve again. I want Vinnie and I to split from the parentals and spend the morning darting from dodgy ride to dodgy ride, hauling the roller coaster buggy up the hill and screaming as we careen down. I want to feel the hot sting of tin on my skinny thighs as we do the giant slide. I want to make her laugh when we ride the seesaw. I want Aggie to still be alive and Vinnie to not be in pain. She might be all smiles for her audience, but I can tell she's holding the grief at bay—squaring her jaw at the world.

"Ruby!" A cherry-cheeked man in a torn undershirt ambles out to collect our empty cups.

"Max!" They kiss each other directly on the mouth. Vin and I exchange glances.

"And who are these two?" he asks. "I want names and details."

Ruby introduces us and explains the connection, skimming over specifics, so she doesn't have to say Aggie's name. I wish she'd just say it: "Aggie."

Ruby tells us she and Max are "friends with benefits," which makes Vin and I laugh.

Max draws up a chair, pushing me and Vin closer. Our knees drift together under the table. I want to press against her. But she gets up, swinging her plastic chair back. It crashes sideways to the ground. I leap up.

"Oops! Sorry!" She straightens the chair and hurries away, her arms clutched over her stomach.

"She's not as sparkly as I remember her," says Ruby. "You two used to be like day and night. Her the day."

“Thanks,” I mumble.

“Ah, come on. I don’t mean it badly! I just mean she used to have a bit more spunk about her. Exam stress, you reckon?”

“Maybe.”

“Stuff with her mum?” she says after a beat.

Since her faux pas yesterday, Ruby is as careful with the elephant in the room as I am, tentatively walking around it. Now that Vinnie’s not here, she has permission to say its name and gently prod its backside.

“I just wish she could talk to me about it,” I say glumly. “About Aggie.”

Her name thumps on the cast-iron table between us. Max eyes us curiously.

“Terrible tragedy,” Ruby explains to Max. “Vinnie’s mum killed herself a while back.”

It sounds so flippant, the way she says it.

Max slurps his coffee. “Holy moley. That’s full-on.”

I don’t know how to add to this conversation so I go find Vinnie, who is staring at three monkeys on a branch. Their cage is too small. They stare back at her. One sticks his finger in his butt then into his mouth. When I laugh, she spins around.

“Monkey just ate bum fluff,” she says.

“Revolting.” This sets her off.

When the laughter trickles out, I say, “Hey, Vin, are you . . . okay? I mean, if ever you want to talk about your mum or anything . . .” I know that dislodging the cork is risky. She stiffens.

Shut up, Roo. Absolutely shut the hell up.

“Sorry,” I say.

She squeezes her eyes tight. When she opens them, they’re filmy.

CHAPTER 64

VINNIE: Love Makes You Do Funny Things

I can be normal, I tell myself. I am a three-act two-hour play on Broadway. Anything is possible when you expend enough effort. Roo doesn't need to know I'm thinking about him in that way, because I am an *actor*.

"Nah, it's okay," I say. "It's really nothing." As long as you can't read my X-rated thoughts. "Should we see if Max wants to give us a special 'friends with benefits' tour?"

"Ew. Gross."

Thank goodness we can move on. Also, I don't want to do this Mum stuff here. Not with the sound of rickety roller coasters, and heat searing my shoulders. Who knows if there's ever a good time or place to tease out everything knotted inside me?

Max is excited to take us around. He tells us we're guests of honor, but I think it's mainly that he's hoping Ruby will invite him over later. He tells us names of the trees and bushes in the oasis garden. A yak eats from my hand. A cockatoo tells Roo he needs a haircut.

The whole time, I am a perfectly ordinary seventeen-year-old *friend*. I stay a healthy yard or so from Roo at all times. I keep blushes to a minimum. I make as much eye contact with Max and Ruby as I make with Roo. I laugh as loudly at their quips as I do Roo's.

I won't lie. The effort is grueling. Every now and then, like when Roo's holding Gary the cockatoo at arm's length so he doesn't peck his ear off, I melt into: *Look at him. He's the cutest. I want to stroke that dimpled cheek so bad.* I squash the thought. Press it deep into the darkest part of my body, lock the door, and throw away the key.

I'm relieved when Roo and Max stride ahead toward the museum. Ruby wraps her arm around my waist as we fall back from the others.

"How's Year Eleven?" she asks.

"You know. I'm not great at academic stuff or anything. But I get by."

"It's great you're still into all that acting stuff. You're good. Always were."

"Thanks," I say.

"And how's your dad doing?"

I eye her. Why's she asking all this? I'm picking up a serious edge to her questions.

"He's pretty good. Oh, do you mean does he have a girlfriend or something?"

"No! Nothing like that. Just making conversation. I haven't seen you lot since—" She's about to say "the funeral," I can tell, but she pauses and says, "My last trip east" instead.

I get this sudden urge to tell Ruby everything. About the exhaustion. The dizzy spells. The double vision. How I am avoiding getting diagnosed because I don't want to hear the truth. I want to tell her I'm having unchristian thoughts about Roo. And about that one time I kissed my best friend's crush. Ex–best friend, if you consider she also stabbed me in the back. And then there's missing Mum—the torn-off limb everyone knows about but no one talks about because where do you even start?

Ruby's not blood-related but may as well be. At the funeral,

I cried so hard when she hugged me, as if a valve had been released.

Wouldn't it be nice to let go?

But I don't open the valve.

"Your back is covered in flies," I say, helping Ruby swat them away.

*

Roo, Ruby, and Max go on the homemade roller coaster. I pretend to have a headache and sit in the shade watching them. Doing the roller coaster at Green Valley was my number-one priority when planning this trip. But I know riding it will spell disaster for my broken body.

The others are hot and sweaty when they approach. Max and Ruby beam at each other like little kids.

"Roo, why don't you take some pictures of Max and the owners for social media," Ruby suggests. "Roo's a good photographer," she tells him.

Roo's cheeks pink up. But he says, "Okay."

Max looks stoked. "I should go freshen up." He wipes sweat from his forehead, which makes his thin hair stand up straight like a toothbrush.

"No, no," says Roo. "You look good like that." When the owners come out, he snaps a few pics of them in the shade, then gets them to take turns using the play equipment.

I smile, watching Roo command the scene. I know definitively that this trip was the right thing for him. Look at him, so confident in himself. He's unapologetic about his craft, like he deserves to be.

This, I think, *is an appropriate friend-like mentality. More of this, please.*

I brainstorm names for his exhibition at the Citadel. "Lens

and Lensibility." "Roo Lens a Hand." "Lensuality." Ha.

Max serves a family at the kiosk, then brings us ham sandwiches made with white bread. Roo doesn't say anything as he plucks ham from his bread and puts it on my plate. I take a few bites of my own sandwich. At some point, Roo's knee rests against mine. My skin lights up like a lava lamp until I suddenly catch on and withdraw so fast, I smash into the table leg. But whatever. At least my leg has reined in its behavior.

Roo shuffles uncomfortably beside me, putting extra space between us, which is the right thing to do.

"I remember something about them making this place for a girl who died?" I say to Max as he sits with us to have a cup of tea.

He looks sad. "Irene died just before she turned sixteen. Her parting wish was that this place was opened to the public."

"So they built her a theme park?"

Max nods. "Yep."

"That's really nice," says Roo.

"They're lovely people," says Max. "Love makes you do funny things."

On the way back to Ruby's, we drive into the sunset, and I think about all the funny things love can make you do. Drive a van across the tablelands. Sleep in a cave. Watch a monkey eat bum fluff. Pretend you don't have MS.

It's risky, but I glance up at the rearview mirror. Roo's smiling at me, which floods my entire body. I let myself smile back. In my lap, I nurse the jar of pickled lamb brains Max gifted us, wondering what other crazy things love will make me do.

CHAPTER 65

ROO: One Song Bleeds into Another

Vin's being super weird as we pack the next morning. She shuffles stiffly around me and flinches when our arms cross, zipping my faulty backpack closed.

I trawl my brain, trying to work out what I've done to upset her. Then I remember that night in the cave. Her body cold and clammy against mine.

"You feeling all right?" I ask her. Ruby's poured us coffee and is going through her pantry to try to find the cereal she swore she bought.

"Yes!" Vin beams at me. "Why?"

"You know, you were up that night at Thunderbolt's, all shivery. Today, you seem kind of . . . off? Still headachy?"

"I'm fine." Her tone is blunt and her beam switches off. She scowls into her coffee before taking a sip. It splashes over the side, pooling on Ruby's table.

"Darnit." She gets up. I grab a sponge from the sink. Our fingers touch, the sponge between us. She snaps away from me. I let go, and the sponge lands on the floor.

"Did I do something wrong?" I ask, picking it up, because now it feels like this is about me.

"No. It's not you—sorry." She summons a small smile. "I'm just being a freak. Ignore me."

She's impossible to ignore.

"Well! I must have chucked it out!" says Ruby, giving up the cereal hunt. "Toast okay?"

*

We leave Ruby's after ten. Vin's asked me to drive again. She assures me it's just because she's tired.

She's quiet during the ride, and I have no idea what to say, so I make dumb remarks like, "Look at that tree!" and "Is that a sheep?"

She mumbles in reply. I keep glancing over, trying to read her expression.

"Can you stop that?" she says tersely as we drive into Guyra.

"Stop what?" But I know full well what she means.

"Being a grandma. You keep looking at me like you think I am going to spew or something."

"Sorry."

"It's fine."

Since we haven't had reception since Tingha, we haven't played music, which is adding to the weirdness of the morning. Now, she puts on a study music playlist that I'd forgotten was downloaded on my phone. The irony of me having a study playlist is not lost on me. The music suits the landscape perfectly. It was made for it.

It occurs to me that maybe Vin's being weird because of stuff with her mum. Visiting the places we went with Aggie must be reopening wounds for her.

I bet, like me, she's remembering the five of us, alive and well, inhabiting this landscape. Her mum striding up Bald Rock, or flicking us with water from her hair as she spins beside the water hole. She's probably hearing the songs Aggie played by the campfire. Sixties stuff, like the Beatles and Bob Dylan. Songs to sing along to.

Part of me feels bad about the pain Vin must be in, remembering it all. Another part is relieved. It would be so much better if we could finally talk about Aggie again. Maybe then, Vin could start to heal. We all could.

"It's kind of weird, isn't it?" I say, keeping my eyes on the road.

"What is?"

"The trip." How do I say it without saying Aggie's name aloud?

"What are you on about, Roo? It's not weird. It's lovely. Are you not enjoying it?" I allow myself a glance. She looks confused. "We can go back, if you want."

"No! No. I don't mean that. I mean—your mum and stuff."

"Oh."

Her mouth bows downward. She stares out the window. The music gets louder. From the corner of my eye, I can see she's pressing the volume button on the phone.

"Sorry," I mutter. "It was stupid. I shouldn't have said anything."

She puts her hand on my arm, the one using the gearshift. I turn. "It's all good, Roo. All of it. Good. Don't worry about it!" And flashes me a grin.

I keep my arm as still as possible, hoping to keep her hand there. It stays for a bit, then she pulls it back. My jaw tightens as I keep my eyes straight ahead.

It's my fault, really. I should have talked more about Aggie these last couple of years. Casual mentions like, "Didn't Aggie prefer crunchy peanut butter?" and "Hey, coral was one of Aggie's favorite colors, wasn't it?"

Instead, a bomb went off in a far-off land and, like everyone else, I didn't say a word. Just imagined the gaping hole it left in the landscape.

"'Celebrity Heads'?" Her words cut through the tension.

"What? Oh. Yeah, sure."

"Great! I have one. Ask me questions."

She turns the music down a fraction, and I keep asking questions until I land on "Am I Dolly Parton?"

"Ha, yep. Thought you'd get it sooner. My turn!"

*

We stop at Ebor Falls to eat sandwiches in the van. There's so much more water and power in the falls than the last time we were here, which is symbolic; like the land is expressing itself in a way we've not been able to.

We keep traveling fifty minutes up the road toward Crystal Shower Falls. Vinnie sleeps the last fifteen. The van's quiet apart from Joy's heaving lungs.

When we park, Vinnie ditches her sandals and changes into sneakers. We look out over the valley from the Sky Walk. I can't say why, but things feel normal again between us. So normal, she makes me recreate the picture of us from when we were twelve. She gives my phone to a nice Korean lady, who happily obliges. She's airborne—Vinnie, not the lady. I'm looking soberly toward Woollumbin.

It rained last night so the path down to the falls is slippery. Vinnie clutches my arm as we walk. It feels like she's using me as an anchor rather than just wanting to be close. While we walk, she describes a movie she saw once at a French film festival. I miss the name of it and, to be honest, I hardly follow what the film is about.

At some point, she makes us stop. She seems puffed, which is odd given how slow we're going and the fact that we're going downhill. Her hand's clammy like it was the night in the cave.

"We can sit for a bit," I say. "There's a stump over there."

She swallows. "Okay, yeah. I'll have a bit of water. Sorry. Just feeling—ugh. It's fine."

She puts her head in her hands and closes her eyes.

"If you're unwell, we can go to the guesthouse early."

"I'm fine, Roo!" she says.

We're out of water. When two girls approach, I hail them over. They're older than us, but not by much. One has faded blue dreads. The prettier of the two wears a wispy skirt and hiking boots.

"Sorry, but do you guys have any water?" I ask. "My friend's dehydrated."

"Course!" says Wispy Skirt. She whips out a metal bottle and hands it to Vin. "Dehydration is the worst, right?"

Vinnie sips gratefully but remains pale.

"Are you sick?" asks Wispy Skirt.

"Sorry," says Vin. The girl makes a point of wiping the rim of the bottle before recapping it.

"Let's turn back," I say.

"No!" says Vin. "We have to do a shot under the waterfall. For the show."

"Oh, you're a photographer?" Wispy Skirt eyes my camera. "That's cool."

"Nah," I say just as Vin says, "Yes! He can take your portrait if you like! He's very good."

The girl beams. She yanks her friend's sleeve. "How great is that? We forgot our phones in the car. I was bummed that we weren't going to get any pics, so it's fate we met you."

"Perfect!" says Vinnie. "I'll wait here and catch my breath a bit. Don't want to slow you guys down."

She puts her head back in her hands. I'm stuck because I don't want to keep going toward the falls without Vin, especially with her looking out of it. But these two girls want me to take their photo.

"I'll be fine. Go!" says Vin without looking up. As usual, I do as she says.

CHAPTER 66

VINNIE: The Rainforest Closes In

The dizziness began the moment I woke up this morning, followed by double vision with a side of exhaustion. Because spending two whole nights staring at the guy who is meant to be your best friend is not only weird, it's also a great way to whip your symptoms into action.

The ground shifts, splits, and swirls.

The rainforest closes in.

With what little sense I have left, I try to manifest another Vinnie Smith. One radiating good health, on a stage preferably. An ordinary Vinnie with Lilah on the sidelines, beaming like we're still friends. And there's Roo. My . . . friend? Boyfriend? It's so hard to know how to even begin untangling the mess inside me.

My breath staggers as I grip the stump to steady myself.

CHAPTER 67

ROO: A Butterfly over Her Head

The wispy skirt girl's name is Maeve. Her friend is Sara. Sara shows me the Orion's Belt tat on her forearm, then lifts up her shirt to reveal an army of inked ants marching across her back.

After I get my shot for Vin of the waterfall, the girls get me to take a dozen photos of them on the suspended bridge. By girls, I mean Maeve. She stands under the waterfall and waves at me to take more. She gestures for me to come closer. I grip my camera with one hand, the rail in the other, and make my way down the rocks toward where they are standing. Maeve asks for this shot, then that. Each time, she does a funny pout that looks unnatural, like she's seen someone do it in a magazine. Each time, I hope it's the last photo. I'm anxious to get back to Vin.

"Can I see?" She grabs my sleeve.

I show her. She grins. "These are great, Roo! Where'd you learn all this?"

I shrug. "I guess I've taken photos for as long as I can remember."

"They're very professional. You don't even need to filter these."

"Thanks," I say, feeling embarrassed. "So, do you think you have enough?"

"Can we just do a couple more, pretty please?" When she grins, her dimples lengthen and deepen. "It's not every day you have an actual photographer at your mercy." I redden at that.

Maeve takes my hand and guides me toward the wet wall behind the falls. It's just the two of us looking through the veil of water. Sara hangs back to read an information sign. I feel awkward still holding Maeve's hand but don't want to offend her by letting it go.

"Okay, so I'm thinking I'll just sit here." She releases me as she lowers herself onto the stone. Her eyes, blue and round, angle up at me. "Take it from up there. Yeah. That's right. Is it good?"

It's actually a pretty decent shot. Better, when she turns to face the falls and light reflects from the bridge of her nose. She's forgotten to pout. The world is a white canvas behind her.

She gets me to pull her to standing. Sara joins us, carrying a butterfly on her finger.

"Wow. An orchard swallowtail. Beautiful." Maeve holds out her finger for the butterfly to climb aboard. It has a gathering of blue and red spots on its tail. Its wings are otherwise white with thin gray vertical stripes.

"You know its name?" I ask.

"Maeve's doing a PhD in Biology," says Sara.

"Actually, it's in Entomology," says Maeve. "So insects are completely my thing. Butterflies are a personal fave. The world would fall apart if it weren't for critters like this little lady. Here, girl—" She holds the butterfly to the sky, and it catches the breeze. I manage to get a shot of it as it hovers above Maeve's hair. I lower my camera and watch as it flutters through the vapor and disappears.

"That's pretty cool," I say. Here I was feeling frustrated at Maeve for being a bit vacuous, with all the posy photos. Goes to show how much I know. I hadn't even heard of entomology until a moment ago.

Sara's also doing a PhD. Hers is in Ancient History. She's studying the intersection between Western and Eastern thinking in classical cultures or something like that. I have no idea what she's talking about but nod along as we head back toward Vinnie. I'm intimidated by their intelligence.

As we turn the corner, I see a group of people huddled on the path. Approaching, I register what's going on.

Vin lies in the center of their worried flower. I run to her, nearly slipping in the mud.

CHAPTER 68

VINNIE: Faces Bearing Down on Me

I open my eyes to see two or three faces bearing down on me. One of them wears an Aussie Digger bucket hat.

"She's okay," one of the faces says.

"Vinnie? What happened?" Roo crouches beside me and tucks a strand of hair behind my ear.

"I-I'm just . . ." I trail off. What can I say? I tried to join the others at the falls. It didn't go well.

"Here." The guy in the hat presses a water canister into my hands when I sit up. Trembling, I try to unscrew the lid. He takes over and shoves it at my lips. It clunks against my teeth. I sip gratefully, the water clearing the passages of my head.

"Take it easy," says an older woman, a red raincoat tied around her waist. "Don't get up too fast."

"I'll call an ambulance," says Aussie Digger Guy, holding up his phone to find reception.

"No!" I exclaim a little too loudly. "I'm okay. Really. Just dehydrated. It's no big deal."

"It *is* a big deal!" Roo seems mad at me, which is a little inappropriate given the situation.

I wave him off and stand. The cluster breaks apart. I need to prove to Roo and everyone else that I'm fine, which I do by squaring my shoulders and standing hip-width apart. A steady and healthy position anyone would assume. His eyebrows raise above his glasses.

"You know what I need? Chocolate!" I lock my arm into his

and drag him up the path toward the parking lot, confident and as steady as freaking Uluru.

*

We arrive at the Belfry an hour or so later, a beautiful colonial-style guesthouse by the river. We stayed here a few times as kids when our parents had enough of setting up and packing down tents. We've been given a room with one double bed. I try to change it, but the lady tells me they're full up.

"Is that okay, you reckon?" I ask Roo.

I know it's completely not okay, as much as I want to share a bed with him. But I want to hear what he thinks. He can be our normal friendship barometer.

He nods. His cheeks flush, though, and I get a weird thought: *What if Roo's struggling with our friendship barometer too?*

"It's kinda awkward," I explain to the lady. "We've known each other since we were born. We probably had baths together and all that, but it's been a while since we shared a bed." Outside Thunderbolt's Hideout, that is. If that counts as a bed.

She beams at us knowingly. "Honey, I get it. If anything comes available, I'll let you know."

With the mess of the day, I have stupidly forgotten to extract cash from Carla's envelope without Roo seeing. The lady waits for me to pay while I process my options.

"Ah . . ." I turn away slightly, bending to conceal the envelope, and slide out two fifty-dollar notes. It won't be enough, darn it. "Can I pay you the rest later? I left my wallet in the van."

"No problem, sweetie," she says, accepting my deposit. I glance at Roo, who is watching me. Did he see the envelope and wonder why I am carrying around so much cash?

I lead us upstairs to room 17. We stand in the doorway, looking at the only bed in the room.

"I can sleep on the floor," I say.

"Don't be silly. If anyone sleeps on the floor, it's me."

"No way! You don't always have to be the martyr, Roo."

"Who are you calling a martyr? You're paying, remember? Well, I'll pay you back. But for now, it's your money. As if I am going to let you sleep on the floor. I'll bring the mattress in from the Kombi. It'll be fine."

"Yeah, good idea." Secretly, I'm disappointed. I don't want Roo to bring in the mattress. I want him to spoon me to sleep.

We eat Yemen street food in the skatepark. Two older guys zoom in the bowl doing cool tricks on their boards. Roo gets me to hold his malawach pastry roll so he can take photos.

"I like that one," I say, pointing to one on his viewfinder of the older guy who's airborne, the setting sun between his board and the ramp. "You're lucky, you know."

"How so?"

"Being able to do that. You don't even have to try."

"Huh," he says.

"Hey, you guys!" The two girls from the walk approach.

"Hey, Maeve. Sara," says Roo.

The beautiful blond girl, who must be Maeve, waves like an overexcited kindergarten teacher. She squeezes next to me. I smell her Herbal Essences shampoo.

"Are you feeling okay, Vinnie?" she asks.

"Totally!" I grin back. "It really was nothing."

Roo shoots me a glare. He's probably still cross at me for not drinking enough water earlier.

"Hey, we bought a tub of Ben & Jerry's we can't finish on our own," says Maeve. I'm trying to think who she looks like . . . Elle Fanning? "You guys want in? I saw you're staying at the Belfry too. We can play board games on the deck, if you want."

"Sounds good," says Roo.

Now I shoot him a look, surprised. It's not like Roo to jump at an opportunity to hang out with strangers. Then again, this very attractive woman is offering ice cream. While I was kinda hoping to go to bed in a few minutes to shake off the veil of exhaustion that's clung to me all afternoon, I nod. "Love me a bit of Ben & Jerry's," I say. "What flavor are we talking?"

CHAPTER 69

ROO: Socks on the Staircase

I watch Vinnie like a hawk. I can tell she's annoyed at me for being too attentive. But that's what you get for collapsing on a rainforest walk.

"Roo, it's your go," says Maeve. She licks the back of her spoon and looks at herself in its reflection.

I study my letters. Mostly, I think about the double bed upstairs and the fact that I am meant to bring the mattress in from the van but haven't yet.

"Ah," I murmur. Vinnie leans over. Throughout the whole game, she's been helping me out, trying to cover for my stupidity. Not for the first time this evening, I wish Scrabble weren't the only game left in the common room.

"Move your *P* there. Yep. Look!" She points to the board. "You get a triple letter!"

I still can't see the word she means so she lays the tiles on the board for me. *P-U-R-E*.

"You're not meant to play for Roo," says Sara.

Vinnie glances up sharply. "Roo doesn't mind, do you?"

"Course he doesn't," says Sara. She yawns, which makes Vinnie yawn. The dark rings under her eyes make her look like someone smudged her with charcoal stick. I hope this yawning circle is a sign that things are wrapping up down here on the deck.

"You know what?" says Vinnie. "I am so exhausted after today. I'm going to take a shower. Roo, you're okay to finish without me, aren't you?"

"Um—" I start, wanting to say, "No, of course, not!" but Maeve grins widely and speaks for me.

"He's going to be okay, Vinnie. Promise. You go have yourself a nice warm shower and get into bed. You've had a tough day."

Maeve tips Vinnie's letters into the green bag, which is Vin's signal to leave.

I sit there staring vacantly at a string of characters on my tray, wishing like hell I could get my legs into gear and walk them up the stairs after Vinnie. Without the mattress.

We play a few more rounds. Without Vinnie, the best I can do is a three-letter word: *W-I-N*, which is so ironic, I nearly laugh. No double-letter points. Nothing. It's a good thing I'm not competitive.

At last, the game's over. I'm about to excuse myself, when Sara asks, "Who wants chamomile?"

"Me, please!" says Maeve.

"I might hit the sack. Thanks, though," I say.

"No! Stay up with us a bit longer!" says Maeve. While Sara goes to the kitchen, she reaches behind her and pries an acoustic guitar from the wall. "Do you play?"

I shake my head. The last song I played was "Hot Cross Buns" on the recorder when I was in Year Two.

Maeve tunes the guitar then strums. It takes me a line or two to recognize the song. It's an image gaining focus. Then my body floods. It's a Bob Dylan song: "Boots of Spanish Leather." One of Aggie's favorites.

I find myself singing along, wishing Vinnie had stayed but also glad she didn't because who knows what this would have stirred for her. Aggie wasn't my mum, yet I feel every organ unstitch.

"Aw, sweet!" Maeve sweeps a soft hand across my face when she finishes. "You're crying!"

"Oh, I am. Sorry."

"Don't apologize, silly. It's lovely!"

Sara returns with three steaming cups and lowers them to the wooden table between us.

"Nice playing, Maeve," she says. I turn away and wipe the last of my tears from my face, hoping Maeve doesn't tell Sara she made me cry.

Sara lodges song requests. Maeve only plays old music, the kind of thing Mum listens to and Aggie could play. No more tears, though.

When she asks me to request something, I can't think of anything she might know. Baker Boy? Telenova? Conan Gray? It'd be cool if she did, but she won't—it's all too recent. She shrugs when I don't answer and starts playing "Sweet Caroline," which is a nice enough song.

Sara goes to bed, and now it's just me and Maeve. I promise myself that I will get my shit together and lift off the couch right after "Leaving on a Jet Plane," but she's into the next song, and I'm still here.

I'm thinking about Vinnie, curled like a leaf on the bed directly above us, when Maeve finally stops playing and tips toward me. Her lips are on mine—powdery and light. My eyes are wide open, staring back. Hers are closed. She moves closer and kisses me again.

Holy crap.

Just as I had no idea how long she was playing, I have no idea how long we're kissing. Well, technically, it's Maeve kissing me, because I'm a frozen statue going cross-eyed.

She drifts away and smiles, opening her eyes. "That was lovely," she says.

"It was?"

I'm in a weird haze, which means I'm not looking toward the staircase. But my spidey senses pick up Vinnie's presence like they've been trained to do for seventeen years. Now, she's just striped socks scurrying back up the stairs.

CHAPTER 70

VINNIE: Bejeweled

If I lie still enough, Roo will think I'm asleep. My thoughts are anything but still, though, colliding, ricocheting, round-abouting, and going crazy. I squeeze my eyes shut so tight it feels like my whole body goes numb.

I had no idea Roo was into Maeve. I mean, of course he is! She's stunning and older than us. A total catch. If I'd had my wits about me this afternoon, I would have realized she was coming on to him. Like, who is that friendly to two random teenagers? Here I was feeling interesting and cool.

The single worst thing about all this is what I now know for sure.

I like Roo.

Not like, "Hey, my friend Roo is super sweet."

Like, "You're all I can think about. *Please* don't kiss another girl. I won't survive."

But Roo is downstairs kissing another girl.

My eyes spring open and I slap the headboard. My palm stings, but I don't care. What I care about is that Roo might come upstairs any minute with the mattress, and here I am acting like a jealous loony.

I lie still, breathing heavily.

The bedside clock reads 11:31 p.m. Great. I have hours left lying awake, hating everything, longing for Roo, knowing he might never come.

I didn't know I could miss someone this hard.

*

Sun slants through the shutters. Birdcalls fill the valley. Of course, I never actually slept, which is going to be the single worst thing for my symptoms, especially after a day like yesterday.

The other single worst thing is that Roo never came back.

Why would he?

I played out every scenario of him and beautiful Maeve in my mind last night. A stop-motion of gritty images, their bodies entwined. Their lips locked. Hands everywhere.

I bury my head in my exhausted hands. I want to cry but am empty.

I'm being a selfish idiot, I know. Isn't this everything I wanted for Roo? Isn't this why we are even here, on this road trip? I wanted him to find himself. Be confident in who he is. What better validation is there than being kissed by a college girl like her?

Under the shower, I try to let it all melt away. I need to be happy for Roo somehow. This is what he deserves.

The last thing he needs is to be romantically attached to me.

Broken, unfixable me.

*

"Hey, you guys!" I say, shining at sixty kilowatts. The three of them, Roo, Maeve, and Sara, nurse coffees in chipped cups as they sit at the same table we gathered around last night. Nearby, a couple huddle together, cradling teacups. They're dressed in yoga pants and wear their long hair knotted into giant buns on top of their heads. A pair of topknot pigeons.

If they squint hard enough, the yoga couple might see the four of us as cool people, hanging together, inspiring one another. They might even wish they were still young like us, with a future stretching ahead of them and so much potential.

Maeve beams up at me. Roo nearly spills his coffee. (Tremble noted.) He can't look me in the eye. I'm determined not to make him feel bad, so I beam back.

"Who won?" I ask.

"Scrabble, you mean?" asks Sara. Roo and Maeve don't reply. I nod. "Oh, Maeve. By, like, ten points. I nearly had it, but she got me on the last word." She pokes her tongue out at Maeve, who retorts with her own tongue poke. I swallow, wishing I could think about anything except Maeve's tongue, which I now know has a lime-green stud through it.

"Are you guys around today still?" I ask the girls.

"Yeah. We booked for three nights. One left. We love it here," says Sara.

My heart sinks. But I say, "Great!" With all the effort I have left, I smile at Roo. He looks so far into his coffee you'd think he's about to disappear into it. "I thought we might head up to the Promised Land, if you're keen to join us?"

Roo doesn't move or look at me. Maeve, on the other hand, does. "Totally!" she says. "It was our plan too. But I'm kinda hoping you'll take us in the Kombi. She's such a beauty."

"She is," I say.

I know this role well. This "Shine for You" performance. I've shone for Lilah and Molly and anyone else who needed my glow. I'll shine for Roo for the rest of my life because that's the kind of friend I am—positively bejeweled.

CHAPTER 71

ROO: Glistening Downstream

Vinnie insists we pick up malawach pastry rolls before heading out to the Promised Land, even though we had them last night. I park mine on my lap, grease seeping through the paper and making a spot on my jeans.

Maeve and I sit in the back. She's the same chatty person she was yesterday and doesn't seem to mind that I froze up like a weirdo and took myself to sleep in the van. I guess college girls have the capacity to move on quickly. I saw her being cozy with a dude in the kitchen this morning. They discussed granola preferences. Maybe I'm one in a string of holiday flirtations.

I do my best to be stiff and unapproachable, keeping a good twelve inches between us. She's making it hard, leaning toward me so she can talk to Sara and Vinnie through the gap between the front seats. She lies her arm along my thigh. When her hair gets in my mouth, I discreetly turn away to pluck it out.

Vin and I have been to the Promised Land quite a few times. As the name suggests, it's a magical glade of mossy rocks beside a crystal stream called Never Never River. This was one of our favorite places as kids. We'd egg each other on, determined not to be the first to dive into the icy water. But then one of us would push the other and, next thing, we'd pull the other person in, screaming our heads off as we let the rapids carry us downstream. We'd bob in the water hole by the bridge, then scramble over the rocks to do it again.

Aggie was usually in the water before any of us, as if she

didn't have cold receptors. She'd emerge grinning, shaking droplets into the sun, demanding we follow her in. Mum only ever went in as far as her ankles. Knee-deep once when I was really little. I went under and she had to fish me out.

When we were old enough, Vin and I would take turns on the rope swing while the adults played music on a sunny rock. They'd pluck oily olives from containers with two fingers. Occasionally, other picnickers would sit with them and sing along.

Maeve's borrowed the guitar from the guesthouse and sits on the same spot Aggie once sat to play folk songs. I pick a nearby sun patch and finally take a bite of my malawach, which is soggy and cold.

Vinnie looks like someone put her inside a Barbie doll and told her to put on her best show. I want to get her out of there somehow. Make her angry at me for kissing Maeve. Make her scream about how unfair it is that her mum died. Make her miserable that we're here, on the same rock Aggie stood on when she challenged us to a breath-holding competition.

I don't know what I'm playing at exactly, but I ask Maeve to play "Boots of Spanish Leather," as if it can do the hard work for me and shake Vinnie in a way I don't seem to be able to.

"Sure!" says Maeve, launching into the song. I glance at Vinnie. Her shoulders straighten and she smiles toward the stream. If something's happening in her chest, she reveals nothing.

I take a photo of her like this, holding her shit together like the world depends on her. She turns when she hears the click and smiles sadly before looking away.

Is she sad about the song or the kiss? That's the trouble with packaged emotions. You can't be too sure about the ingredients.

Vinnie pushes up from the rock, yanks off her T-shirt, and

steps out of her jeans. Wearing a purple bra and striped undies, she lowers herself, not even wincing as she hits the cold water.

She floats downstream.

I didn't plan to swim. Yet I undress down to my boxer shorts and follow her in.

"Gah, it's cold!" I say, breaststroking to catch up with her, quietly proud of myself for not drowning. I float beside her for a bit until it's just us in the water hole, dog-paddling. Maeve's singing is a murmur in the background.

"Do you remember that breath-holding thing we did last time?"

"Yeah," she says, disappearing under the water. She's gone for ages. I sink to join her, paddling madly to keep myself down here. Her cheeks are full, with little bubbles trickling out her nose. Just as my head is about to explode, we break the surface and she blows a stream of water into my face. I laugh in surprise.

I feel twelve but not twelve, because look at us, all grown up. Me, loving Vin in a way twelve-year-old me would never have been able to imagine.

"You okay?" I ask.

"Course! Why not?" She dolphin dives under the water, two feet flicking like a tail. When she emerges, she squirts water in my face again. I get her back. She freestyles away from me. I catch up. This time she splashes me with palms flat against the water.

"So, did you and Maeve have fun last night?" she asks, smiling.

"You know nothing happened, right?"

"I know you kissed, Roo. You don't have to be shy. Are you guys going to kiss again? Like, if you need space or anything,

I'm happy to go read in the room. Or the Kombi, if you want the room. I don't mind!" My heart sinks. She wants me to be with Maeve, not with her. I can't tell her how I feel because she'll think I've lost my mind. "If you want to keep going with those guys, I'll understand," she says. "Whatever you want, Roo. I'm just happy to see you like this."

She splashes me again.

"Like what?" Messed up?

"All confident and everything. You were never like this at school. You're only like this—"

"With you," I cut her off. I try to hold her gaze to make her believe me.

She doesn't say anything. Just smiles. A sloping, sad sort of smile.

"Maeve's really nice, but—"

"Go for it, Roo! She's great. You are too! You need to back yourself, you know." Water glistens off her biceps as she lifts herself out of the water. She has goose bumps and is purplish from the cold.

Sun bleaches her out as she picks her way over the rocks. At some point, she stumbles and props herself up by holding one of the bigger rocks. Her honeyed hair is darker now that it's wet and slicked against her back. I watch her go. I let her go. Once more, I have no idea how to tell her how I feel.

When did we get so tongue-tied? I wonder.

CHAPTER 72

VINNIE: Dead on Account of No Charge

Dark clouds gather, sending us back to the Belfry, where Sara tells us she's going to visit a friend. Maeve suggests that the rest of us eat together.

"I have everything we need for a green curry. Maybe you could chop ginger, Roo?"

I want to grab the knife she holds out for him and do the chopping myself. Send Roo to his room so he's far, far away from Maeve. But I know that's stupid and jerky. I need to be okay with all this and give them space. Also, I don't really want to be the third wheel.

"I might head out for a walk, if that's okay. I'm a bit headachy and need air. You guys go ahead!"

"You can't go. It's raining," says Roo.

I'm out the front gate when he jogs up behind me.

"I'll come with you," he says.

"No, silly. Stay with Maeve. This is your chance to have her all to yourself." I summon a smile.

"I don't want her to myself. What are you talking about?" He looks cross. He wipes raindrops from his glasses with his sleeve.

"I'm talking about you two! It's lovely! She's so hot! I'm really, really happy for you."

"My god, Vin, you're so far off the mark—"

"Bye, Roo! I'll see you later!" I sing out as I cross the parking lot.

"Wait up!" he calls. "I'll get our jackets!"

I don't look back and continue hurrying down the street.

It's dark and the rain's getting heavier. I yank down my hood and cross my arms tight across my chest, walking fast so I don't get too wet. There aren't too many people out, because it's a weeknight. Just a few dribbling in and out from the supermarket. The rest of the shops are closed.

I get an insane urge to ring Lilah. I want to tell her everything that's happened. That I've somehow fallen in love with Roo, but now he likes another girl and I feel really horrid about it, but I also feel happy for him, and I'm a total jerk and yeah . . .

I duck under an awning and fish out my phone. It's still dead, on account of never being charged. I sigh. Even if it wasn't, I don't think I'd have the guts to actually call her.

Her face, when she saw Freddie in my house. I'll never forget that hurt.

I miss her so much, I realize. Not just her. I miss Dad too.

I miss Mum.

I wipe a few droplets from the screen, put my dead phone in my pocket, and head into the rain.

"Watch it!" says a man in an oilskin coat.

"Sorry." I dart out of his way. The path is slippery. I use a post to catch myself from falling. Despite the rain, I slow down, so as not to slip, which means I'm getting drenched. I have no idea where I am heading. Who cares, as long as I am not huddled in my room feeling sorry for myself.

I use the pedestrian crossing and launch away from the shops, toward the houses. The door to one is ajar and light spills out. I hear voices. A handwritten sign beside the door reads COMMUNITY THEATER. I push the door open and step inside.

The stage is smaller than at the Citadel. There's a smattering of plastic chairs through the hall. It smells like sausage rolls and sounds like raucous laughter. Onstage, the actors wear cat ears. They're immersed in one of the last scenes from Andrew Lloyd Webber's *Cats*. Without invitation, I slide against the back wall to watch, hoping no one will notice me.

It's just a rehearsal, so the director stops the actors every so often to give them feedback. Mr. Mistoffelees cracks me up because he keeps asking the director for a minute, then turns away to burp. There's an argument going on between two cats offstage, each claiming the other has more lines.

Finally, my favorite character, Grizabella, comes out. She shuffles onstage to sing "Memory," a song that never fails to make me gooey. My eyes are wet, watching. It's Andrew Lloyd Webber's alchemy, sure. But it's mainly remembering that time Mum played Grizabella all those years ago.

It's not a stranger up there, belting out "Memory" like her life depends on it. It's Mum.

I am sucked back to that moment when she pulled me under her musty Grizabella jacket. We were in the stage wings, watching the show; the smell of her jasmine perfume overpowered the mustiness.

"Isn't this the best, Vin?" she whispered into my hair.

"You're the best," I whispered back.

"*We're* the best."

We laughed silently and lip-synced the song that was happening onstage.

Now, tears roll down my cheeks, and I'm missing her with every particle.

CHAPTER 73

ROO: The Moments Beat Past Us

I have no idea where she's gone. My call goes straight to her voicemail.

I weave through the rain across the street and back again. The only place open is the supermarket, which I have already been through three times, up and down aisles. I asked several of the staff if they'd seen a beautiful girl in a green hoodie. Her long hair is probably wet, I said. They said they weren't sure. Good luck finding her.

I've checked the van. Joy's still there, but Vinnie isn't. I checked the pubs. The restaurants. She's nowhere.

I imagine her body, lifeless, in an alleyway. *She's collapsed*, I think. Blacked out and now has pneumonia because I have taken too long to find her. Or she's been found by the EMTs and is in the hospital.

I check my phone to see if I can walk to the hospital from here because Vin has the van keys with her.

I'm halfway there and drenched to the bone, when I see a few people in costume, gathered under the striped awning of a small hall, smoking. I hear singing inside. On a normal night, this is a place I'd cross the road to get away from. But tonight, I approach.

The singing is off-key. But I ignore it, thinking of the job at hand. Sure enough, there she is, sitting with her back to the wall, her knees pressed against her chest.

"Why'd you disappear like that?" I say. My voice is sharper than I intended. Her head snaps up. She frowns.

"Hang on. Why are you mad?"

"I was worried. I looked everywhere!" She wipes her cheek. Her face is puffy and raw, her hair slicked to her skin like she's a seal. I knew she wasn't right. I knew it, and I let her go anyway.

"You didn't need to be worried. You're meant to be having fun!" I go to sit next to her, but she's already up. "Why aren't you off having fun?"

"You're so bossy," I say. "You can't make me go have fun, especially without you."

This time, her frown is spiteful. A man in an undershirt looks over at us and lifts a caterpillar-shaped eyebrow. Vinnie grabs my wet coat sleeve and drags me from the hall.

"Did you just call me bossy?" she says.

"Yeah, I did. You keep telling me to be with Maeve. *Have fun!*" I mimic in a high-pitched voice. "I keep telling you—I don't want to!"

She sighs, all put out or something, and marches away.

"Why are you so cross?" I call after her.

"I'm not!" she throws back, without turning. "You are!"

I jog to catch up. "Me? I'm not cross! I'm worried!"

"You're mad at me. You called me bossy."

"But you are! You're making me do an exhibition I don't want to do. You even direct all the photos you want me to take. Now, you're forcing me onto some twentysomething-year-old girl. You dragged me on this trip, and you don't even want to hang out!"

She turns, her face crumpled and rain streaked. She pushes hair from her eyes. The moments beat past us.

"Now I know how you really feel." She strides away.

"Wait, Vin! I'm sorry, okay? I didn't mean to say that. I love the trip and everything. It's just—argh, you can't force me to be someone I'm not."

"I'm not forcing you!" She stops and turns to face me. "You're self-sabotaging. Again. You don't believe you deserve Maeve. Or your own exhibition. Or a decent future. So you're mucking it all up."

"I'm not self-sabotaging! It's just not my choice. I'm not into Maeve because I'm into you!"

She blinks. Wipes her face with her sopping sleeve.

"What did you say?"

"I fucking love you, Vinnie Smith. That's what I said."

The next moment, we're closer than we've ever been before, practically one body. She kisses me. Our wet faces press together, her lips on mine. My hands cup her face. They're in her hair. I can't pull her close enough.

CHAPTER 74

VINNIE: Falling into This

Roo smells like butterscotch and tastes like home. I want to kiss him forever. I press into his body so fiercely I may disappear. I don't care that we're drenched.

He loves me. I love him.

I pull away, remembering that I'm not meant to do this, as much as I desperately want to. Loving Roo is letting him go. He can't love me. He doesn't really know what he's loving.

"What is it?" he says, his head tipped slightly, his lips soft.

"Sorry." I squeeze my eyes tight. When I open them, he's still gazing at me through fogged lenses.

He presses his forefinger to my lips. "Don't be sorry. It was amazing." But when he leans toward me, I pull away. Hurt crosses his face.

"I see," he says. "I'm sorry, Vin. I shouldn't have said that. Done that." He shoves his hands in his pockets and marches up the street, toward the guesthouse.

"Roo!" I chase after him. My balance is off. It's dark, so I miss the side of the path. My knee buckles, and I land in the grass. Roo's too far ahead to realize.

Water seeps through my jeans. I push myself to standing and hurry after him, trying to keep my footsteps certain.

He gets to the guesthouse before me and yanks a blanket from the double bed.

"I'll sleep in the Kombi. I just need this," he says, holding it up. "So sorry, Vin. I'm the worst."

"Stop, Roo." I hold both his arms to pin him there. "Please, stop. Listen, okay?"

"I'm an idiot. I shouldn't have said that."

"Because it's not true?"

He's quiet. All I want to do is kiss him again and let him hold me, his body wrapped around mine so perfectly. I exhale, long and hard.

"I love you, Roo. I guess I always have." I push aside his wet hair, which is draped across his glasses. His eyes are distorted through the droplets that gather on each lens. "That's what this trip's all about. I'm sorry I'm so bossy about it. I just . . . I just want you to be happy. And I thought photography made you happy."

"You . . . love me?" His mouth lifts at the side.

I nod, smiling. I should let him go. I need to let him go. But when he drops the blanket on the bed, I can't help falling into this.

*

We bump into Maeve and Sara at reception the next morning. Maeve drags her blue suitcase.

"There you guys are! You disappeared on me last night."

"Yeah, sorry," I say. Roo grins at me sheepishly. I wonder if Maeve notices.

"We're heading back to Sydney today. I have an appointment with my supervisor first thing in the morning. E-mail me if you're ever in the city." She reaches for a pen on the reception desk and writes her e-mail on the back of a Belfry business card. "Oh, and send me those photos, will you? All of them?"

"Yeah, sure," says Roo.

"You could come to Roo's show," I say. "We'll have an

opening night. Maybe there'll be a photo of you in the exhibition, if you're okay with that?"

I ignore Roo's stern expression, the one he gets every time I mention the show.

She beams and nods. "Absolutely! More than okay! Though I don't think I can be there in person. Good luck with it!" I flinch when she kisses Roo on the cheek.

"You coming, Maeve?" calls Sara from the gate. She waves at us, her other hand gripping the case.

"See ya," says Maeve.

"I can't believe you want me over her," I say, watching her leave. "She's a Woodstock goddess."

"Are you crazy?" Roo pulls me against him.

CHAPTER 75

ROO: That's Her All Broken Down

Vinnie can't stop smiling. Neither can I. She leans against me, and even lets me put on my playlist, cleverly titled: Roo's Favorite Songs. The top favorite, "Bones," by Telenova, reaches every nerve ending. Morning sun and blue sky. The thought of us huddled together in the middle of the bed. Bellingen will never feel the same again.

We stop for donuts and coffee on the side of the road. I buy her a packet of raspberries because they're her favorite. She eats them in three fistfuls. She still has berry smudges on her cheek. I want to kiss them off, but I also want to leave them there because they make me happy. *She* makes me happy.

Unlike the two of us, Joy's cranky today. She had a cold, wet night, so her exhaust has taken a while to warm up and she's got a lot of complaining to do. Halfway down the highway toward Woody Head, she coughs ferociously then staggers to a stop by the side of the road.

Vin's eyes are closed. She's fallen asleep against the window, but she wakes when I poke her arm softly.

"We're here?"

"We've broken down."

"Damn."

We climb out to inspect the damage. Sure enough, Joy's butt is smoking. It's not a pretty nor a comforting sight.

"Should we give her some space, in case she blows?" asks Vinnie.

"I think we should."

We walk as far up the shoulder as we can without getting back on the highway. Meanwhile, Joy puffs. From here, we hear a pathetic wheeze.

"That's her all broken down, I'm guessing," says Vinnie. "Don't get too close, Roo." She pulls me back.

We use my phone to call roadside assistance using her dad's account. The guy tells us he'll be here in half an hour. We sit on our suitcases by the side of the road, taking turns to give each other shade, while we play "What Am I?" Vin has me stumped on a human-made item, which turns out to be an RV. It's surprisingly hard to guess, despite the four hundred RVs that pass us.

Ed the mechanic arrives nearly two hours later. The donuts have worn off. I'm famished. I feel the bridge of my nose peeling. Vinnie's freckled nose is also crimson.

"I'm not hopeful," says Ed, his face wizened with sun and age.

"Like, not hopeful at all? Or this is a good two grands' worth of work?" says Vin.

"Like, she's a goner. The engine's overheated. I'll have a proper look for you. But don't get your hopes up."

"I'll call Mum to come get us," I say.

Vinnie looks concerned. "And go home?"

"Yeah, what else?"

"Then it will be over."

"Yeah."

"You guys need a lift somewhere? I'm going to tow your van to Coffs Harbour. We can sort you out with a rental."

"Let's do that," says Vinnie.

"We can't afford a rental, Vinnie." I'm imagining the giant pile of money I have to pay Vin back if and when I ever have a proper job.

"It's fine, Roo! Trust me." She stands on tiptoe and kisses my cheek. I sigh, thinking about the debt I'm incurring.

"We'll take that lift," Vinnie tells Ed.

CHAPTER 76

VINNIE: The Stars Come Alive, One by One

Ed offers us a seven-seater Nissan X-Trail, which is all he has left. It's $159 a day, which is a lot. I look up bus timetables on Roo's phone but there's nothing heading Murwillumbah direction until Saturday. X-Trail it is.

After paying him to tell us Joy's a write-off, plus towing back to Murwillumbah, and two days with a rental, we've eaten so far into Carla's money, I'm worried I'm not going to have enough to print Roo's photos, let alone enough for the hall hire.

We take the cheapest cabin at Woody Head campsite. The afternoon's cooled, which is a welcome relief after a day spent baking on the side of the road.

"I can't believe Joy's broken," I say as we unpack our stuff. "I hope it doesn't take too long for them to tow her home."

"You're keeping her? Why don't you sell her to help pay for all this?"

"I can't," I say.

"Because she's your mum's, right?" He says it carefully.

I suck the inside of my cheek. "I guess." Once Joy goes, there's not a lot to hold on to. "Surely we'll find someone around home who can fix her. I refuse to accept that she's a write-off."

"Your endless optimism."

It looks like Roo wants to say more, and I'm scared he's going to bring up Mum again. It's not that I don't want to talk about her. I just don't know how.

"Should we go for a walk?" I say. "The sunset's pretty beautiful on the north beach. You remember?"

Roo takes my hand. Tingles shoot up my arm.

We wade through the shallows. There's not much beach left these days because the ocean is eating into the coast and eroding the shore. Melaleuca trees are fallen soldiers on the sand. We stumble over the giant trunks, getting caught on branches.

We give up climbing over them after a while and sit on a log facing the sunset. This point is pretty special because from here you can see the sunrise and the sunset. The bay is deep enough for whales to come close to shore.

Tonight, there seem to be loads of them. Roo says you call a group of whales a celebration of whales, which I love. A mama and her calf flap their fins against the surface.

"Apparently, that's them telling other whales where they are," says Roo.

"Or it feels good." I trail my fingers along his palm.

Somehow my lips find his, and soon my hands move down his back like it's the most natural thing in the world. I'm strict with my brain, telling it to shut the hell up and not worry about the future for five whole seconds so I can just enjoy this. For once, it behaves itself in a way my hands will not. I slide off the log and onto the sand between the fallen trees.

"Come here." I pull him down with me.

We lose track of time, skin pressing skin, moving without thought but making more sense than anything, ever. The sound of our breath is swallowed by the ocean heaving beside us. The sky glows marmalade and fades to violet.

"Why did we wait so long to do all this?" I ask Roo. I lie

against his shoulder, no space between us, tracing my fore-finger along his jawline toward his chin and back again.

"I have no idea." He smiles gently, glasses askew and foggy. He draws small circles on my hips with his fingertips.

I grin back, then turn to face the sky and watch the stars come alive, one by one.

CHAPTER 77

ROO: Trumpet Player in the Dunes

I could do this for the rest of my life—lie with Vinnie in my arms. It's everything I ever allowed myself to imagine and more. I'm floating. Soaring. Elevating. Nothing can pin me to Earth. Nothing but her.

I get Roo-typical thoughts like, *Why me?* and *Has Vinnie gone mad?* But I let the thoughts trail into the void. Why not just enjoy this, while I can?

We must have fallen asleep, because I'm woken by waves licking my bare feet.

"Vin, get up. Or we'll be in Ballina by morning."

She murmurs. The whites of her eyes glisten with moonlight. She sits up, adjusting her top. She's shivering.

We take our time, picking our way over logs, helping each other across. There's movement in the bracken. I worry it's a snake. But as my eyes adjust, I see it's a turtle. It pushes itself back into the water and disappears.

Back at the cabin, I try to warm Vinnie's body with mine like we did that night in the cave. She's so cold. She tips out of bed, races to the bathroom, leaning over the toilet like she's going to throw up. I follow her, pinning back her hair, which is wet and full of sand. Nothing comes up. She slumps against me, small and vulnerable, which I'm not used to.

"You're not well, Vin," I say, pulling her into me, my little bird. "Should I take you to the hospital?"

She shakes her head. "No. I'm okay."

"You keep saying that."

I walk her back to bed and fill a glass of water, which she sips tentatively, before lowering onto the mattress. I lie against her. The trembling has slowed, but her skin ripples intermittently.

"Vin, are you sure you're okay? You don't seem good."

Her eyes are shut, but I can tell she's still awake.

"Vin?"

She peers at me in the dark and strokes my cheek. "Shhh," she says.

"I should take you to the hospital," I say again. "They can run tests. See what's up. Maybe you've got low iron or something. Or a virus?"

She shakes her head. "Please don't," she whispers.

I stroke her hair until she's asleep. I, of course, can't sleep. Images from the last week form a police lineup in my mind.

Her slipping on Bald Rock.

The coldness and clamminess of her skin as she shivers against me.

The fatigue.

Her unsteadiness on the path to Crystal Shower Falls.

Something vague whispers at the corner of my brain so faint, I barely hear it.

Aggie dealt with these kind of symptoms plenty. They came in bouts. Most of the time she was fine. But then, she'd have a flare. She'd lose her balance. Her vision would go. Multiple sclerosis isn't hereditary, I don't think. But what if there's some familial connection? Have I been ignoring the signs, blinded by my feelings for Vinnie?

I know we should go straight home the next morning, get Vin to a doctor. But she's dragging me onto the beach to take photos.

She insists we still need more for the exhibition. I haven't the heart to tell her I don't want to do the show. It's the last thing in the world I want right now.

"Try it from that angle," she says, directing me onto the sand dunes.

A woman wearing stretch pants and a beanie plays trumpet on the dunes. We stand awkwardly. She stops until we pass.

"Nice playing!" says Vinnie. The woman smiles warmly and lifts the trumpet to her lips. The effect Vin has on people always amazes me. Even when she's unwell, she's luminescent and we all are drawn to her glow.

We head farther up the beach until we're close enough to hear the woman play and far enough to not be weirdos. Vin drags me down to sit next to her on the dunes. We interlock fingers while we listen. I'm drawn to the way shadows and light make her almost abstract.

"I wonder if she'll mind if I take her photo," I say.

"You can always ask."

Her name's Meredith, and she doesn't mind. I ask her to keep playing. Sun bounces off the trumpet, causing a glimmer I know will look amazing against the horizon.

CHAPTER 78

VINNIE: Delicate Bubble

Roo's still asleep the next morning when I use one granule of reception on his phone to log on to the internet. We're meant to go home today. I promised Roo. But I'm not ready. I don't think I ever will be.

The place we went most often as kids was Lake Ainsworth in Lennox Head. Most spring and summer holidays, we did at least a week at the lakeside campsite. Roo and I would take turns using Mum's paddleboard. In the afternoons, we'd all walk into town for ice cream, then keep walking up the headland to watch the sunset and the whales.

We can't finish this trip without going to Lennox. It would be like eating ice cream and throwing out the cone.

The campsite is fully booked. So I check out Airbnb and even hotels. There's one room. It costs more than what I'll be paying to hire the Citadel for Roo's show. But I book it before I can change my mind.

I'm already in the driver's seat when Roo emerges from the cabin with his backpack.

"Don't be silly. I'll drive," he says. "You're not well."

"I'm fine!" I say brightly. It isn't entirely true. But I'm good enough to drive.

We head north for an hour or so. On the highway, I take the Ross Lane exit toward Lennox.

"Vin, where are we going? We should just head home." Roo taps the dashboard with all fingers, like he's been doing the whole way.

"We will. But I have one last surprise."

His eyes widen, worried.

"Chill!" I say. "You'll like it."

I'll like it, I know that. In fact, if I had the money, I'd stay with Roo in Lennox Wave Motor Inn for the rest of my life, because going home is putting a pin in our lovely bubble. When we go home, the van goes to rust forever in the garage. I'll have to deal with Freddie. Find a way to talk to Lilah.

On this trip, Roo and I float in a liminal space only we need to understand and don't need words to explain. When we go home, who are we? I'm scared to find out.

Roo still doesn't look pleased as we sit side by side on the world's comfiest bed. It's everything four stars promises and more. "We can't afford this," he says plainly, cradling leaf-shaped guest soap in his palm. He lifts it to his face and sniffs.

I fall back on the mattress and pull him with me.

"We can. I have money. I keep telling you! This is my gift to us. Let me spoil you."

I tickle him, to try to get him to smile. He pulls away but at last succumbs. We laugh. He tickles me back. I'm laughing so hard I roll off the bed onto the carpet. I bang my head against the bedside table, but I don't care. He rolls after me, and we lie together.

"We should get rafts," I say, eventually pulling him to standing. My vision blurs slightly. I figure fresh air will help.

"You sure, Vin? Don't you want to rest? You may as well get the most out of this expensive bed you've just taken out a mortgage for."

"What's not restful about rafts? Anyway, I thought you loved me. If you love me, you have no choice."

He groans and messes up his hair with his hand.

We borrow rafts from the hotel and float on Lake Ainsworth, looking up at the clouds. Later, we fall asleep, entwined under the paperbark trees. It's cool when I wake, and the brightness of the day has eased. My flesh is goose-bumped. Roo's propped on his elbow, smiling down on me.

"See? You're happy I made you come here," I say. "I always know what's best for you."

"You do, do you?" He smirks. I push up his glasses for him. He's so darn cute.

My vision's still a bit blurry. Roo wafts side to side. Now there are two of him.

Stuff it.

"Yep. Ice cream and a sunset walk," I say.

CHAPTER 79

ROO: Padlocks over the Ocean

Vinnie seems pretty fine again today, thank goodness. If she does have MS like her mum, and the disease progresses like Aggie's, the symptoms will come and go.

Tomorrow, we go home. I'll drive her to the hospital myself if I have to. Slam the doors and lock them so she can't escape. None of this booking us into fancy hotels. Once she has a diagnosis, she can get proper help. I bet treatment options are improving day by day. Even since Aggie's diagnosis, there'll be more options. As soon as we're home and I have decent reception, I'll research.

Now, though, I play along. I want Vin to be happy. It's all I've ever wanted. And if ice cream and sunsets make her happy, I'm in.

Purple bleeds into a velvet sky as we walk toward the lookout. I glance at the grass shivering by the footpath, looking for snakes. That's all we need. Death by king brown.

We don't talk as we watch the sun melt against the ridge, then keep walking up the hill toward the padlock fence. Hundreds of padlocks glint. A flight of locks. Memorials to couples like us, locked in a moment they never want to forget.

I untie one of my Vans then unlace it.

"What are you doing?" asks Vin.

I weave the lace through the wire. "It's not a padlock, but it'll do. It's a sign we were here."

She laughs. "Too bad it'll blow away in the next storm."

Yeah. Damn. Hadn't thought of that. I've basically signed the contract that ensures we have no future. All we have is this single moment. Then we flutter away when the storm descends. Depressing stuff.

I squeeze her hand. She squeezes back and rests against my shoulder.

"Come on, let's keep walking. I'm not ready to go back," she says.

"It's pretty dark, Vin."

She threads her arm through mine and leads me down the other side of the hill. The track here is practically invisible. If there are snakes, we won't see them, which is a horrifying thought.

I shine my phone flashlight, but Vin makes me put it away.

"The moon's bright. Your eyes will adjust," she says.

And they do. By the time we get to Boulder Beach, I can see clearly. Three women gather around an unlit fire pit.

"Having a good night, kids?" says one.

"Sure are!" sings Vin.

"We should go back," I say to her. But she ignores me and strides on, along the track through the marsh.

After the boardwalk, we get to Iron Peg, Boulder's smaller, rockier sister.

"Vin? Let's head back."

But she either doesn't hear me or doesn't listen. She's stepping out of her sandals and walking across the stones, toward the water.

"Vin!"

A memory untucks itself and steps into my brain. Aggie, going out as far as she could. Past where the fishermen stand. Past where anyone should stand. I remember feeling sick about it, watching her. Vin's dad called her back, but that was Aggie—always doing things *extra*. More roller coaster rides than everyone else. More hikes up impossible trails. More laughter. More singing. More pain.

"Vinnie! Don't go that far out. You know it isn't safe!"

Either the wind's swallowing my voice or Vin's ignoring me. Either way, she keeps going. Just like her mum.

CHAPTER 80

VINNIE: Wild and Unleashed

The ocean sprays my face. You can't feel this kind of freshness anywhere. It's wild and unleashed. I laugh, intoxicated.

"Vin!"

I look back. Roo's hobbling across the rocks, one foot bare, a shoe dangling from his fingers.

"You should feel this. The world. It's amazing." I close my eyes as a wave breaks on the outermost rock.

"Come back, Vin. Please," he pleads.

I climb to higher ground and tuck my knees against my chest. He approaches and hovers over me. "Sit!" I say, pulling him down.

He relents and burrows into me, his long arm clasping my shoulder. His hair is damp with sea mist. So's mine. I stroke his cheek, laughing. "Amazing, right?"

"Stupid, right. Will you come back to land now?"

"In a bit. Just let me sit for five minutes, okay? I want to feel this."

He's quiet.

"I wish we didn't have to go home," I say, after a while.

"I figured that's what this is all about."

"What's it all about?" I ask.

"You. Running. From everything."

"Oh, right." I stiffen. "That's harsh."

"Yeah, it is. Sorry. I didn't mean it to sound like that."

I could forgive him, but I don't want to. A flame licks my insides.

"You think I'm running from the Lilah stuff, you mean?"

He's quiet. Then, "Yeah. And your illness. Stuff with your mum."

A wave crashes, loud enough that I could pretend I didn't hear him. But I did hear him.

"Shit. Sorry, Vin," he says. He must notice my anger.

I don't reply. Instead, I get up and climb over the last few rocks until I'm as close to the black ocean as I can get. It's a monster, reaching for me.

"Vin! Get back from there! It's dangerous."

"Yeah, it's dangerous. Life's dangerous. You call this 'running'?" I sweep my arms wide like a crucifix, close my eyes, and face it all. The wildness. My mum's suicide. Her illness. *My illness*. My fragile future with Roo. "I don't know about you, but I call this Facing My Fucking Problems." I turn to him now, the ocean's fury racing through me.

"You're just like Aggie," he says, shaking his head.

"What, running?"

"Yeah. Wild and running."

"You think she ran?" I yell. "She wasn't running. She was suffering." My voice is jagged. "How would you feel, being in all that pain? Who are you to judge? Well, you might not run. But you sure as hell hide."

He crouches. He's no longer reaching for me, calling me back.

"Who am I hiding from, exactly?" A wave crashes. My shirt, my jeans, are soaked through. I don't care. I can't feel cold anymore.

"Yourself."

"Sure," he says. "Just because I don't want a show, you mean. Just because I'd rather do stuff for other people than myself. That's hiding? Right."

I turn to face him. He wipes his glasses with his sleeve. His hair is chaos. "You tell yourself it's for other people," I say. "But really, you're just scared. Meanwhile, you're wasting your talent. Do you know how frustrating that is? For me? For Carla?"

"What's Mum got to do with this?"

"She's as frustrated as I am. Why else would she pay for our trip?"

The words are out before I can catch them. Maybe he doesn't hear me over the ocean. But his face is stricken. He heard me, all right.

"*She* paid for this? But you told me—"

"Forget about it, okay?" The wildness seeps out of me. I step back from the last rock. Collapse onto my haunches so I can crawl back safely from the edge. I look at him and know he won't forget about it. Ever, probably.

"This is all from the Extra money? All that money in your envelope. That's Mum's? For the car? For the hotel? What the hell, Vin. That money is for Mum. Not me."

"She wants you to have it, Roo. She wants you to start looking out for yourself, for once. We all do."

My eyes are bleary. My throat is thick with salt and emotion. I wish I could take it back. All of it. I want to start at the very beginning with Roo. Do it again, beautifully, perfectly, and make zero mistakes.

He turns away and stumbles toward the path. He flings his sneaker. It bounces and disappears between the rocks.

"Roo!" I call after him, right before a wave reaches up from behind and pulls me into the ocean.

CHAPTER 81

ROO: Water for Miles and Miles

How dare she? How fucking dare she?

I can't believe Vin would take Mum's money. She knows how hard we've had it all these years. Vin kept me company lining up for food donations when Mum was off work for six weeks with back pain. She was there the night the landlord told Mum we had no chances left—the next time we miss rent, we're out.

Who is Vin to decide how and when my mum helps me? She's forever trying to direct my life, like I'm an actor in one of her stupid plays. I am so livid, I want to take the X-Trail and drive into the bush without her. She can walk home, for all I care.

Who am I kidding?

"Argh!" I scream into the sky. Stars vibrate back, mocking me.

She has me stitched up because, no matter how mad I am, I still love her like crazy, and I'll never leave her. She knows that. I know that.

I turn, wondering how to apologize. How to go back in time, before all this. I don't see her in the blackness.

"Vin!" I call.

She doesn't reply. I stumble back over the rocks, slipping, nearly breaking my damn leg, desperately searching for her.

"Vin!"

I can't see her anywhere.

I kneel at the edge and lean toward the ocean, searching for her. For anything. But all I see is water for miles and miles.

"Vinnie!"

I fumble with my phone, trying to get it to turn on, to call for help. Emergency services. Whoever you call in these freaking situations. God?

"Shit! Shit!" It's dead. I chuck it against the rocks. It smashes and slides into the water. I stare desperately over the ocean, scouring the waves, tears bleeding over my face. The surf trying to drag me in.

I can't let it. I need to find her. I need to make her safe. It's all I ever needed to do.

CHAPTER 82

VINNIE: Drifting out to Oblivion

When I give up screaming, I paddle. When my body no longer has the energy to paddle, I float. I lie on my back, trying to keep my lungs full, my mind clear. The ocean heaves me in different directions. But I need to stay calm. I can't let it pull me in. I can't fight it. But it can't defeat me.

Time drifts. I could be miles from the shore for all I know. The waves are less intense. Undulating, as they lift me up toward the stars and down again.

I finally open my eyes and take in the sky. There's so much of it. I see Roo's emu, the Milky Way, and the moon halfway to being full.

I feel weirdly calm, drifting out to oblivion.

Is this what Mum felt, the night she took the pills? Was this the relief she was hoping for?

Thinking of her, especially her on the last night of her life, makes me howl.

I wish she hadn't left me. There was so much ahead of her. Sure, she had a chronic illness. But there were so many options!

I wish like hell everything was different.

The tears eventually slow. I'm cold. Freezing, in fact. My limbs have bypassed numbness to what feels like a permanent state of nothingness.

I ache for Roo. His warmth. His arms. His lips on mine. Thinking of him makes the tears start again. But I need to stop and save energy. There's not much left.

A bigger wave heaves and buries me. I splutter, trying to bring myself back to the surface. But I am so tired. So goddamn tired . . .

CHAPTER 83

ROO: The Current Is Going This Way

"You all right, kid?"

I turn. It's one of the women from the fire pit. She looms over me, her patterned dress fluttering.

"My friend. She's—disappeared. In the ocean," I somehow manage. I point.

"Beth!" she calls over her shoulder. "Lois!"

The other two women make their way over the rocks.

"Kid overboard. Call surf rescue," commands the biggest of the women, the first one to approach. Another woman pulls out her phone and dials.

"The current is going this way," says one of them, pointing north.

She helps me up. I stumble after her, half crying, half dying, trying to stay with it, for Vinnie's sake.

Surf rescue is on its way. They'll find Vinnie. They have to. I just hope her body's strong enough to hold her.

There's only one car in the parking lot. Theirs, I'm guessing.

"How long . . . will they be?" I stammer.

"Come. Walk," says one of the women, pulling me, dragging me along with her. She's sturdy and calm. Smells like earth.

On Boulder Beach, she points.

"There. Look."

I sprint toward the water, falling over myself, not able to run fast enough. I can't see her at first but then I can—

A long body drifts in the shallows, faceup.

I run so hard, my body nearly breaks. When I fall into the sand, I push myself up with both arms, wipe sand out of my eyes and mouth, and keep stumbling forward. It's her. It's her.

CHAPTER 84

VINNIE: Glowing in the Dark

"Vin!"

I hear his voice. Thin. Far away.

"Vinnie!"

My eyelids flicker open. His shape emerges.

"Thank fucking god." He collapses onto me, dragging, pulling, crying.

I splutter, trying to get rid of the water. I need to breathe. A woman is there with him.

"You're okay. It's okay." Her voice is low and calming. I breathe slower. Roo's expression clears as I lift my head out of the water. The woman tucks an arm under my shoulders and drifts me properly to the surface. She uses her body to guide me.

I'm lying on sand with Roo panting beside me, stroking my face feverishly.

"Vinnie, I'm sorry. I'm so sorry," he murmurs. "I'm sorry."

"It's okay," I whisper. My throat is scratchy. It hurts to talk.

We lie, quietly, the woman crouched nearby. I think there are two more women. Siren colors whir. I hear its blare. The women disappear. Voices murmur. The siren fades. The voices fade.

A rescue team checks my pulse. They talk in calm voices. Get me to sit up.

"I'm okay," I keep telling them. "I'm okay."

All I want is for them to go away. All I want is to be with Roo, holding his hand, leaning against him, the night around us.

Eventually, they leave. It's just us. We sit for a while in silence, him warming me.

"I'm so sorry, Vin," he says again.

"Don't be," I say. "I'm the idiot who went to the edge. You have nothing to be sorry for. I'm sorry about the money from your mum. I shouldn't have said anything. She didn't want me to."

"Yeah, that." I don't know what he's thinking, so I press his hand. He looks at me, his face a silhouette against the beach.

"She was meant to spend that money on herself. Not on me. She was going to do an art course."

"But she wanted to give it to you, Roo. You have to let people help you sometimes."

"Speak for yourself." I face him. His mouth is turned up at the corners.

"Okay. Fine. You're right. I have to let people help me. Like you, for example. The emergency crew. And those nice women who helped save my life."

"And you're going to get tested, right? For MS?" He says it very quietly.

"You know?"

One shoulder lifts into a shrug. Of course he knows. How could he not?

I nod, defeated. "Yes. I'm going to get tested. I know I've been avoiding it, but I need to know for sure. If it is MS, I need to get support. And if it's not, I'm going to have to keep getting tested until they know what's going on. I'm still probably going to need support. Whatever's going on, I can fight this."

"*We* can fight this. So you admit you need help?"

I snort. "Yes, Roo. I admit I need help. If you admit you need to stop doing everything for everyone else. We're doing that exhibition. Everyone is going to come. You're going to be rich and famous. Hey! You can donate the proceeds to your mum for her art course. It'll be amazing!"

He cocks his head. Smiles.

I don't have much strength left. There's not much night left, either. There's enough of both, though, for me to drag him toward the ocean, even though it nearly killed me.

The waves light up like magic. Bioluminescence clings to my ankles, making them glow. Roo wades next to me.

"You understand we can't be together, though, right?" I say.

He doesn't reply.

"Roo?" I stare at him. His features are soft. His hair ruffled by the light breeze.

"Because I'm a loser," he says.

"What? You're not a loser! You're amazing. Because you deserve someone intact like Maeve. Not me."

He grins. Pretends to press buttons on an imaginary phone. "Just one sec. I'm e-mailing Maeve now. Dear Maeve, Vinnie tells me you're intact and we should be together. Love, Roo."

I laugh. "You know what I mean."

"The trouble is, Vin, you don't really get to choose who you love. And there's no way any of that can stop me from loving you." He reaches for my hand. Our fingertips graze against one another then lock together.

Glowing in the dark, an emu in the sky above us, I kiss him. He kisses me back.

Part Three

Off Track

CHAPTER 85

VINNIE: No End of Days Bolognese Needed

It takes a few days to feel okay again when we get home. The ocean really did a number on me. I can barely get out of bed, I'm that tired. It's good, though, being home, with Dad. Letting him look after me. Having lots of time to research MS. Seems like there are lots of options. With the right support and medication, you can live pretty well.

When I tell Dad I think it might be MS, I don't even need End of Days Bolognese. He's the perfect person to tell. Of course he is. He's done this before. Also, he's the balancing weight on every cantilever that ever existed. He rubs his beard with his palm and studies me, his eyes liquid.

"Now you mention it, I'm surprised I didn't notice earlier" is all he says, before pulling me into the biggest hug he has. Here, I feel safe. Always.

We talk too about Mum. He tells me about the day of her diagnosis. Mum had had symptoms for a while, but like me, she was good at masking them. It was one of her colleagues, actually, who also had an MS diagnosis, who insisted she get tested.

"Did she cry? Was she scared?" I ask.

"You know your mum. She pushed back her shoulders and marched on. Actually, pretty sure she performed that night. *Evita*, was it? Gosh. I can't remember. I should remember. Probably had one or two other things on my mind."

Mum's neurologist isn't available for another two weeks. I'm glad I have Roo's show to keep me busy until then.

I spend the first couple of days after our trip going through his photos on the camera, trying to select the best. It's hard. There are so many. Roo is that good.

When we did scriptwriting back in Year Nine, Ms. Montague told us that a good play needs a theme. Something to hang the imagery from, even if the associations are subtle. I think the same should be true for an exhibition.

We can't theme it just as landscapes, though. That won't be enough to distinguish Roo from every other photographer. It has to get the audience in the heart, like a good play does. Stir them from the inside out until they can't not buy Roo's work or hire him for their next big event.

On the third day back, I find what I am looking for. It's an old photo, actually, that makes me realize that the heart of this show was here from the very beginning.

Roo mightn't agree. I decide I'll pitch the idea with a side of waffles. Who can say no to waffles?

First, though, I bike down Condong Street and hover outside Lilah's house. It's just after four p.m. on Tuesday. She doesn't have activities on Tuesday, and both her mums' cars are parked in the driveway. There's every chance she's home.

It takes me five whole minutes to gather the courage I need to knock.

"Vinnie!" Kathomi's hug is comforting and homey. It's like she's oblivious to everything that's happened between Lilah and me. "How was your adventure? Lilah mentioned you went on a road trip?"

"She did? Oh yeah. Roo and I were working on his exhibition. You guys should come. Next Friday. Six p.m. at the Citadel."

"Would love to! Lilah's upstairs with Molly. Go up! She'll be excited to see you."

I love the way Kathomi assumes Lilah and I are the same kids we've always been, bouncing up and down for each other.

Lilah's not excited to see me. Her expression is blank when I appear at her doorway. She's lying tummy-down on her bed. Molly's slumped in her beanbag, wearing headphones, and doesn't see me at first. When she does, she grins cautiously. I bet Lilah's given her every gory detail. I bet Molly thinks I am the worst.

"Can I come in?" I ask.

Lilah pauses, then motions toward the computer chair. An invitation to sit. I do.

I twirl side to side for a bit.

"How was your trip?" she asks, breaking the silence.

Fell in love with Roo. Nearly lost my virginity. Almost died. Faced my demons. You know.

"Great!" I smile as hard as I can.

"Good." She unlocks her phone screen, taps out a message, then looks back at me. This is Lilah, asserting her priorities—i.e., not me.

"Er, how's it all going, as Drama Captain, and everything?" I ask.

Her beam is as forced as mine, when she says, "Great! Ms. Montague thinks she's found the perfect monologue for me to do for the audition."

My heart slides down a notch, thinking of the audition I'll never do.

"What is it?" I ask.

"She thinks I should go classic. So I'm doing Tennessee Williams."

"Streetcar?"

"Yeah."

"Good choice," I say because it is. Lilah will do a great job. "What about a song?"

"Still undecided."

"I keep telling her she should do the song from *Frozen II*," says Molly, still wearing her headphones but clearly listening in. "She's a total Idina Menzel. Don't you think?"

I laugh a bit, imagining Lilah auditioning for the best performing arts school in the world with a *Frozen* song. Molly's right, though. Lilah would be a good stand-in for Idina Menzel, which is a compliment if ever there was one.

I tell them about Roo's show, and my curatorial plan. I ask if either of them would be interested in singing while the crowd gathers. For atmosphere. I don't want to sing because I have another plan for myself—and I can't let this turn into *The Vinnie Show*. This has to be *The Roo Show*. Well, mostly.

Lilah looks at Molly, who grins. Lilah shrugs. "Yeah? Sure. Sounds fun." We brainstorm song ideas. We land on songs Mum used to sing, like "Boots of Spanish Leather." Molly and Lilah decide it should be an a cappella duet. They're totally right.

I take a big breath. I need to apologize. To explain.

"Look, Lilah. About Freddie—" I start, my heart hammering.

But she waves his name away. I exhale, relieved.

I don't want to talk about him, either. All I want is for Lilah and I to be friends again in our last year of school together.

CHAPTER 86

ROO: Shining Under All That Pressure

It's been more than twenty-four hours since I saw Vinnie, making this the longest day of my life. I had to work at Myrtle's last night, tonight, and I have another shift tomorrow night. I'm not complaining, especially not after all my groveling to Sonia, telling her how much I need the money, like for a new phone and life and everything. Also, I like working here. I like the gang. I like having a boss who doesn't treat me like crap. But I'll always miss Vin when I'm not with her.

Elbow-deep in greasy water, food scraps clinging to my skin, all I can think about is her. Her lips. Her eyes. The curve of her jaw. Her body. I can practically feel her beside me, everywhere I go.

"What are you smiling at?" asks Tarek, grinning in a way that makes his eyes bright. "You gonna spill?"

"Nup."

"I bet you found yourself true love."

Ha; found. Discovered. There was no finding. She was always there.

I want to tell Tarek everything. I want to describe the great Vinnie Smith and the depth of feeling I have for her. But I can't put any of it into words. Also, it feels too good to share. So I just shake my head and smile like a goon.

*

I'm still asleep the next morning when I hear her voice. She's right there on top of me.

"I smell waffles," I say.

"You do." She floats a Styrofoam container over my bed. A glob of maple syrup ekes out the corner like sap.

"Don't drip that on my quilt." I get up and direct her toward the kitchen.

I've eaten half already when Vin pipes up about the exhibition. She leads by showing me the photo I took years ago of Aggie. The one of her calf and shadow against the rock.

"I'm thinking the show needs to be about Mum," she says. "It's a memorial, kind of. But a road trip. We'll sequence the photos not by time but by place. The audience will travel along with us as they walk through the show. What do you think?"

I chew slowly, my eyebrows raised, watching her talk. It takes forever to swallow.

"Ah, yeah? Sure. Sounds like a plan."

I was kind of hoping Vinnie preparing to see the neurologist would mean she hasn't got the headspace for me and my show. I'm worried about spending the last of Mum's Extra money on printing and hall rental. I also don't want to be there for it. When I think about standing in front of my photos, shaking hands with potential buyers, talking crap about some idea behind the photos or something, I want to throw up.

"You don't like it," she says glumly.

"It's not that. I do. But—what if we just made a book or something. A postcard."

She's gutted. Damn. I take another bite, even though I don't feel like waffles anymore. "You want some?" She shakes her head.

"I just thought . . ." Her eyes well up. I push the container away and grab both her hands with both of mine. Mine are sticky. "I kind of thought it was a good idea," she says. "People love all that . . . tragedy, you know? It won't be full tragic. It'll be bittersweet. Hopeful, sad. That kind of thing."

Well, I did want her to talk about her mum. This is more than talking. This is showing. And sharing.

"It sounds really good, Vin." I want her to be happy. I want her to be proud. She should be. I'm proud of her. Everything she's gone through? She's a champion. No one else could have borne the weight she did and come out of it so bright. She's a goddamn diamond—glittering under all that pressure.

She smiles and finishes what's left of my waffles.

CHAPTER 87

VINNIE: Flying Foxes Perforate the Peach Sky

"I don't know." I tip my head to one side. I've got half of my hair pinned up so you can see my turquoise dangling earring. Actually, it's Mum's, but hey. She's not here, so now it's mine. "I reckon move it to the left a bit. Yep. That's pretty good."

Carla climbs down the stepladder and moves it to the next hook. I pass her the photo of the light dancing in Girraween. I found the frame for this one at Goodwill this afternoon. It couldn't be more perfect.

Roo's managed to pick up magic in every situation. So much more than I noticed was there.

The exhibition is not just about the landscape. It's mainly landscapes, sure. But it's also people forming the landscape. Mum's leg against the rock. My silhouette against the falls. Carla's shadow by a eucalyptus. Mum, a crucifix against the terrifying ocean.

I check my phone again to see if Roo's messaged. No missed calls. Just a Snap from Lilah to say she and Molly are getting sushi but will be here soon to warm up.

I haven't told him yet about the monologue I've prepared about Mum. I guess I wanted to make sure it works before asking if I can weave it into the show. I wrote and rewrote it four billion times and have practiced it so much since, I swear the words have welded to every cell in my body.

It makes me cry. But it works. And it's short enough that I

(hopefully) won't be casting too long a shadow over Roo's big night.

I want to give Roo the heads-up before everyone starts arriving so he doesn't freak out when I launch into a dramatic poem about my mum suiciding and all the ways it's changed me.

"Have you heard from Roo?" I ask Carla. She's sitting on the steps, drinking Coke from a can. Her hair's tied up in a yellow bandana.

"No?" She puts it like a question.

I try him again. No answer. Great. As if I'm not nervous enough.

It's not that I'm worried about forgetting my lines. Impossible. I'm worried about cutting myself open and being exposed in front of people who know me. Know us. Most people probably know how Mum died, but somehow saying it aloud, to an audience, is menacing. I don't want to damage the idea people have of her or tarnish their memory of her in any way. But I also need to say the truth, from my perspective.

I distract myself by checking the price list again. Roo will be here. He has to be. Like me, he's just feeling butterflies.

*

"You guys were incredible," I say to Lilah and Molly when they finish their set. "Man, like, *really* good. You should go into business."

Lilah laughs. "Yeah, if Molly wasn't ditching us for Melbourne." She pokes Molly's waist. She smiles back.

Lilah and I turn and look at the door. And there's Freddie wearing the same button-down he wore the opening night of *Gatsby*. I snatch a look from her. Why is Freddie here? Has he no receptors?

"I'll tell him to leave," I say hurriedly.

She looks hurt. "No. Can you, like, not?"

"Are you sure?" I grab her hand. "I mean, it's not exactly *appropriate* for him to be here."

Molly and Lilah exchange a glance. Neither of them says anything as Lilah crosses the hall to greet Freddie. I hang back with Molly, watching. I feel ill.

Molly takes my hand, pressing gently, as Lilah reaches on her tiptoes and kisses Freddie. It's a deep, passionate kiss.

"Oh!" I utter, surprised.

"You okay?" whispers Molly.

"Yep! It's just—wow!" I have no actual words, clearly. Molly shrugs as if she owes me an apology, which she definitely does not. "Seriously," I assure her. "I'm happy for them. If that's what Lilah wants, then . . . it's great!" I mean, I think it's great. I hope he doesn't hurt her again. But I guess this is Lilah's life and she can make her own decisions.

I haven't told either of them yet about Roo and me. Not that it's a secret. Not really. I just feel so protective over us still. I figure everyone will be able to work it out after tonight, anyway. If Roo decides to turn up.

It's ten past six, and still no sign of him. I breathe, trying to calm myself. A woman arrives, wearing a plaid shirt and sensible shoes. I recognize her from Myrtle's website. It's Sonia—Roo's boss. I phoned her at the restaurant earlier this week, and she said she would make it if she could.

I hurry over. "Sonia?" I say. "Hi."

"You must be Vinnie." She smiles fondly, like she already knows me. I shake her hand and walk her through the show, taking her in the direction you are meant to go. There are quite a few people already gathered. Carla's slapped a few red dots on the wall. I'm hopeful my monologue will help sell more, making people feel a part of our journey.

“He’s pretty good,” says Sonia. “Would it be okay if I let you know in the morning how many we can commit to?”

I swallow. How many? Like, more than one? “Ah, yeah!” I say, professional as ever. “Of course! We’ve limited the prints to editions of five, but I have no doubt you will be able to take your pick. Is it for the restaurant?”

“Yes. For the restaurant. A small edition is always a good idea. Means you can ask more. I’m liking this one.” She’s standing in front of Ruby’s place. The whole garden is lit up. No filter needed.

“Yeah, it’s great,” I say.

“I have to get back to Myrtle’s. But tell Roo congratulations.”

“I will! Thanks!”

I wave her off at the door, looking for Roo. I’m starting to feel slightly irritated. Where *is* he? More than anything, I don’t want to do the monologue if he’s not here. There’s no point.

“You okay, Vin?” Dad hands me a mineral water. A sprig of rosemary bobs up and down among the bubbles.

“Just wondering where Roo is,” I say.

“Hm.” He never bothers with unnecessary words. Now’s no different.

Our principal, Ms. Parker, interrupts and asks me to tell Roo he should be proud.

“I bought one for my office. He’s excellent. I’d love to have him do my portrait if he’s taking clients.”

I take her through the commission price list, which I have had printed on the back of a photo of Joy against the sunset.

Seven p.m. comes and goes. Seven thirty. A few people leave. A group, including a real estate agent and a guy who works at the bakery, head off, leaving a wake of red stickers.

I should do the monologue. But I can’t—won’t—without Roo.

Lilah and Molly do another brief set, to distract from the fact that the man of the hour decided to be a no-show. I thank them from the back of the hall with prayer hands.

When they finish, I head toward the stage and fumble for the microphone. "Ah, hi," I say, my voice squawking. I pull the mic away slightly. I avoid Freddie's encouraging smile. "Thanks for coming, everyone. Sorry Roo couldn't be here himself. He had a . . . turn. Anyway. We're grateful for all your support. We have a price list here if you need it." I drop the pile. Scramble to pick it up, which is pointless, as they're scattered across the stage. Carla scurries over to help. I stand, flustered. "And ah, yeah. It also has details about commissions. Thanks for coming!"

The applause is deservedly pitiful, like drought rain.

I phone him again. No answer. I should stay until the end. See this thing I have created through. But I can't.

On Hospital Hill, he texts.

Out on the street, flying fox bats perforate the peach sky, and I run.

CHAPTER 88

ROO: She Makes Her Own Light

I wait for her, holding the book against my chest. I watch, as the flying fox cloud ebbs across the sky then disappears. A cauldron of bats.

"Where were you?" she yells, still fifty or so yards off. "Why weren't you there?"

She's red-faced and panting. I'm suddenly regretting all this—what if the stress of this situation exacerbates her symptoms? What if she ends up in the emergency department?

"How could you do this to me?" She slams against me with both palms. I hold the book for protection but stumble back. She's too strong for me.

"I'm sorry, Vin."

"Sorry? You're always sorry. Why can't you just be there for me?"

I don't reply. I sink into the overgrown grass. Place the book beside me. It bends the grass aside.

She refuses to sit. "What's that?" She points. There's a photo of her on the cover. The one of her at the Promised Land.

"It's for you. I made it."

She exhales deeply, trying to slow her breath. At last, she slumps into the grass next to me, the book between us. She pulls it into her lap and flips through. The light is dull. I hold the phone flashlight so she can see.

Photos of Jack and his dolls.

Photos of the kids singing on Bald Rock.

Photos of Ruby and her crystals.

Of Max and the owners of Green Valley Farm, their crazy rides glinting behind them.

Of Maeve and her butterfly.

Meredith and her trumpet.

Vinnie and the world.

"Well?" I ask.

"Obviously, they're really good. But you already know that. Why, though?"

"I came," I say. "To the show. I stood out front. I saw you there with everyone, glowing like Venus in her freaking shell. You're so good at all that, Vin. I'm just . . . not."

"But you are . . ." She trails off.

"I'm not. It's not me. I hate it. It makes me feel sick. I wanted to do it for you. But I know you don't want me to do that anymore. Do everything for everyone else, that is. So I came here instead. I know it's a jerk thing to do."

"It's not . . ." She's quiet, then looks at me sternly. "It's actually quite cool." Her smile is small.

"Cool? Me? Are you sure?" I elbow her gently.

"Yeah, you doofus. You're cool. Okay? Are you happy?" She elbows me back. "By the way, you're still basically doing what I want you to do. By not doing everything I want you to do."

"Ha. Good point."

She's quiet, looking over the town.

"What is it?" I ask. "You're still mad?"

She stands and faces me. The sky's darkening but, as usual, she makes her own light. I wait, wondering what's happening.

When she speaks, her voice is clear. It's her performance

voice—the one that comes from deep in her belly. The rest of the world dissolves, and the only thing in focus is her.

We cross the sky.
The land.
The sea.
We cross. Her. Us.
You.
Me.
Once, when we were kids, we played tag in long grass
and laughed in steel structures made with love until we
couldn't laugh anymore.
Once, when we were kids, we raced each other on the rock,
our parents taking their sweet time.
I remember us. Do you?
Our parents.
Our net.
Until the net broke and let us fall.
That was Mum. That was all.
She told us she had MS long ago. That was okay.
We could do that.
We had each other and everything in between. The sunsets.
The campfires. Everything that made us *Us*.
Then, against the sunset, the smoke in our eyes, she said
she thought about dying.
We let her talk, eyes stinging, hearts sore.
The words made no sense, then.
They make no sense, now.
Do you still hear them like I do, echoing around your skull?
We made up this landscape and this landscape made us, but
then we retreated because, like her, we couldn't. Anymore.

She reaches up, the stars at her fingertips, her chin facing the sky. I'm holding back tears. She lets her arms fall, her head fall, and holds herself tight.

We couldn't and can't and won't and didn't.
My mum made her choice.
And we made ours, to run and hide, and that is okay because choices are all you have.
We still couldn't. We still wouldn't. We still didn't.
Then we found the landscape again.
Here.
There.
Sunsets forever.
Oceans deep.
We found us there too. You. Me. Broken. But together.
Together, we're more beautiful.
Together, we hold more.
Each other.
The world.

She looks at me briefly before sinking into the grass, as if her performance used the last bar of battery. She doesn't look up—her head hangs limply. Her arms are like fabric beside her.

I take her hand. Cup her chin and kiss her, hoping it's enough.

She smiles. I can't say why, but somehow, I know it is.

Author's Note

If you're familiar with New South Wales, Australia, you'll probably recognize many of the names and landmarks. You might also wonder why some names have been changed. I haven't messed around with names for natural places, such as Bald Rock and Crystal Shower Falls. But yes, most of the business names have been fictionalized.

I was running in the Promised Land behind Bellingen when Vinnie and Roo first formed in my mind. Vinnie's mum's story also emerged.

I knew several people in my younger years who lived with MS. One, tragically, took her life far too soon.

Perhaps this was the whisper in my head that urged me to train as a suicide counselor for Lifeline. Most calls were from lonely people checking in with someone—anyone. Several, though, were suicide interventions. It was disconcerting not knowing what happened after the paramedics were notified and the call had ended. All I could do was hope. Losing someone I grew up with to suicide years later made the importance of this work even more profound.

If you or someone you know is struggling or in crisis, help is available. Call or text 988 or visit 988lifeline.org.

If you are looking for more information about living with multiple sclerosis, you can visit this site: www.nationalmssociety.org.

Acknowledgments

Every story needs a map of some sorts. This map has been lovingly held together by some very important people.

I would firstly like to acknowledge the traditional custodians of Bundjalung, Gumbaynggirr, and Ngarabal country who gently and respectfully care for the lands featured in this story. I pay my respects.

Thank you to dear Kiah Thomas for reading chapters as I wrote them, feeding me encouragement, pointing out signposts, and waving me toward the finish line. You were the first person to know and love Vinnie and Roo as much as I do and somehow managed to convince me that they're real. There's an obvious reason this book is dedicated to you.

To my writers group: Sarah Armstrong, Lian Tanner, Tristan Bancks, and Deborah Abela—your thorough chapter reads sent me on my way and made me see plot holes I might have missed. Also, you're darn good company.

Thank you to my agent, Lori Kilkelly, who believed in Vinnie and Roo from the beginning, shepherded their journey, and showed their story to the right people. This would not be a book without you, Lori.

Thank you to my wonderful editor, Jennifer Thompson, at Scholastic Press, and to my Australian editor, Jeanmarie Morosin, at Hachette Australia, for taking this story under your wings. I knew from the minute I first spoke to you both that Vinnie and Roo would be in safe hands.

Thank you to all the wonderful people at Scholastic Press and Hachette Australia for your scrupulous edits, your design, and your expertise in sales and marketing. A book is not a book without the hardworking team behind it.

Thank you to Muhammad Mustafa for bringing Vinnie and Roo to life on the cover.

Writing about sensitive topics takes care and precision, a great deal of research, and a lot of nerves. I am endlessly grateful to Pamela Jones, a graduate professor of education, who read this story for mental health sensitivity and provided thorough notes and reassurance. Thank you, too, to Sarah Anderson from the National MS Society, who helped me more accurately portray the experience of living with MS. Jessie Barry, who speaks publicly about her own MS experiences, kindly read Vinnie and Roo's story for credibility and advised based on her own experiences. It is necessary to note that MS varies widely from person to person, but Sarah's and Jessie's help has been invaluable.

Award-winning author, Maggie Hutchings, who has years of experience as a counselor as well as living with a disability, read this manuscript in its final stages. Thank you for your comforting notes, Maggie.

To Elka, my wonderful eldest daughter, and now, most important reader. Your keen insights are so necessary and are delivered in such a sensitive, thoughtful way. I'm wondering now how I ever wrote stories without you.

Thank you to the booksellers, parents, teachers, and librarians who devote your lives to placing books in hands. Authors are indebted to you.

Thank you as always to my parents, Richard and Margaret, and my loving husband, Gregor, who celebrate every moment of my career and provide the guardrails needed to keep me on track. To my youngest daughter, Eve, and of course Elka . . . this journey wouldn't be half as much fun without you both.

A special thanks to my late aunt, Hendrika, who wrote over seventy books in her time, spoke openly and passionately about living and dying, and lived with a fierce authenticity that inspires me to be a better person. I will think of you always.

Finally, to you, dear reader, I hope your journey is bright. But even on days when it's not, may this book shed some light along the way.

About the Author

Amber Melody

Zanni L. Arnot has published over forty trade books for kids under the moniker Zanni Louise, including bestselling board books, picture books, chapter books, and middle grade. She tours the world, visiting kids in schools and running writing retreats for grown-ups. She's also a proud ambassador for Room to Read, an organization that gives kids access to books.

In her free time, you'll likely find Zanni trail running in forests. Zanni lives with her family of four on the east coast of Australia.

To find out more, visit www.zanniarnot.com.